The adventurers had come to the end of their game.

Paolina walked slowly out into the Long Gallery, her heavy veil trailing behind her like a train, her gown, stiff with the diamond and pearl embroidery, rustling over the polished floor like ghostly fingers. Below, rocking a little on the tide, was the glittering golden gondola—the ceremonial vessel of a thousand brides.

She thought of how she and Sir Harvey, traveling as sister and brother, had fooled the finest families of Verona and Venice with their little intrigue. Even when all their money was stolen they had managed to carry off their scheme grandly so that no one ever guessed their plight.

But now the masquerade was over, the goal accomplished, and Paolina was to be married to the richest nobleman in Venice—today! It was what they both wanted—until they fell in love.

THE
GOLDEN
GONDOLA

Barbara Cartland

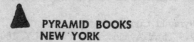

PYRAMID BOOKS
NEW YORK

THE GOLDEN GONDOLA

A PYRAMID BOOK

Pyramid edition published February 1971
    Second printing, September 1971

Printed in the United States of America

PYRAMID BOOKS are published by Pyramid
Communications, Inc. Its trademark, consisting of
the word "Pyramid" and the portrayal of a pyramid,
are registered in the United States Patent Office.

Pyramid Communications, Inc.,
919 Third Avenue, New York, N.Y. 10022.

1

He awoke and for a moment thought he was still at sea. He could feel the waves rising and falling until suddenly he realized that they existed only in his mind. The bed on which he lay was still.

He opened his eyes—the room was entirely strange to him. It was bare and poverty-stricken and the sunshine coming through the uncurtained, unshuttered windows illuminated the rough, uncovered wooden floor.

He stirred and was instantly conscious of an aching head and a body that felt as if it was bruised all over. Someone came quickly from a corner of the room and laid a cool hand on his forehead. He looked up into the kindly, dark eyes of a middle-aged woman.

"So the *Signor* is awake," she smiled.

"Where am I?"

He found it difficult to enunciate the words. His mouth was dry and his lips cracked.

"You are safe, *Signor*. My husband rescued you last night from the storm. You must thank the Mother of God for your safe deliverance."

"The storm!"

He repeated the words slowly and now it all came back to him. The sound of the ship breaking against the rocks, the cries of the sailors, the shrieks of the passengers, the wind and rain which seemed to whip the very skin from off his back, and then the bitter cold of the water as he dived into it.

"You are lucky, *Signor*," the woman was saying. "No bones broken. You must be a very strong man to have been through such a storm and to have survived."

5

"Yes, I am strong," he repeated, catching at the words almost like a child who was learning to talk.

But then he remembered something else.

"The girl! Is she safe?"

"She is safe, *Signor*. Thanks to you. My husband saw you struggling with her in the water. You held her on to a piece of floating wood and then, as you came near to the shore, he waded in and rescued you. You do not remember?"

"No. I can only remember holding on and trying to persuade her to do likewise. She was unconscious, I think."

"The poor lady. Yes, she was unconscious. If it had not been for you, *Signor*, she would have been drowned."

"Who else is saved?"

"No-one, *Signor*. No-one at all."

"No-one!"

He sat up despite the pain which seemed to shoot through his body at the effort.

"But that is impossible! Incredible! What happened to the Captain and the crew?"

"They are all drowned, *Signor*; every one of them. Some of the bodies have already come ashore. The rest must be in the ship or at the bottom of the ocean."

"It seems unbelievable."

"It is the good God who save you, *Signor*, or His Blessed Mother. No-one else could have kept a man alive in such a storm as there was last night."

"Surely you must be mistaken?" he insisted.

"No, no, *Signor*. You will see for yourself when you are better. My husband and the men from the village are all down at the shore now. Soon they will go out to the ship to take what they can from the wreck."

The man's eyes narrowed.

"I must get up," he said. "Where are my clothes?"

"But, *Signor* . . ."

The woman's protests were silenced before she could speak them.

"My clothes, I said, and quickly."

"*Si, si, Signor*."

She hurried from the room. He could hear her wailing all the way down the stairs that it was crazy for him to move when he should rest.

With a tremendous effort he got off the bed, throwing aside the thin blanket which had covered him, and then, as

6

his feet reached the floor, dragging it off the bed to wrap around his nakedness.

His legs felt as if they were too weak to carry him. With an effort he walked to the window. The sun was shining, but there were still clouds over the sea. He had a glimpse of the waves, white-crested, but there was no doubt at all that the sea was dropping.

He was still standing at the window when the door opened and the woman returned. She carried his clothes over one arm; in her other hand was a tray containing a bottle of wine and a hunk of rough, black bread such as the peasants ate.

The man at the window turned to her with a smile.

"That is what I need," he said, and taking the bottle he poured half its contents down his throat.

He felt the rough wine bring new life to his tired body. The woman watched him appreciatively.

"I will cook something for the *Signor*. It is early. The *Signor* needs food for his strength."

"Later," the man commanded. "I must get down to the ship. Leave me now so that I can get dressed."

"Ah! The *Signor* is in a hurry to see if anyone is alive," the woman said. "You will find that I have spoken the truth. They are all drowned—every one of them."

She went from the room. The man finished the wine and for a moment played with the idea of eating a piece of the dark bread. But he felt it would choke him, and instead he busied himself dressing.

His clothes had been dried, but they were sadly cockled and creased. The smart breeches, too, were torn. Two of the jewelled buttons on his coat were missing. He was, however, quite indifferent to his appearance. It was only when he was dressed that he realized that his shoes were missing, and remembered kicking them off before he dived overboard.

He swept his hair back from his face and having no ribbon with which he could tie it, left it to hang untidily about his ears as he prepared to walk downstairs in his stockinged feet.

The stairs which led to the top of the house were little more than a ladder. He negotiated them carefully, feeling the splinters in the wood prick his feet through the torn and laddered stockings.

When he had descended he found himself in a huge

7

kitchen furnished almost solely by a large table. The woman who had attended to him was cooking over a fire. She straightened her back as he appeared and smiled at him as if he had achieved something miraculous.

"You are, indeed, a strong man," she said in terms of heart-felt admiration.

"I need shoes," he told her.

"*Hélas, Signor,* I have none. My husband wears his only pair; and mine—mine would be too small for your big feet."

She laughed as she spoke and then he heard another, gentler laugh come from the far corners of the room. He turned and saw a girl lying on a roughly improvised mattress beneath a small window.

Oblivious of his strange appearance he contrived to give her an almost courtly bow.

"You are alive, *Signorina!*"

He spoke in Italian, but she answered him in English.

"I am told it is entirely due to you, Sir, that I am."

He walked towards her and looked down at her.

"You are English?"

"Like yourself."

"I had no idea. I did not see you on board."

"No. I kept to my cabin. My father was ill and it was impossible for me to leave him."

Her eyes clouded as she spoke, as if she suddenly realized that her father must be dead.

The man stood looking down at her in amazement. He would certainly have remembered her had he seen her, he thought. Her face was pale as she lay back against the coarse pillow, and her long, golden hair fell over her shoulders. He had never seen such hair. It was the true colour of gold and even in the dingy atmostphere of the kitchen it seemed to glitter and glisten almost as if it were alive.

"Have you found out who else has been saved?" she asked in a low voice.

He saw then that her eyes were dark, almost purple in their depths, and fringed with dark eyelashes. A strange combination, he thought to himself, and then realized that she had asked a question.

"The woman tells me that everyone was drowned save ourselves."

"She told me the same thing," the girl answered. "It cannot be true, it cannot. There must be others."

"That is what I am going to see for myself."

"Please, see if my father . . . But, no, I know he is dead," the girl said. "He died before I left his side; before the ship hit the rocks. It was the constant buffeting and his seasickness. I think it must have affected his heart. I was just about to tell the Captain when the crash came."

"I believe it is still impossible to get to the ship," the man said. "But I will do my best."

"Thank you."

She moved one of her hands towards him and he realized that they had taken her clothes away, too, to dry them. She must be naked beneath the covering blankets, and he saw the whiteness of one shoulder peeping from beneath the cascading golden hair.

She was lovely, he thought, and as if she was suddenly conscious of his thoughts she raised the blanket a little higher towards her chin, while a faint flush spread over her white cheeks.

"I will go and see what I can discover," he said abruptly, and turned away.

"Please, one moment! Will you tell me your name? I should like to know to whom I owe my gratitude—and my life."

"My name is Harvey Drake—Sir Harvey Drake, Baronet, of Watton Park, Worchestershire. And yours?"

"I am Paolina Mansfield. My father was Captain Mansfield, late of the Grenadier Guards."

"You have an Italian name."

"My mother was Italian."

So that, he thought, explained the dark eyes that were such an unusual contrast to the gold hair.

"Your servant, Miss Mansfield."

He bowed and was gone, hurrying from the house over the roughly cobbled path despite the discomfort of walking without shoes.

Fortunately it was not far to the beach. A narrow, winding path led him down the cliff-side where he could see a group of men standing at the water's edge. As he reached them they turned towards him eagerly, full of expressions of good-will and congratulations that he had defeated death the night before.

He was introduced to Gasparo, the big bearded fisherman who had saved him and to whose house he had been taken.

"Thank you," he said. "And I am more grateful than I can say. I hope to reward you more suitably when I can reach the ship and perhaps salvage some of my personal belongings."

"That is doubtful, *Signor*," one of the fishermen said. "The ship has been battered continuously against the rocks. We cannot get to her. If the waves do not subside soon she will sink, and once that happens nothing can be saved. The sea is very deep around the rocks."

Sir Harvey looked at the ship. It was only a short distance from the shore and yet the rocks which constituted the small island of peril also caused a water race which surged between them and the high cliffs.

He could see that the fishermen were right. The ship was being lifted with every fresh wave and battered down against the rocks. Already all the superstructure was gone and it looked as if in another hour or so nothing would be left.

He could see the jagged tear in the ship's side which had let in the first influx of water. Wreckage was strewn about all over the sea, and each piece, as it came near enough to the shore, was eagerly salvaged by the fishermen. One piece of wood, skimming the waves, bore the ship's name—*Santa Lucia;* beneath it was inscribed: *Naples, 1740.*

"Only ten years old," a fisherman remarked as he waded in and pulled it out of the water. "Not a long life!"

"She had a lot of good stuff in her," another man answered. "Come on, let's get at it."

But it was still too rough and too dangerous for them to put out their boats although over a dozen of them were waiting on the sand.

"Can any of you swim?"

Sir Harvey asked the question and before they spoke he knew the answer.

"No, no, *Signor*."

It was what he might have expected. He gauged the distance between the shore and ship and then began to take off his coat.

"What are you doing, *Signor?*"

"I am going out to see what is left," Sir Harvey answered.

A babel of sound arose immediately. The fishermen tried to persuade him to change his mind, pointing out the dangers, telling him of the risks he undertook.

He paid no heed, laying first his coat and then his shirt and torn stockings on the dry sand. Then, wearing only his

10

breeches, he walked towards the sea. He braced his muscles. He was still stiff, his head ached, but nothing worse than that was wrong with him. Without further comment he plunged into the water.

It was not so cold as it had been the night before and somehow it seemed invigorating. The tide was with him and carried him swiftly towards the wreck, and not for one moment did he feel afraid or even overwhelmed by the lashing waves which carried him down into their green depths then swept him up towards the sky.

He reached the wreck and with difficulty prevented himself from being dashed against it. It was dangerous, but he managed to squeeze himself round the shattered hull without being crushed between the ship and the rocks. And then, with the agility of a cat, he clambered up the ship on to what was left of her deck.

The tide was going out fast and he thought it would not be long before the fishermen would be able to get their boats alongside. He glanced back at them and realized that he was only just in time. He was well aware that anything salvaged from the wreckage of ships which ran on the rocks along this dangerous coast was considered the lawful property of those who first laid hands on it.

Crawling along the heaving deck he made his way to the companion-way. He had to move immediately after a wave and before another came to create more damage. Somehow, instinctively, he got into the rhythm of it. And then, moving below into the bow of the ship filled with water, he began to grope and feel his way.

There was just enough room for him to move and breathe although every wave splashed the dirty water against his face or pinioned him to the mass of loosened wreckage. It was dark and yet the holes in the ship enabled him to see enough.

There was one cabin for which he was searching, one that was his objective. It was on the opposite side of the ship to the rocks and was therefore comparatively undamaged. The porthole had been burst in and in the sunlight he could see what he had expected to see.

It was the body of a a woman lying on the floor under about four feet of water. She was being rolled slowly backwards and forwards by the movement of the water. He could see her quite clearly with the sunlight percolating through the open porthole. She had long dark hair which floated in the water and her lips were red even in death.

Backwards and forwards she rolled, and then, peering through the water which covered her, Sir Harvey saw that she held something tightly in her hand. It was a velvet box, padlocked and with silver corners such as women use for their jewellery.

Even the battering of the waves had not caused her fingers to loosen. White and somehow tenacious, they still held on to the box as she rolled.

Taking a deep breath Sir Harvey bent down. He took the box from the thin fingers. Her hand, when it relinquished the box, fell away limply as if she no longer had any interest in the only thing she had tried to save.

Sir Harvey straightened himself, being, as he did so, flung backwards against the cabin wall by a rush of water pouring into the ship from a mountainous wave.

But the box was his! Holding it in one hand he breathed deeply. Then he bent down, before the water came flooding in again, to take the pearls from the dead woman's rounded neck—three rows of them, perfectly matched and with an elaborate clasp set with rubies and diamonds. Her hair entwined itself around his arm, and gently, as if he feared to hurt her, he disentangled it.

Up again, he slipped the pearls into his breeches' pocket and made his way slowly and laboriously back to the companion-way. He paused as he reached his own cabin which was near to it, hesitated for a moment, and then a sudden wave went to his head crashing against the wall so that for a moment he was almost stunned.

He did not leave hold of the box he held in his hand, but in a sudden pause he stumbled up the companion-way. When he reached the deck he was half exhausted and very nearly collapsing for want of breath, fighting against the waves that kept splashing over him, blinding him and half choking him with their spray.

He heard shouts from outside. The fishermen were approaching. He glanced round and saw a coat floating towards him. He snatched it up and wrapped the box in it, and tucking it under his arm jumped from the deck of the piled-up ship into the water below. As he rose to the surface of the water he found himself near a boat and hauled himself aboard.

"You are a fool, *Signor*," one of the fishermen said. "You might have killed yourself. Did you get anything?"

"Only an old coat," Sir Harvey said disgustedly, throwing it down beside him in the bottom of the boat.

12

"And you risked your life for that?"

The fisherman spat over the side.

"You would risk your life if you realized that everything you possessed was in that broken hulk of wood," Sir Harvey answered.

He cupped his hand round his mouth.

"Ahoy, there! I will reward any man who salvages my clothes for me. They are in the second cabin below the companion-way, and there is money, good money, in the pocket of a coat you'll find there."

He saw the interest his shouts had aroused. But the fishermen were still wary of climbing on to the ship.

"Money is all very well," his own boatman told him. "But there's no knowing if it will be useful in Paradise or, indeed, if you can get it there."

"Think how sought after your widow would be with it," Sir Harvey parried with a smile, and his sally evoked a roar of laughter.

One of the fishermen, braver than the others, was now trying to emulate Sir Harvey's effort in clambering up the side of the ship on the deck. But he got his arm crushed between the rocks and the moving ship and fell back into the sea with a great gash from wrist to elbow. He was hauled aboard one of the boats, bleeding and cursing, and the other fishermen drew their boats further back and waited.

The tide was running out quickly; at the same time the ship was disintegrating. Great pieces of wood began to fall from the rocks into the sea. There was a noise all the time of splintering and crashing which had an almost pathetic sound as if it were some live creature that was being destroyed.

The fishermen were all the time filling their boats with anything that was flung within their reach by the waves—a cask of wine; a chair, broken but still recognizable for what it had been originally intended; some clothes; and a number of cooking utensils; all of which were snapped up eagerly.

"Won't anybody else try their luck at getting inside the ship?" Sir Harvey asked.

"Why don't you try again?" a fisherman suggested.

Sir Harvey shook his head.

"I would," he said, "but I am still weak from last night."

"That must be true," one of them said. "You are a strong man to have survived it all."

Sir Harvey smiled at his naive admiration.

"It is not always strength which counts," he answered. "Sometimes it is brains."

"It was strength that kept you alive last night," the fisherman said. "Or else the devil looked after his own."

He spoke as a joke and then, to make sure, crossed himself for fear that his joke should have disastrous results.

Sir Harvey laughed, and then pointed to where one man had apparently achieved the impossible and reached the deck of the ship.

"Well done!" he cried. "Wait for the rise and fall of the waves. Move as soon as one is past."

Emulating Sir Harvey's own feat, the young fisherman scrambled and crawled to the companion-way, then disappeared. It was some minutes before he reappeared again spluttering and spitting, but holding an armful of clothes which he chucked over the side.

"Well done!" Sir Harvey shouted. "Well done! All that my pockets contain is yours."

He paused and then bellowed again.

"I want a pair of shoes. Don't forget a pair of shoes."

Encouraged by the fisherman's success the other men managed to board the ship. There was blood all over the deck from the cuts they received against the jagged rocks and the splintering wood, and yet now things began to come from the cabins in quick profusion—bedding; clothes; candlesticks; glasses; and even pieces of carpet. All to be snatched from the sea by the men waiting below in their boats.

One man was supported out with a great gash on his forehead and lowered down to the men waiting below; and just as they finished getting him aboard there was a sudden shout.

"She's breaking! Look out, she's breaking!"

The remaining men left inside the ship jumped from the heaving deck into the water just as the ship split in two and the pieces slowly began to sink.

There were more pieces of wreckage floating on the waves and a wild scramble to pick them up, and then the men clambered or were hauled into the boats and they all pulled away.

The hull of the ship, the last to remain on the rocks, began to whirl round and round, was flung against the rocks and sucked back again. Now it was getting lower and lower until finally it disappeared altogether and there was

14

only a broken assortment of wood, straw, bottles and filth to show where once it had been.

Still picking up all they could along the route, the fishermen pulled for the beach. Sir Harvey, picking up the coat he had thrown in the bottom of the boat, stepped out on to the sand. He tucked it under his arm and walked along to where another boat was being hauled in shore, filled with a miscellaneous collection of damp objects, amongst them his own clothing.

He picked his things out one by one and put them over his arm. A coat of blue brocade; another of cherry red satin; breeches looking lank and colourless in their wet state; and, last but not least, a pair of shoes.

He put these on quickly, squelching the water out of them with his bare feet, and then feeling in the pockets of the coats found in the one of blue brocade a purse.

"There are not many crowns in it," he said, "but what there are I give to you with my most sincere gratitude."

"You are welcome, *Signor*," the fisherman grinned. But Gasparo's eyes were fastened on the buttons of the blue brocade coat.

They were glittering in the sunshine and looking uncommonly like diamonds. Sir Harvey saw his glance and taking up the coat threw it across Gasparo's shoulders.

"They are, alas, only crystal," he said. "But accept the coat as a gift; you saved my life."

The big fisherman's rough hand went out to stroke the silk material which even though it was wet seemed to retain its sheen and colour.

"You are letting me keep it, *Signor*?" he asked incredulously.

"It is yours," Sir Harvey answered.

He turned and walked away up the beach, carrying only two garments besides the black coat he had himself salvaged. He had gone quite a little way before a shout behind him made him turn his head and he realized he had left behind his shirt, coat and waistcoast which he had removed before swimming out to the ship.

Laughing at his absent-mindedness, he walked back and picking them up added them to the bundle in his arms. The sun was shining now. He could feel it beating on his bare back as he climbed laboriously up the cliff towards the village above.

There were only a handful of cottages and the one in

which he had been sheltered the night before was by far the largest and the most impressive. He walked up the path and opened the door of the kitchen.

Paolina Mansfield was standing at the table which was laid for a meal. She glanced up as he entered and hurried towards him.

"What did you find?" she asked.

She was dressed, but her long golden hair was unbound and fell down her back to her waist. She was very pale and her eyes seemed unnaturally big in her little oval face. It struck him before he answered her that she was the most beautiful girl he had ever seen in his life.

"There is no-one alive," he answered.

He walked past her towards the ladder leading to the upper room. She hurried after him.

"But are you sure?"

"All that was left of the ship is now at the bottom of the sea," he answered.

He saw the hope die from her face and felt he had been a brute.

"No-one could have suffered," he said. "Those who were below decks were drowned almost instantaneously when the water rushed in on them. Those who were on deck must have been swept overboard."

She covered her face with her hands.

"It is too horrible to think about," she whispered. "Those poor people!"

Sir Harvey paused yet another moment before climbing the staircase.

"You must be thankful you are alive," he said. "For us there is always the future."

She took her hands from her face and looked at him.

"Yes, but what sort of future?" she enquired.

His eyes took in again the golden hair, the wide beauty of her eyes, the fullness of her red lips.

"For someone as lovely as yourself," he said, "could it be anything but fair?"

She made a little gesture of impatience as if the compliment annoyed her.

"You do not understand," she said coldly, and walked away from him towards the open door.

He hesitated and then climbed up the stairway to the room above. He shut the door and would have locked it, but a rough latch was the only sort of fastening it had.

Throwing his wet clothes down on the floor, he pulled

16

the velvet box from beneath the coat. For a moment he stared at it and there was a strange expression on his face. Then he looked round for something with which to open it. A knife lay beside the bread which was still left on a table by his bed. He picked it up and skilfully forced the lock.

The box lid flew open. Sir Harvey made a little sound between his teeth. Inside there were brooches, necklaces, ear-rings and rings, all set with diamonds, emeralds and some very dark, very magnificent sapphires. They lay there glittering in the sea water which had percolated into the box.

Sir Harvey stared at them for a long moment, then very slowly he drew from his pocket the three strands of pearls he had taken from the dead woman's neck. They were almost flawless and as he held them in the warmth of his hands they seemed to glow with almost a supernatural light.

Very gently he tipped the water from the jewel case, placed the pearls on top of the other glittering gems and shut the box lid. Thrusting it beneath the mattress of his bed he threw off his wet breeches, wrapped himself in a blanket and pulled open the door of his room.

"*Signora! Signora!*" he called.

He could see below him in the kitchen that Paolina Mansfield was looking up at him, but he ignored her.

"*Signora!*" he called again, and now the fisherman's wife came running from the outhouse where she had been plucking a chicken

"What is it, *Signor?*" she enquired.

"I want my breeches dried again," he said. "And these other things too. And hurry, for I am wet and hungry and how can I eat if I cannot join you at the table?"

She chuckled at that.

"They shall be dried, *Signor*. Never worry, they shall be dry in a few minutes."

She hurried down the stairway with them. Sir Harvey closed the door after her, then he flung himself on his bed and stretched his hands behind his head. He could feel the jewel case below the thin mattress. It was hard and uncomfortable and stuck into his back, but he didn't mind. He was smiling as he lay there, smiling at a future which suddenly seemed bright and very different from what it had been first thing that morning.

Downstairs Paolina helped the Italian woman to spread the wet clothes in front of the fire. They both exclaimed

17

over the damage to the breeches Sir Harvey had been wearing when he boarded the ship. They were torn at the knees and the buckles had been wrenched away and looked as if they would really be of little use to him again.

The pair that had been salvaged from the ship were intact. Of white satin, they were unblemished save that they were wet, and the red satin coat was the same. It was of excellent material and the pearl buttons were undamaged as was the embroidery on the pockets and on the deep, turned-back cuffs.

"The *Signor* must be rich," the fisherman's wife said in awe. "His clothes are those of a nobleman."

"He is a nobleman," Paolina answered.

"And I have been addressing him as *Signor*, instead of Excellency," the fisherman's wife said. "But how was one to know? All men who are half drowned look the same."

"That is true," Paolina said. "And women, too, I suppose."

"Except when they are as beautiful as you," the Italian woman smiled. "When Gasparo carried you in, I thought you must be an angel come to visit poor sinners like ourselves."

"Hush, hush!" Paolina exclaimed. "I am only a woman like you. I wish that I were an angel. Then I should have no worries, no troubles."

"Wait until His Excellency has been fed and then you can discuss your problems with him. But take my advice and wait until after the meal. Men are never at their kindest when they are hungry."

Paolina laughed.

"No, that is true," she said.

"And now, *Signorina,* if you will watch the clothes, I will finish plucking the chicken or it will never be ready."

"I will do that," Paolina said. "And when they are dry I will take them up to him."

The woman hurried away. Paolina turned and re-turned the steaming clothes in front of the fire. They were not long in drying. The fire was hot and the material being thin they were soon completely dry if a little shrunk. She picked them up and put them over her arm and climbed, with a little difficulty, up the rickety stairway.

She knocked on the door. There was a moment's pause before there was an answer and she wondered if Sir Harvey was asleep.

"What is it?" he asked.

18

"I have brought your clothes," Paolina answered.

She heard him get off from the bed and she could hear him moving about before finally he came to the door and opened it. He was wearing his shirt and waistcoat, but the blanket was draped round him so that he looked so incongruous that she wanted to laugh. Nevertheless, it was with a serious face and downcast eyes that she presented him with his coat and breeches.

"Thank you," he said. "I am afraid I shall have no stockings, although at least I have managed to procure a pair of shoes."

"I am luckier than you are," Paolina answered. "My gown is torn, but at least it is intact."

She tried to smooth it with her hands as she spoke and he saw that she wore a simple, inexpensive dress which might have been chosen with good taste by someone who could not afford to spend a great deal of money. For the first time he wondered about her plight.

"What are you going to do?" he said. "Can I help you make arrangements to get away from here?"

She raised her eyes to his and he saw that they were troubled.

"I was going to ask you if you would advise me," she said.

"But of course," he replied. "Wait a moment while I get dressed and then we will talk about it. Tell the woman I want something to eat quickly and also a bottle of the best wine that the village can procure. Whatever it is, I expect it will be undrinkable."

"Can you afford to pay for it?"

The question surprised him and he answered:

"Of course! Do you imagine I should order it otherwise?"

"I am glad. . . . I mean, it seems so hard on them that we should accept their hospitality and be able to give nothing in return."

"You mean—you can give nothing in return?" Sir Harvey asked.

"I have not a single *sequin*," Paolina said. "Oh, please! What is to become of me?"

He saw that she was near to tears, and walking across to her laid his hand kindly on her shoulder.

"Go downstairs," he said. "Do as I have told you and tell the woman, too, that I want the village barber to come here and shave me."

He saw the trouble on her face and added, more kindly:
"Do not worry. We will think of something for you."

She flashed him a smile and then was gone.

Sir Harvey finished dressing; then, drawing the velvet box from beneath the mattress, he filled the big, voluminous pockets of his satin coat with its contents.

When the box was empty, he turned it upside down to be quite sure and going to the window he flung it as hard and far as he could out into the maize field which lay just beyond the narrow garden of the house. The box disappeared into a sea of green and then, with a little sigh of satisfaction, Sir Harvey, in waterlogged shoes, climbed slowly down the staircase to the kitchen below.

It was some time before he was able to talk to Paolina. The barber had come hurrying at his command, wine was brought for him to taste, and by the time he was shaved the chicken had been cooked and was ready to be eaten.

They sat down at the long table with Gasparo, his wife and his three sons; and, as if that was not enough, neighbours came peeping through the door and dropping in on the most feeble pretences merely to look at Gasparo's guests and to marvel how they had been saved from the terrible tempest of the night before.

Finally, however, the meal was finished, the bottles were empty. Gasparo and his wife settled themselves for their *siesta*. Even the dogs in the village seemed too drowsy to scratch. Everyone was asleep except Sir Harvey and Paolina.

They went outside and, leaving the village, walked a little along the cliffs until they were out of earshot of everyone except the seagulls.

"Now we can talk," Sir Harvey said, settling himself comfortably while Paolina sat down with a billowing out of her wide skirts, her little hands clasped in her lap, her face turned anxiously towards him.

From where he half sat, half lay, her head was silhouetted against the sky. Her hair was so golden, her skin so white, that he found himself staring in open-mouthed admiration. He had seen too many women to find his breath taken away by a new beauty. It had to be someone really startling, and he knew that unless he was still stupid from the buffeting of the night before, Paolina's beauty would, in the right setting, be absolutely sensational.

"Now we can make plans," he said after a moment,

realizing that she was expecting him to take the initiative. "We must not be long, for I have arranged with Gasparo, as soon as the *siesta* is over, to take me in his cart to the nearest town, where I can hire a carriage to carry me to Ferrara."

"And what are you going to do there?" Paolina asked.

"Well, the first thing I am going to do is to buy myself a pair of stockings," Sir Harvey smiled. "And after that a new suit. This one has shrunk until I can scarcely move my arms."

She said nothing, and after a moment he went on:

"If I can give you a lift as far as Ferrara, I shall, of course, be delighted. Where do your relatives live?"

"I have no relations."

He looked at her in surprise and then said:

"You mean you have no relations in Italy?"

"I have no relations anywhere."

"But that is absurd. You must have aunts or cousins, or even friends."

"I have nobody."

She made the statement simply, without self-pity.

"I cannot believe that."

"It is true. You see, my father has been ill for a long time. For reasons of his own he . . . he could not return to England."

Sir Harvey made a mental note that Captain Mansfield's past was a subject best avoided, but he said nothing except to remark:

"But you told me your mother was an Italian."

"Yes, but she died many years ago. She had been cut off by her family. My father ran away with her and they disowned her."

"But all these years you must have made friends, you must have met people."

"As I told you, my father has been ill. He had grown querulous and his friends drifted away. He had a few acquaintances, but none to whom I could turn for help."

"Well, let us get this clear," Sir Harvey said. "You mean that you have no money and nowhere to go?"

"That is it exactly."

"But dammit all! You must have some plans."

"I was hoping you would suggest something."

"Well, what can I suggest? What do you propose to do?"

"I do not know. You see, when I was with my father we

21

had . . . well, we had a little money, but it had nearly all gone. We just had enough to get to Venice, and after that . . ."

"Yes, after that?" Sir Harvey prompted. "What did you intend to live on?"

There was no answer, but Paolina turned her head away so that he could only see the lovely curve of one cheek, the sudden trembling of her tiny chin.

"What were your plans in Venice?" he insisted. "You must have had some idea of how you were going to manage?"

Still there was no answer and after a moment he said almost impatiently:

"You must be frank with me. How can I help you if I do not know the truth?"

"My father was . . . a . . . gambler." The words were only a whisper. "He lived by gambling, that was why we could never stay long in any particular place. Sooner or later he could not pay his debts."

Sir Harvey was silent. He knew only too well without words the precarious existence she must have lived, the recriminations, the rows, the insults she must have endured, as well as the terror of having to keep running away, to slip out unbeknownst before their debtors could catch up with them.

"An unfortunate story!" he said aloud. "You have my sympathy."

"Thank you," she answered with dignity.

"The difficulty is, of course, to suggest what you can do now. Have you any accomplishments?"

Paolina made a little gesture of helplessness.

"I can sew," she said. "I had thought that perhaps I could do a little embroidery when we were in Venice. That was unless . . . my father was unusually . . . successful. He seldom was."

"And if he was, it would not last long!" Sir Harvey said brutally. "How well one knows the story, and yet every gambler lives on hope, every gambler believes that things will change for him, if not today, tomorrow."

"I know, I know," Paolina said, and her head sank lower on her chest.

"She is exquisite," Sir Harvey thought, watching her. "Every pose, every gesture is more beautiful than the last."

"Would you like to go to England?" he asked.

Paolina raised her hands.

"How can I?" she asked. "And even if I went there, I know no-one. I have not been in London since I was five or six years of age."

"Then it appears you must stay in Italy."

Paolina clasped her hands together.

"I only wish I had died last night," she said. "How much better me than some of those other poor creatures who had so much more to live for. Why, why did you save me?"

She looked at him with eyes brimming with tears.

"It was instinct more than design," Sir Harvey said. "And now, having rescued you, I suppose I am responsible for you. There is a legend, isn't there, that if a man rescues another from death he must keep him for the rest of his life?"

His lip curled a little at the corners.

"Don't," Paolina begged. "Don't joke about it. I do not think I can bear it."

"But I am not joking," Sir Harvey replied. "I cannot allow you to starve. But before you throw in your lot with me I had best be frank about myself."

He paused a moment and waited. Her big eyes met his. He could see in them a sudden flicker of hope, and something else. Was it a question or merely a glint of curiosity?

"You see, my dear," he said drily, "I am what is known as an adventurer!"

2

"An adventurer!"

Paolina echoed the words and stared at Sir Harvey in amazement.

For the first time she noticed how good-looking he was—dark hair swept back from a sunburned face, grey eyes which, deep set beneath winged eyebrows, seemed to be permanently twinkling as if the whole world amused him. He had a firm chin, and his mouth, which curved slightly up at the corners, had a hint of steel about it.

"Yes, I am an adventurer," Sir Harvey repeated.

"But . . . I don't understand," Paolina insisted. "What does it mean?"

"It means, my dear," he said with a smile, "that I live on what wits it has pleased God to give me. Sometimes I live well, at other times my wits fail me and I sink to an almost unendurable poverty. Yesterday was one of those times—today everything is changed."

Paolina's smooth white brow wrinkled a little.

"But how can it have changed?" she said. "I must be very stupid, but it seems to me that you must have lost nearly everything you possessed in the storm, even as I have."

Sir Harvey laughed.

"That is where my wits have been most obliging. That and the fact that I could swim, which, fortunately, these fishermen have never learned to do."

"I do not understand," Paolina said.

"Then do not try," Sir Harvey answered. "But let me repeat that I will look after you. We will go to Venice together."

"But I cannot batten on you like that," Paolina protested. "If you will help me to find employment, then I shall be very grateful to you."

"And what could anybody as beautiful as you do?" Sir Harvey asked.

She flushed a little at his words and looked up to meet his eyes. The blush grew deeper.

"I have the perfect solution for your problem," Sir Harvey said as she did not speak. "You must get married."

"It is easy to say that," Paolina replied a little bitterly. "It is what my father used to say to me. But no-one in this country wants a bride without a dowry. So it is not surprising that during these years of flitting from one place to another no suitor has made me what one might call an honest offer."

"But doubtless there have been plenty of dishonest ones," Sir Harvey smiled. "Do not worry, my dear. I have told you that I will look after you."

Paolina put out her hand and laid it on his arm.

"You are being kind," she said. "I know that. And though I dare say it is wrong to confide in a stranger, I am telling you the truth. But you must tell me what you are suggesting I should do. It is frightening to be kept in the dark."

Sir Harvey laid his hand over hers. His fingers were strong and warm and Paolina resisted a temptation to cling to him.

"It is all very simple," he said quietly. "I am going to present you in Venice. You will meet the most influential and illustrious nobles. Venice is a city which appreciates beautiful women and one of them will undoubtedly offer you his hand in marriage."

"Until he learns that I am nobody, that I have no money . . ." Paolina said.

"He will not learn that until it is too late," Sir Harvey answered. "It may be unnecessary for him ever to learn it. You will go to Venice as my sister."

Paolina stared at him wide-eyed.

"Why?" she asked at length.

"Because, my dear, although I may be an adventurer, I come of a very decent family. The Drakes, dating back to my revered ancestor Sir Francis Drake, are respected in

25

Devon. The doors of Society will be open to me, and where I go you will accompany me."

"But . . . supposing . . . supposing they find out?" Paolina asked.

Sir Harvey shrugged his shoulders.

"There is no necessity to be fearful of that," he said. "One has taken greater risks in one's life. And besides, to put it bluntly, there is no other way in which we can travel together."

Paolina blushed again and her eyes fell before his. For a moment there was silence, but when she looked up at him again she found that he was still staring at her.

"In the right clothes you will be sensational," he said reflectively. "Blues and greens will be your best colours, though sometimes a touch of pink is effective with gold hair."

"How do you know all these things?" Paolina asked, bewildered.

"A rolling stone sometimes does gather moss," he answered. "A year or so ago I lived in Paris. A very beautiful and very famous actress honoured me with her favours. She graced the stage as no other woman has ever managed to do before at the *Comédie Française*. She allowed me to accompany her when she chose her gowns. I learned a lot of what is important if a woman would look her best."

"How clever you are!" Paolina exclaimed.

"I am honoured that you think so," Sir Harvey answered, and his eyes seemed to twinkle more merrily than usual as he added: "That is just the right tone of voice in which to speak to a man. Admiration is, of course, the sincerest form of flattery!"

"You make it sound as if I were doing it for effect," Paolina retorted a little petulantly.

"Don't you understand that is exactly what you must do?" Sir Harvey answered. "My dear, you are already very lovely, but real beauty is a thing of art. I am going to take the raw material which God has given you and turn you into something so exquisite that a man will be prepared to pay any price for the privilege of possessing you."

Paolina looked away from him to where the sea shimmered blue beneath the warmth of the sun.

"Will love have anything to do with it?" she asked in a very low voice.

26

"Love is something which invariably flies out of the window when poverty comes in at the door," Sir Harvey answered, and his voice was harsh. "For love one needs comfort, luxurious surroundings, soft music, perfumes, wines and well-cooked food. When you have all those things, Paolina, you can think of love."

She did not answer, but there was something in the sudden drooping of her shoulders and the wistfulness of her eyes which made him say:

"Do not be afraid. I will not force you to marry someone who is repulsive to you. But once you have a rich and noble husband you will find you have plenty of time on your hands to seek for love."

"I would wish that I could marry the man I loved, or love the man I must marry," Paolina said.

Sir Harvey threw back his head.

"You are asking too much. Like everyone else in the world you are greedy. Nature gives with one hand and she takes with the other. She has given you beauty but no money with which to deck it. She has endowed me with poverty but has given me wits to make the most of every opportunity. We must be content with what we have. Dream your dreams if you must, little Paolina, but remember that wealth, security and a good position mean more in old age than all the heartbreaks of an unsubstantial love."

"You are cynical," Paolina accused him.

"I do not think so," Sir Harvey replied quite seriously. "It is just that I have loved so many women and found that sooner or later they all begin to pall upon me. It is easy for a man in those circumstances to take up his hat and go. But for a woman, she has only a few years in which she has something worthwhile to sell in exchange for a ring upon her finger."

Paolina jumped to her feet.

"You are horrid!" she stormed. "Love is not like that. It is not cruel, hard and ugly, grasping greedily for payment. It is gentle, sweet and tender. And when it comes, then the world is well lost. Kisses cannot be calculated in cash. Nothing will make me believe otherwise. I . . . I will not go with you."

She stood trembling with the intensity of her feelings. Sir Harvey rose slowly to his feet. Then he reached out his hands and held her by the shoulders.

"So fiery, and all about nothing. If you will not come

27

with me, what will become of you? Will you stay here? Your beauty will not last long if you work among the vines."

"You are laughing at me," Paolina said with a sudden sob in her voice.

"For your own good," Sir Harvey replied. "You have got to awake from your dreams and face reality. Let us be sensible about this. I have told you the truth; I have told you what I intend to do. If you will not accept it, then our ways must part."

"Would you leave me here alone?" Paolina asked tremulously.

"I am afraid so," he answered. "You see, as I have already told you, I am an adventurer, and quite ruthless if people interfere or do not co-operate with me. I am going to Venice. I am prepared to take my sister with me, but I am not interested in encumbering myself with any other sort of relationship."

Paolina shook herself free of his hands and stamped her foot.

"You are impossible," she said. "Do you think I am suggesting that I should go with you as . . . as . . ."

Words failed her. Sir Harvey laughed and put out his hand to lift her chin towards his.

"You grow lovelier every moment," he said. "Even in a rage you are entrancing. But we must be rid of those badly made clothes, and I cannot believe that the sun is good for your skin. Come back to the house. We will be able to leave in another half-hour."

"You are quite sure that I will come with you, aren't you?" Paolina asked.

He laughed again.

"You have little alternative," he answered. "If you change your mind when we get to Ferrara, I can leave you there. Perhaps you would find enough sewing to keep body and soul together, but I cannot help feeling that having once set eyes on you the gentleman of Ferrara might have very different ideas."

"I must come with you, I see that," Paolina said. "And I am grateful even though I am afraid."

"Of me or of the future?" Sir Harvey asked.

"Of both," she answered. "But mostly of you, I think."

"Perhaps I have been unkind to you," he conceded. "But I wanted you to face facts and I would not insult you by trying to pull wool over your eyes. I shall, to put it bluntly, sell you to the highest bidder, and I assure you I, personally, shall do extremely well out of the deal."

"But, supposing . . . supposing after all this I am a failure?" Paolina asked. "Supposing nobody wants me and I am left on your hands?"

"Then I must find another way of getting rid of you—" Sir Harvey said. "I can, of course, always drop you into the Lagoon on a dark night."

His smile and the twinkle in his eyes told Paolina that he was teasing her. She had a sudden feeling that beneath all his cynicism and flippancy he was kind and that whatever else happened he would not abandon her completely.

They were now walking towards the village and she laid her hand on his arm.

"I trust you," she said. "I do not quite know why; and though you may not believe it, it is not entirely because I must. Something in my heart tells me that I can really trust you."

"Then, of course, you should follow your heart," Sir Harvey said. "Except where it interferes with my plans for your marriage."

"I . . . can only pray that you will choose me someone I can at least . . . respect," Paolina faltered.

"Venice is filled with nobles of every sort and description," Sir Harvey replied. "Yet from what I have heard it is not a place where one would go looking for great nobility of character. It is a city of merry-making and of amusement. I will promise you a gay husband—someone who will make you laugh, someone who will make your life one of endless entertainment. You will travel gaily in the great golden gondola in which every bride goes to her wedding—but I cannot promise that you will respect your bridegroom."

"It sounds better than I imagined," Paolina said.

"Stop imagining anything," Sir Harvey commanded. "Women always imagine the worst and never the best. Be like me and take things as they come. Who knows what adventure or what excitement tomorrow may bring? Why, who knows, you may fall in love with the Doge and he with you."

"But, surely the Doge is always a very old man?" Paolina answered quickly, and then said accusingly: "You are laughing at me again."

"That is because you are too serious," he answered. "If you are going to be a success in Venice, you have got to learn to find everything, including yourself, a joke."

"The whole idea terrifies me," Paolina said.

She walked into the house where they had stayed the night, to find Gasparo and his wife arousing themselves from their *siesta*. And yet, even so, it was some time before the cart, drawn by an under-nourished mule, was ready; and then quite a time was passed in saying a farewell.

"I am afraid I cannot pay you in money for your hospitality," she heard Sir Harvey say to Gasparo. "All I possessed was lost in the ship. But will you accept this precious stone? It is a sapphire of good quality and will, if you sell it to a reputable dealer, provide you with a decent sum to save against your old age."

"You are more than generous, *Signor*," Gasparo cried, taking the stone in his hands. "The ship has brought a wealth to the village, which is very welcome. Any hospitality that I have been able to offer you in my poor house was given without a thought of reward."

There was a final exchange of courtesies and finally they were off. Only as they rattled away from the village down the rutted road did Paolina turn to Sir Harvey and whisper:

"Is it true that you have no money? What shall we do for food and accommodation?"

"You must leave such matters to me," Sir Harvey answered. "And you need not whisper, my dear. The man who is driving us has no knowledge of our native tongue."

Paolina smiled.

"I forgot that I was talking English," she said. "I have grown so used to speaking both languages."

"It is useful," he said, "that you can speak Italian. It would have complicated my task a good deal had I escorted an English girl who had not a word of any language save her own.

"How did you learn to speak so well?" Paolina asked.

Sir Harvey looked at her out of the corner of his eye and then said:

"My instructress was very attractive!"

Paolina blushed.

"Oh, I understand," she said hastily. "So you learnt French and Italian in much the same way. Have you also a knowledge of German?"

"No, I regret my German is not very fluent," Sir Harvey

30

answered. "But I am extremely grateful to a certain lady who sang German opera like an angel in that she has made certain things possible both for you and me."

"What do you mean by that?" Paolina asked, puzzled.

Sir Harvey did not answer but sat with his hand deep in his coat pocket running the diamonds and pearls slowly between his fingers.

Their journey to Ferrara was tiring but uneventful and they reached the city just as it grew dusk and its great spires and towers were silhouetted against the deepening sky. Its history seemed to be written in the narrow mediaeval streets around the Cathedral, while the magnificent buildings made Paolina stare about her in wonder. She had not expected anything so impressive.

"Where are we going?" she asked in a low voice as the coach in which they now travelled turned down a busy street.

"To the best hostelry," Sir Harvey answered. "And remember that your name is Mistress Paolina Drake."

The coach came to a standstill. He descended and walked into the inn calling imperiously for the landlord. A man came running and stared with astonishment at Sir Harvey's rather disreputable appearance.

"Your very best rooms, my good fellow," Sir Harvey said in a voice of authority. "My sister and I have been shipwrecked upon your accursed shores. Our baggage has been lost, we have been drenched with sea water and carried here in the acme of discomfort over your execrable roads."

"What a disaster, Your Excellency!" the landlord exclaimed.

"Show us to our rooms, and pray Heaven the beds are comfortable," Sir Harvey commanded. "Cook a meal which is palatable and bring up the best wine you have in your cellar. I also require the attendance of the most reputable tailor and the best dressmaker in the city to attend upon us immediately."

The inn-keeper was obviously impressed by Sir Harvey's manner.

"*Si, si, Excellency*," he answered. "Everything shall be as you have ordered. My best rooms are fortunately empty. They are large and comfortable. The Duke of Parma himself occupied them only last week and praised their luxury. If your Excellency will condescend to follow me. . . ."

Sir Harvey and Paolina followed him up the narrow staircase and were shown into two well-furnished and airy rooms on the first floor. There was a sitting-room opening out of them, but when Paolina was about to exclaim that they were charming Sir Harvey silenced her with a glance.

"Are these your very best?" he enquired in tones of disdain.

"Excellency, they are the finest rooms in all Ferrara. Everyone who is of importance stays here if they are not the guest of Her Highness the Princess d'Este or His Grace the Duke of Ferrara. Only last month——"

"That will be enough," Sir Harvey said. "If this is the best you can do, then we shall perforce have to accept them. Hurry now with the wine, and do not forget that I require the most skillful tailor in the city."

"To hear is to obey, Your Excellency," the landlord said. Then as he reached the door Sir Harvey said:

"I wish also to see a jeweller. Is there one you can recommend?"

"But *si, Excellency*. There is no-one who has not heard of Farusi. Everyone consults him when they come to Ferrara. The Princess d'Este's diamonds were recently re-set to his design. He is famous—famous, Excellency, over the whole Plain of Lombardy."

"Then tell him to attend me within an hour," Sir Harvey commanded.

"But, Excellency, Farusi does not always come from his shop. Clients go to him."

Sir Harvey drew himself up.

"Tell Farusi that if he wants business with Sir Harvey Drake of England, he must come here. Otherwise I shall take my custom elsewhere."

"Very good, very good, Excellency."

The landlord bowed and hurried from the room. As he closed the door, Paolina turned towards Sir Harvey.

"You were magnificent," she said. "But why should you want the jeweller?"

"Do not ask me that question," Sir Harvey answered. "The dressmaker will be here soon and we must concentrate on choosing gowns which will make even the Venetians stare."

"It is all going to cost a great deal of money," Paolina said in an awed voice.

"A sprat to catch a mackerel," Sir Harvey answered.

"The mackerel being the rich nobleman who is to ask for my hand in marriage," Paolina said, and there were two dimples in her cheeks. "I wonder if he has any premonition what fate, or rather you, have in store for him."

"Now you are beginning to enjoy this adventure!" Sir Harvey smiled. "I am glad of that."

"I think it would be difficult for me not to enjoy it," Paolina answered. "It is only that I find myself trembling because I am so afraid that I shall fail you."

"You will not do that if you leave everything in my hands," Sir Harvey answered. "All you have to do is to look beautiful and do as I tell you."

"What you need is a doll, not a woman," Paolina retorted.

He laughed at that and then taking her hand raised it to his lips.

"You are far more amusing than any doll could possibly be," he said. "Nevertheless, such an idea has its points."

Three hours later Paolina began to wish that she was, in fact, a doll and did not have the ordinary feelings and fatigues of a young woman. Her head was drooping with weariness, her body still ached from the buffeting that she had experienced the night before; but while her bed waited invitingly for her in the next room, Sir Harvey would not let her go.

She must stand while rolls of silk, satin, brocade, lamé and gauze were draped over her shoulders, twisted round her waist and tried against the texture of her skin.

The conversation between Sir Harvey and the dressmaker had long since ceased to make any sense to her. She was so tired that she felt if she lay down on the floor she would be able to go to sleep.

Yet still they talked on, looking at sketches and then discarding them, deciding on this coloured satin and then finding another which they declared was of a better hue. There was talk of shoes, silk stockings, of mantles and petticoats, of bonnets and gloves, until Paolina's head whirled and the whole conversation became an unintelligible jumble of words.

The whole business of choosing gowns had taken so long because Sir Harvey was continually being called away. His tailor had been given instructions which had not taken long, but which had also involved the showing of brocades

33

and satins, of embroidered waistcoats, the choosing of sparkling buttons and antique lace.

Then, when once again he had returned to Paolina and the dressmaker, a servant had come to announce that Farusi was waiting to see him. Sir Harvey had gone from the room and Paolina had wondered again why he should want a jeweller. Surely he was not so crazy as to expend the money about which he was so mysterious on anything so extravagant as jewels?

And yet where was the money? she wondered. One moment he said he had it and the next minute spoke as if he had not a *sequin* to bless himself with.

On thinking it over she realized that she had not seen him expend even the smallest coin since they first met. She had expected that he would stop for food along the road to Ferrera, but he had made no suggestion of it and there had been no question of their eating or drinking until they arrived, at nearly eight o'clock, at the hostelry.

She had been forced to admit that the meal had then been worth waiting for and the wine was good enough to make Sir Harvey order another bottle after the very first sip.

"How strange it all is!" Paolina thought to herself as she sat on the stiff sofa and looked at the sketches the dressmaker showed her and waited for Sir Harvey to return.

He came back in about twenty minutes and she knew by the expression on his face that something had pleased him greatly.

"And now, my dear, to concentrate on your wardrobe," he said.

"It is getting late," Paolina answered. "Would it not be better to postpone it until tomorrow?"

"No, no. We have no time to waste. We want these gowns as soon as possible. We cannot stay in Ferrara indefinitely. Now for another evening gown."

He pulled out a length of silver lamé which Paolina had set aside as being far too expensive and insisted on ordering a whole gown of it.

"But, how can we afford it?" she asked in English, almost beneath her breath.

"You would be surprised at what we can afford," he answered.

The dressmaker, with an order which made her eyes protrude and her lips wet with excitement, packed up her materials and was ready to take her leave.

"I give you just one week," Sir Harvey told her. "Anything that is not ready in that time will be cancelled. Is that understood?"

"Perfectly, Excellency. All shall be ready. It is a pleasure to dress anyone so beautiful as your lady sister."

The woman curtsied and withdrew and Sir Harvey turned to Paolina who had sunk down upon her bed.

"You are tired," he said. "We shall both sleep well tonight and with an easy conscience. The first step is accomplished. We can afford to take all the others that lie ahead."

"It is all right, then, about the money?" Paolina asked.

She felt it was indiscreet to ask the question and yet she could not help it. She was so used to worrying over her father's finances, and she was half afraid that Sir Harvey would tell her that this was all a dream. Suppose, she thought in terror, they must slip away in the dead of the night because they could not pay for what they had already ordered?

"I have told you not to worry your little head about money," Sir Harvey said.

He drew something from his pocket and held it out towards her. She looked at it through eyes dull with fatigue and then suddenly gave an exclamation of excitement.

It was a string of pearls he held between his fingers—a single row, perfectly matched, with a clasp that seemed somehow too big for it.

"Pearls!" she exclaimed.

"For you," he said.

"For me!"

With a cry of sheer delight her hands went out towards them, and then dropped to her sides.

"But, I cannot take them," she said. "They must have cost a fortune, and you will need the money."

"If we need it, then our capital is there safely round your neck," he said. "And think of the impression they will cause. They are pearls of the very finest quality. I have it on very good authority."

"They are beautiful," Paolina said. "But . . ."

"There are no buts," Sir Harvey answered. "They are yours and I want you to wear them."

"Is that why you sent for the jeweller?" Paolina asked.

35

"One reason," he answered. "But do not waste time asking questions. Let me put them round your neck."

She bent her graceful head towards him and he clasped the pearls round the warm ivory column of her throat. They shone there against her skin—warm, slightly pink, with that subtle lustre which reminded her of the first fingers of dawn in the sky. She put her fingers against them wonderingly, then walked across the room to look in the mirror on the dressing-table.

"I never thought I would ever wear pearls," she said wonderingly.

"They become you," he answered.

She turned round and ran towards him with a little impulsive gesture.

"Oh, thank you! Thank you!" she said.

She stood, sparkling and almost dancing with excitement before him, all her fatigue forgotten, her eyes alight with the thrill of her first jewels.

He stood staring at her and, surprisingly, his expression was grave. Then he bent his head and kissed her cheek.

"Good night, little sister," he said, and walked from the room, shutting the door behind him.

Paolina went back to the dressing-table and stared at the pearls. She had a feeling they were suddenly heavy and that if she were wise she would tear them from her. She imagined for a moment that she was a helpless prisoner and that they were chains dragging her at a chariot wheel. Then she shook her thoughts from her and concentrated on seeing how well the necklace became her, how it seemed to make her beauty even more precious because of its own intrinsic value.

Slowly she undressed, glancing every other second into the mirror; then finally she slipped between the cool sheets of the curtained bed and laid her weary head down on the pillow.

She should have slept at once, but now that she was able to rest she no longer wanted to. Her thoughts were going round and round in circles.

She found herself remembering her father; the last long year when he had been ill. She tried to think of him with affection; instead, she could only remember his querulousness, his impatience, his raised voice, the times when he cursed her again and again because she did not do exactly what he wanted.

Before that she could remember only the long days and

nights when she was alone in some lodging-house or disreputable inn, locked in her room, waiting for his return from the club or casino.

How miserable her life had been, how utterly empty of friendship or kindness! Those awful times when they must creep away without paying people who trusted them; perhaps people who had been kind because they had been sorry for her.

And her father had never cared. It seemed as if the cards had killed every spark of decency in him so that he had gambled away not only their money but his very soul. They journeyed to town after town, some big, some small, chosen only because there were facilities for gaming; and as their money ran out, their lodging became more and more squalid and more disreputable.

And then had come her father's illness—a kind of rheumatic fever which had left him semi-paralysed so that his hands could not hold the cards. That had been more terrible than anything, when the only thing he craved for, the only drug that could alleviate his sufferings, was denied him.

They had gone from physician to physician, paying none of them, hurrying on when the bill got too big or when they were pressed to meet their debts. And then at last her father had decided that he must go to Venice. Someone had spoken to him of how amusing the gambling was, how high the play.

He had fretted and fumed until, quite unexpectedly, a letter had arrived from England containing money. It had been a very small legacy from a distant cousin which had been following them around for some months. It was not a very large sum and Paolina had suggested that they should spend it cautiously. Unfortunately the only thing which her father could think of was that the money would at least pay their fares to Venice.

"What will happen when we get there?" she had asked.

"I shall make money, do not worry about that," he answered confidently.

How well she knew that tone of voice, that eager hope, that greediness in his eyes, that utter indifference to anything and everything except the game which lay ahead of him!

She had pleaded with him, she had even gone down on her knees to beg him to see reason; but he had cursed her and told her to obey him. She knew now that it was im-

37

possible for her to mourn him. Even when he died last night, before the storm became really dangerous, she had not been able to force herself to feel anything but a sadness that he had died without a prayer or a priest to help him.

She thought perhaps the misery she had suffered these past years had numbed her heart. She wondered why she had ever bothered to speak to Sir Harvey of love. What did love mean to her? She felt as if her whole being had dried up and turned to ice inside her.

As a child she had desperately wanted to love. She had tried to love her father because he was all she had. She had lavished all her childlike affection upon him, believing that he must reciprocate because she loved him so deeply. Gradually she had begun to realize that it had meant nothing to him.

In her childhood she was just a tiresome encumbrance that he must take about with him because he could think of nothing else to do with her. As she became older she became of more use to him. She could cook when they could not afford to eat at restaurants; she could mend and press his clothes; she could even clean his shoes and go hurrying to the pawn shop when they were down to their last penny and money had to be procured from somewhere.

He had never loved her! Never! Never! Paolina found her pillow was suddenly wet with tears. She tried to laugh at herself for being so stupid. She ought to have got over this long ago. She had cried about it often enough and finally had told herself that she would weep no more but would grow as hard and indifferent to the world as the world seemed to her.

And yet how grateful she should be. If Sir Harvey had not taken her under his wing, what would have become of her? She thought perhaps she should have died in the storm, and then knew, because she was young, because she was afraid of death, that she was thankful to be alive.

She felt the thought tingling through her body, down to her very toes—she was alive. There were excitements ahead of her and Sir Harvey to protect her.

"I am grateful, I am," she whispered, and wiped her eyes fiercely in the darkness, ashamed of her own weakness.

Then she put her hands to the pearls that she wore round her neck. He had given them to her. It was the first present she had ever had from a man, the first jewels she had ever owned. Pearls—and worth a king's ransom!

She felt as if her heart was overflowing with something

that was warmer and more responsive than ever gratitude can be. Why had she not thanked him more fulsomely? Then she remembered that she had had an irresistible impulse to fling her arms round his neck and kiss him.

She felt herself blush in the darkness. Thank goodness she had not done so. It would certainly not have been the behaviour he would have expected from his little sister!

3

Paolina awoke feeling as if she had slept so deeply that she might have been drugged. But even as she stirred she knew that her tiredness had, for the most part, vanished.

Her legs were still a little stiff from the buffeting of the waves and she had seen last night that there were a number of bruises coming out on her white body. But otherwise she was unharmed, and with the elasticity of youth she was suddenly gloriously and joyously thrilled to be alive.

As she lay there letting the events of the past day seep into her mind, she heard a church clock strike the hour. It was midday.

With a sense of guilt she jumped out of bed and ran to the window, throwing back the heavy shutters to let in the sunshine.

Outside she could see the great, round cupola of a church ornamented with statues, and around it were the colourful tiled roofs of the high houses which bordered the narrow streets. Above them flew, fluttered or perched hundreds of grey and white pigeons.

She stood there entranced, forgetting for a moment her haste. She felt in that moment that her spirit was one with the birds winging into the blue of the sky. She was alive and there was adventure just around the corner.

She crossed the room, rang the bell for hot water, and when it came started to bathe herself. The maid who attended her also brought her a cup of hot chocolate. When she had drunk it, Paolina asked:

"Where is His Excellency . . . my . . . my brother, this morning?"

She flushed as she spoke the lie. The maid's eyes lit up.

40

"His Excellency has gone out, *Signorina*. He called for a carriage and four horses. We all felt it must be to make a visit of great import."

Paolina, knowing that Italians loved to romance about any action, however trivial, did not think that the fact that Sir Harvey had asked for four horses was of great significance. She was only thankful that he was not waiting for her, angry at her laziness in sleeping so late and already finding her a nuisance.

When the maid had left, she dressed quickly. She found herself pondering with a clear brain the amazing trend of events which had brought her to where she was. It seemed incredible, somehow, that yesterday she should have been orphaned and utterly penniless, and today she had a protector who asked nothing more than that she should pose as his sister.

Paolina was not ignorant of the world. She had lived too long with her father, meeting undesirable people, listening to Casino gossip, not to know only too well to what depths women must sink rather than that they should starve.

As she fastened her gown, she thought how lucky she was to have found someone so kind and understanding as Sir Harvey. She was still thinking of him when she heard a noise in the sitting-room and guessed that he had returned.

Hurriedly she opened the door and saw him standing there, resplendent in a new coat of turquoise blue velvet over breeches of an almost dazzling whiteness. He also wore a sword, the handle of which glittered and shone with every movement he made.

"Oh, but your clothes have come!" she exclaimed, forgetting in her excitement even to make him a curtsy or to wish him a courteous good morning.

She liked the smile which twisted his lips and twinkled in his eyes.

"Do women ever think of anything but clothes?" he asked teasingly. "One of your gowns will be here within the hour."

"Oh, how did you manage it? How could they have made it so quickly?" Paolina asked.

Sir Harvey crossed the room and poured himself a glass of wine from a decanter which stood on a side table. She noticed that he wore his hair in the new fashion, unpowdered and tied simply with a black ribbon.

"You will learn, my dear," he said, "that anything is possible if one has enough money."

Paolina gave a little exclamation.

"That was something which I wished to speak with you about last night," she said. "But I was too tired. I wanted to protest about all the things you were ordering for me. I do not dare to think of what the cost will be. I should not . . . I cannot accept so much."

"What I am spending on you," Sir Harvey replied, "is in the nature of an investment. I am but loaning you that which I shall expect you to repay."

Paolina went a little pale.

"And suppose I cannot do that?" she said.

"You will be able to," he answered confidently. "Have you not looked at your face in the mirror this morning?"

She glanced up at him wonderingly, realized that he was paying her a compliment, and blushed.

"You are very kind," she said. "But suppose no-one offers for me, what then?"

"They will," Sir Harvey said. "I shall make sure of it. I have this morning left my card on the Duke of Ferrara. I expect we shall have an invitation to the Castle."

Paolina clasped her hands together.

"Do not speak of it," she begged. "Can you not understand that in such places I should be entirely out of my depth? Yesterday you swept me off my feet; when I listened to this fantastic, wild plan of yours, you made everything sound so easy. But today I can see sense. It is impossible. It would never work. Please send me away before I disgrace you."

Sir Harvey carried a glass of wine across the room and put it in her hand. Then he raised his own glass.

"Let us drink," he said, "to your marriage, and to the comfort it will undoubtedly bring both of us."

Paolina stared at him and made no attempt to raise the glass to her lips.

"I am . . . afraid," she whispered.

"Forget your fears," Sir Harvey said. "We have many more important things to do at the moment."

"What sort of things?" Paolina asked.

Sir Harvey drank off the wine and put his glass down.

"We are about," he said, "to start your lessons."

Paolina stared at him and he continued:

"You are quite right to feel afraid that you might do the wrong thing. Anyone who has not been educated in the highest Society would naturally find it impossible to know all the rules and regulations, the curtsies and the etiquette

42

that distinguishes someone of noble birth from the mere commoner."

He made her a courtly bow.

"It is these things, my dear, that you have got to learn—and quickly. I let you sleep late this morning so that you should be particularly clear-headed. But this afternoon we have to work."

"Tell me exactly what I have to learn," Paolina begged timidly.

"You must know how to enter a drawing-room," he replied; "how to curtsy to a lady of rank, to a nobleman, to a Duke or a Duchess or a Princess of the Royal blood. You have got to learn to extend your hand in just the right gestures to someone you would encourage and to someone you wish to discard. There are a hundred ways of using a fan, of speaking without words. And there are also a dozen ways of saying good-bye to your hostess when you leave a party—but only one is the right one."

"Shall I ever be able to learn all these things?" Paolina asked.

"You have got to," Sir Harvey answered, and his voice was grim.

Immediately after their midday meal the instruction began. And in all her life Paolina had never met such an exacting taskmaster. For hours she walked across the room, entering through the door, curtsying to Sir Harvey who sat at the far end, and then bidding him farewell and leaving by the way in which she came.

Again and again he sent her back to repeat it until her back ached and her eyes filled with tears at the humiliation of being so incompetent as not to portray immediately what he required of her.

"No, no! Your curtsy to the Princess would be deeper, much deeper. Keep your chin up! Your hands are extremely ungraceful."

Up; down; down; up. And always his voice commanding her to do it again and yet again. When she felt her knees would crack if she curtsied once more, he allowed her to sit down and started to instruct her in the right methods of address. And after that came a lesson in using a fan as only a Venetian woman would use it.

"How do you know all these things?" Paolina asked at length when the afternoon was far advanced and still there were other things for her to learn and other actions she must practise.

"I was a page at the Court of King George," he replied briefly. "My father was Lord-in-Waiting to His Majesty, and almost before I could walk I learned to bow in the correct manner."

"They did not teach you to use a fan," Paolina said with a little hint of laughter in her voice.

"No, that I learned from a very lovely Venetian woman the last time I visited Venice."

"Is that a long time ago?" Paolina asked.

"A long time," he replied. "But I have always wanted to go back to the City of Pleasure, the city where anything can happen and everybody laughs all the time."

"And yet they are so particular about etiquette," Paolina said.

"I would rather they laughed with you than at you," he answered.

She made a little grimace at that and once again ran through the modes of address for an Abbé, a Cardinal, the wife of a reigning Duke, the Dogaressa. She stopped suddenly.

"Do you really think I am likely to meet all these people?" she enquired.

"Most certainly," Sir Harvey answered. "That is the very reason why we are going to Venice."

Paolina made a little gesture of despair.

"I shall fail you, I am sure of it," she said. "And then someone will be clever enough to guess that I cannot possibly be your sister but am an imposter, someone you have picked up out of the gutter—or, rather, out of the sea."

Sir Harvey bent forward and put his hand on hers.

"You are doing splendidly," he said. "But you are tired of learning so you shall now have your recreation. Go and put on the gown that is waiting for you in the other room."

"May I?"

Paolina sprang to her feet, her eyes alight. Woman-like she had been bitterly conscious as she walked backwards and forwards across the room of the drabness of her gown, which was faded and cockled after its bath in the sea. And, anyway, even if it had been fresh and unsoiled it would have contrasted badly with Sir Harvey's new magnificence.

She felt her heart jump with excitement as she saw what was lying on the bed. It was a gown of stiff blue satin, embroidered with tiny flowers, and the wide frame which held out the panniers on either side made her waist seem

44

tiny and accentuated the gentle swelling of her breasts. There was a fichu of exquisite lace and the gown was ornamented with tiny bows caught with little diamanté buckles, each of which also held a silk rose.

It transformed Paolina and when, with the help of the maid whom she had summoned to assist her, she had got it on, she stared at herself in amazement.

"It is beautiful, *Signorina!* Really beautiful!" the maid exclaimed, not once but over and over again, and Paolina could not but agree with her.

There were shoes to match the dress and little lace ribbons to fall from her hair at the back.

"Bella! Bella!" the maid murmured.

And then Paolina crossed the bed-chamber to return to the sitting-room. As she put her hand on the door, she hesitated. Somehow she was shy—shy of showing herself, and she knew the real reason was that she wanted Sir Harvey to be pleased with her appearance.

"His Excellency will think you beautiful," the maid was murmuring behind her, and with an effort Paolina pulled open the door and entered the room.

She had expected to find Sir Harvey sitting in the chair where she had left him. She planned to herself that she would walk in exactly as he had instructed her to do, with her head held high, and then proceeding until she faced him, she would sink at his feet in the deepest curtsy of all—the one reserved for a Royal Prince.

When she entered the room, she found, to her consternation, that Sir Harvey was not alone. He was, indeed, sitting almost where she had left him. But there was another man beside him and both had glasses of wine in their hands. She would have withdrawn the moment she realized that Sir Harvey was engaged, but he looked up and saw her and it was too late.

"Ah, Paolina!" he said. "We have a visitor."

He beckoned her forward and then, as she reached his side, said to the man who had risen:

"Your Grace, may I present my sister?"

As if manipulated by a master hand, Paolina sank down in a deep curtsy, and as she rose Sir Harvey said:

"The Duke of Ferrara has most graciously invited us to sup with him tonight."

"That is very . . . kind of Your . . . Grace," Paolina managed to stammer.

"I was sorry to hear that your ship was wrecked," the

Duke said kindly. "When I learned of your misfortune I came in person to see if there was anything I could do to assist you. I am only so glad to see that neither of you are injured. I was ready to put my personal physician at your disposal."

"We are, by the grace of Providence, unharmed," Sir Harvey said. "My sister must, of course, take things easily for a day or two. After that we shall proceed to Venice."

"I, also, am going to Venice at the end of the week," the Duke said. "I hope you will honour me by travelling with me in my *burchiello*—and I assure you that every precaution will be taken to see that we all get there safely."

"That is indeed kind of you," Sir Harvey murmured.

Paolina, meeting the Duke's eyes, lowered her own and said nothing. She felt a sudden stab of fear. Was this the man, she asked herself, whom Sir Harvey was choosing for her as a future husband? If so, she knew that she could not go through with it.

It was not that the Duke was repulsive. He was tall, with clear-cut, aristocratic features, and although he was middle-aged he still had a slim figure. But there was something about him which for no tangible reason Paolina disliked.

"I cannot do it! I cannot do it!" she wanted to say aloud, and then thought how ridiculous she was being. Was it likely that the Duke of Ferrara, one of the most important and distinguished men in Italy, would even so much as look at her, whoever she might pretend to be?

The Duke was making his farewells.

"I shall see you both this evening," he said. "My carriage will be at your disposal and I shall look forward to welcoming you to my Castle."

Paolina curtsied, still without saying anything, and then Sir Harvey escorted the Duke down the stairs to where his carriage was waiting in the courtyard. When he returned he was frowning.

"Can you not be a little more gracious?" he asked. "Surely you could have told him with your eyes, if not with words, how much you were looking forward to seeing him again."

"But I wasn't," Paolina said simply.

"Odds fish! But isn't that a woman all over?" Sir Harvey said in an exasperated tone. "Here we have the chance of dining in one of the most magnificent Castles in Italy—the

46

place is a veritable treasure-house, I am told—and you say you would rather not. What is the matter with you?"

"I have told you, I am afraid," Paolina answered.

"Then forget your fears. There is nothing worse than a woman who is so gauche or so stupid that she cannot make herself pleasant to a man who is obviously attracted by her."

"That is the whole point," Paolina said. "I do not want him to be attracted by me."

Sir Harvey put back his head and laughed.

"Good lord!" he said. "I had no idea you were so conceited or so puffed up with yourself. Beautiful you may be, but even I, in my wildest dreams, never aspired as high as the Duke. Why, he has been the despair of every match-making mamma for the last twenty-five years."

He put his hand under her chin and turned her face up to his.

"No, you can consider yourself quite safe there. He has, as a matter of fact, a fair charmer in Rome to whom I believe he is devoted. She sings at the Opera House. When she is not singing, I believe she proves a very expensive plaything as far as the Duke is concerned. At any rate, the emeralds that he gave her last time I was in the Eternal City were fabled to have cost more than the whole income from the Duke's vineyards the previous year."

He released her and Paolina felt her spirits lightening. At the same time, she was ashamed at having been so stupid.

"I am sorry," she apologized. "I was afraid and that was why I behaved so stupidly."

"Afraid of what?" Sir Harvey enquired.

"That you would make me marry the Duke whether I wanted to or not," she answered almost tearfully.

He laughed.

"No, no, my dear. We will not set our cap so high as that. That would be a prize beyond prizes. But there are plenty of less difficult suitors and we hope that maybe you will learn to smile at them with just that hint of an invitation on your lips and in your eyes."

"More things to learn," Paolina pouted.

He turned away almost as if he were irritated.

"If you really regret what we are doing," he said, "you are, of course, always free to leave my company."

Paolina stood very still. Then suddenly she was at his

47

side, her hand on his arm, looking up at him with the face of a frightened child.

"You do not really wish to be rid of me?" she asked.

He looked down at her but his expression was grim.

"If you stay, you must do what I want of you," he answered. "I am gambling everything on one throw."

Paolina twisted her fingers together.

"You mean . . . that you are . . . spending all your money on the chance that I shall . . . marry well? Is this risk fair to you?"

"I am prepared to take it," Sir Harvey answered.

She thought of the Duke and the expression she had seen in his eyes and felt herself shiver. If it was not to be him, would she feel any different about another man whose only eligibility in Sir Harvey's eyes would be that he was wealthy?

Then she remembered that she had no alternative. Either she went with Sir Harvey, throwing her lot in with his, or she went alone to discover what sort of living she could make with nothing but her looks to recommend her.

"Either way it seems I sell myself," she murmured beneath her breath.

"What's that?" Sir Harvey asked.

"Nothing," she answered.

She saw the expression on his face and realized for perhaps the first time that he was wondering whether he had been wise to take her under his protection. She knew then that she must restore his trust in her, that somehow she must wipe away that first feeling of uncertainty.

With what was less of an effort than she had expected she smiled up at him almost flirtatiously.

"You have not mentioned my gown," she said. "Are you pleased with it?"

He stood back a few paces to examine her. She turned round, lifting her wide skirts for his inspection, glancing at him laughingly over her shoulder, her eyes suddenly alight, her lips parted, her curls swinging with the quickness of her movements.

He watched her and she knew she had captivated him. The uncertainty had vanished from his eyes. He stepped forward and raised her hand to his lips.

"You are enchanting," he said. "Just as I knew you could be."

"You approve?"

She was forcing compliments from him, but somehow she wanted so desperately to hear them.

"You look very beautiful," he said. "Is that what you want me to say?"

"But, of course," she answered. "Every woman wants to hear that."

"But I am your brother," he said abruptly, "and brothers are not expected to pay fulsome compliments to their sisters."

"No, of course not," she answered, feeling as if in some manner he had slapped her for something she had not done.

He stood back and was frowning a little.

"Your hair must be done again before tonight," he said. "I will send for a coiffeur. I have explained that we have only the clothes in which we stand up, but you will need a mantle. Is there anything else?"

"Not that I can think of," Paolina answered. "Will there be a party?"

"There are sure to be a number of people there," Sir Harvey answered. "Someone of the Duke's importance does not often choose either to dine or live alone."

"Did you know him before?" Paolina asked.

Sir Harvey shook his head.

"Only by reputation," he answered. "But I knew the story of our arrival and what we had suffered by shipwreck would already be round the town. When I called at the Castle this morning I happened to mention to the Major-domo to whom I spoke that my father was Lord-in-Waiting to His Majesty and had known the Duke's father intimately."

"And had he?" Paolina asked.

Sir Harvey shrugged his shoulders.

"I have not the faintest idea," he answered. "But it is impossible for a man to assess who were his father's friends and so I took a chance on it."

Paolina laughed.

"You are incorrigible," she said. "I suppose really I should be shocked because of the lies you tell."

"When I do things that are reprehensible," Sir Harvey answered, "I always say to myself, 'Needs must when the devil drives.' I feel then, in some way, that it is the devil who is responsible and not me."

"I am afraid we cannot avoid our sins as easily as that," Paolina said severely.

"It depends what you call sin," he answered. "Personally, I only consider it a sin if I am hurting or injuring some person weaker than myself. We are certainly not hurting the Duke by taking a good dinner off him—in fact he is really in our debt. I shall amuse him and you will decorate his Castle. He must be prepared to pay for his entertainment."

"And will he?" Paolina asked simply.

Sir Harvey slapped his pocket.

"I am hoping there will be a game of chance after dinner," he said. "If there is, you must be prepared to make yourself pleasant to any gentleman who is not at the tables or to any lady who is forced to keep you company."

"Be careful how you play," Paolina begged.

She had a sudden vision of all their plans going awry, of their fine clothes being returned because they could not pay for them, of being forced to leave the hotel and seek cheap lodgings in a less fashionable part of the town. She had known it happen so often. Was this to be the end of their adventure—a gaming table which had so often before caused her unhappiness and privation?

Sir Harvey saw her expression and put his hand on her shoulder.

"Do not be afraid, little one," he said. "I never play when I am losing."

"It is easy to say," Paolina answered unhappily.

He smiled and walked across the room to his own bed-chamber.

"You must try and not be apprehensive," he said. "Half the miseries in life are suffered long before they happen. One punishes oneself by worrying. I promise you one thing; I have been looking out for myself for so long that I shall find it quite easy to look after you."

"I will try not to worry," Paolina said humbly. "But I should hate to lose all this." She paused a moment and then added almost beneath her breath: ". . . and you."

He turned back and looked at her.

"I will be very careful, I promise you," he answered. "I, too, am enjoying this adventure, as you call it."

Without waiting for her reply he went into his bed-chamber and shut the door. Slowly Paolina went to her room and sat waiting for the arrival of the coiffeur. She felt a sense of excitement creep over her.

It was a long time since she had been out to dinner in a grand house, let alone a Castle. She had a new dress, there
50

was a fortune in pearls around her neck, her hair was to be dressed by skilled hands rather than by her own, and, most of all, she had someone to escort her.

She had wanted to tell Sir Harvey how well his new clothes became him, how handsome he looked. But she had somehow found no words, and now she thought how tiresome and irritating she must have been to him—complaining and finding fault when he was doing so much for her.

She put her hands up to her face, ashamed at her own stupidity. She would not be so tiresome again. If the Duke flirted with her tonight, she would flirt back. She would meet his dark eyes with that hint of invitation in her own which Sir Harvey had asked of her.

She felt somehow safe now that she knew that the Ducal affections were engaged elsewhere. Whatever Sir Harvey might say, it was frightening to encounter admiration—or was it something more demanding?—from someone like the Duke.

The coiffeur came and arranged her hair high on her head, the curls falling on to her white shoulders. She looked different and yet, even to her eyes, infinitely more beautiful.

She was only just ready when the carriage arrived. Sir Harvey, anxious not to be late, hurried her downstairs after producing a mantle of satin and velvet which he wrapped around her shoulders.

The carriage was the last word in luxury, with padded seats, accoutrements in embossed gold, and a foot-warmer for their feet even though the evening was not cold. There was also a sable rug and footmen in resplendent gold and scarlet uniform to ride behind the carriage to open the door when they arrived at the Castle.

"For goodness' sake talk," Sir Harvey admonished her as they drove quickly through the cobbled streets. "It doesn't matter if you have nothing to say. Nothing is more boring or damping than a silent woman who looks as if she might disapprove."

"I thought men only liked women who listen," Paolina managed to say.

"Clever men may prefer that because they wish to speak of themselves and their achievements," Sir Harvey said. "But men like the Duke wish to be entertained. Remember he is used either to the society of the most intellectual and brilliant people in the Province, or else to the gay chatter

51

of his opera singer and her friends whom he entertains in Rome."

"It seems to me I fall between two stools," Paolina said; but Sir Harvey was not amused.

"To be a social success you have only to be gay and sparkling," he said. "With a face like yours no-one wants you to be intellectual. At the same time, no Italian wants a woman who appears gloomy or out of spirits."

"I will do my best," Pallina said as the horses swung over the drawbridge and into a magnificent courtyard.

There were at least twenty people in the big *Salon* to which they were shown. Their host hurried forward and it seemed to Paolina that he held her hand longer than was necessary. She knew that the other women present were watching her curiously and speculating both on her gown and her jewels, and for perhaps the first time in her life she knew she need not be ashamed of either. She was their equal in appearance and certainly in looks, if not in breeding or wealth.

"What lovely things you have in your Castle," she said to the Duke.

"After dinner you must permit me to show you some of my pictures," he answered.

Paolina glanced at Sir Harvey and saw the slightest, almost imperceptible shake of his head.

"If you are gambling, Your Grace," she said after a moment's pause, "I shall hope to watch you win. I do not play myself, but I like to watch a good game of chance."

She realized that by her answer she had, in some subtle way, avoided some pitfall that had been waiting for her. It also seemed as if the other women warmed to her. She was escorted into dinner by a charming young man who told her he was the Compte de Gaumont and was staying in the Castle as he was a distant relative of the Duke.

Paolina was surprised when they reached the dining-room to find that she was sitting on the Duke's left. There was a lady of title on his right; and although the other ladies present were more important, he explained, with a charming smile, that Sir Harvey and his sister were the guests of honour that evening and that was why he wished Miss Drake to honour him with her company.

Before the end of the meal Paolina was well aware that the Duke was interested in her. Whatever Sir Harvey might say about the difficulty of catching him in the matrimonial net, there was no doubt at all that he was prepared to go out of his way to flatter and pay attention to her even if he had no intention of offering her a wedding ring.

"When can I see you alone?" the Duke asked Paolina under cover of the general conversation.

She pretended to misunderstand him.

"I do not know what my brother and I intend to do tomorrow," she answered.

"I am not interested in your brother," he said. "Will you let me take you driving in the morning?"

"I do not know," Paolina answered vaguely. "As I expect my brother has told you, we are busy trying to obtain clothes to replace those which were lost in the ship."

"You look entrancing as you are. Why should you want to wear anything else?" he asked.

She laughed at that.

"Would you like to have to wear the same coat day after day?" she asked. "Even as magnificent as the one you are wearing tonight?"

The Duke looked pleased.

"Do you like it?" he asked. "I chose it hoping it would find favour in your eyes."

"I am afraid I do not believe a word you say," Paolina said. "I have always been told that Italians are flatterers and you, Your Grace, are no exception."

"I speak the truth!" he expostulated. "And I promise you that when I was told that a lady as lovely as an angel had arrived at the inn I was all agog to see her, even before your brother's call gave me an excuse."

"I am sure you are making that up," Paolina answered.

"It is true, I swear to you. Have you not found that my countrymen think that anyone with golden hair must come direct from Heaven? But, of course, there is no mistaking that you were made in an angelic mould. The trouble is—can you stoop to be kind to someone who supplicates your kindness?"

His voice was low but Paolina was uneasily aware that his conversation, almost whispered in her ear, was causing the other women at the table to look at her with something like indignation.

Quickly she turned to the young man on her left and started a long conversation with him about the terror of being wrecked at sea. She could feel the Duke's anger on her other side, but she paid no heed to him.

It would do him no harm, she thought, not to get what he wanted for once. The result was not exactly what she expected. Being repulsed made the Duke all the keener, and as the ladies rose from the table he clasped her hand.

"I have got to see you alone some time this evening," he insisted.

Paolina shook her head and moved quickly away from him. To reach the door she had to pass close to Sir Harvey and looked up at him apprehensively.

All through the evening she had been afraid of doing the wrong thing. But as she had been seated on the same side of the table as he was, she had not been able to catch his eye or tell by his expression whether he was incensed at anything she had done.

Now she gave him an almost despairing glance and was relieved almost beyond words to see only approval in his eyes. She moved past him, but not before she had caught two words which he breathed rather than spoke between his teeth—words which made her sweep through the door with her head held high and her heart beating a little quicker.

"Well done," he said.

Outside in the *Salon* the women arranged themselves on the sofas and talked in an affected, gushing manner which meant that they cordially disliked each other and were filled with envy and hatred of each other's looks and possessions.

"I adore your gown," one woman said to another, only to be answered by the reply:

"And I have adored yours for years."

Paolina sat silent, feeling that here, at least, Sir Harvey would not expect her to assert herself. Because she had had a success with the Duke she was well aware that the others were punishing her by ignoring her. But she was content to let them do so.

Only after some time, feeling that the reprimand had been obvious, one of the older women turned to her.

"You must tell us about the shipwreck, Miss Drake," she said. "How strange that you and your brother were the only people who were saved!"

"I think it good fortune rather than strange," Paolina said.

"Perhaps you were cleverer than the others," another guest suggested.

It was, Paolina thought, as if they sensed there was some mystery about it and yet could not quite put their fingers upon it.

"How good-looking your brother is," someone said. "How is it that he has never married—especially as I hear he is so rich?"

"Who told you that?" Paolina asked.

"Now I come to think of it it must have been your brother himself. But you are rich, aren't you?"

It was a direct question and Paolina knew that she had to make some answer.

"I have never met anyone who thought they had enough money," she answered. "I, personally, leave all such things to my brother. I do not trouble with anything other than making him happy."

"How virtuous," a woman drawled, then turned the subject to other matters as if realizing there was nothing to be gained in plaguing her.

Paolina was thankful, however, when they were joined by the men. The card tables were put out and the women with little cries of joy moved to their places. Paolina was waiting, wondering what she should do, when she found the Duke beside her.

"Come and see my pictures," he said. "They are well worth a visit, I assure you."

She shook her head.

"I would rather stay here," she answered.

"I think you are the first person in years who has refused to visit one of the finest art collections in Italy," the Duke said.

"Could we make up a party?" she suggested. "My brother has often told me how interested he is in the Italian masters."

The Duke stood looking at her, his lower lip protruding a little.

"I cannot quite make you out," he answered. "You look so beautiful and yet you are hard and cold—or is that only a façade that I must break down?"

"I do not think we know each other well enough to say what we think or what we feel," Paolina said.

"You are right there," he answered. "But we have a long time to get to know each other before we reach Venice."

"Yes, that is true."

Paolina felt her heart sink at the thought.

"And now, if you will not look at my pictures, may I show you my Library which opens out of this room?"

There was that look in his eyes which Paolina detested.

55

She looked up at him, her eyes meeting his fairly and squarely.

"I think it would be more proper, and certainly more correct, Your Grace," she said, "if both you and I stayed here with your other guests."

Without a word the Duke turned and walked away. He stumped up to the card table in an obvious ill humour, and threw himself down into a chair.

Paolina stood where he had left her, trembling a little. Then she looked across the room at Sir Harvey and felt her heart sink. He was frowning at her.

4

"More flowers!" Sir Harvey ejaculated as one of the servants of the inn staggered into the sitting-room carrying an enormous bouquet and a basket of rare fruits.

"No need to ask where they came from," he added and rose and walked towards the table on which the servant had set them down. "At the same time, you might like to read the *billet-dous* which I see is nestling amongst the blossoms."

"You can read it if you want to," Paolina answered without looking up. "Oh, look at this exquisite stitching! I do think we might have searched the whole world without finding better seamstresses than we have found here."

She was looking down at two of her new gowns which had just arrived, touching them with fingers that seemed to thrill at their elegance and beauty.

She had been too tired that first night to appreciate the richness of the materials which Sir Harvey had chosen for her. Now she found unexpected delight in the embroidery, the skillful application of the lace, the sheer richness of the brocade and velvet.

Sir Harvey was reading the note which he had opened without apology.

" 'To the fairest face that has ever graced Italy,' " he read aloud, " 'and may the giver of these humble gifts be rewarded by a smile.' Poetical, isn't he?"

"I do not like him," Paolina replied.

"All the same, he is a Duke," Sir Harvey reminded her. "And we want to save ourselves a journey to Venice by

57

more uncomfortable means. The Duke's *burchiello* is, I am told, the swiftest and most luxurious craft around the whole coast."

"What is a *burchiello*?" Paolina asked.

"It is a kind of floating house," Sir Harvey answered. "It has a long chamber in the middle, small cabins at each end and a place for the servants on the prow and the poop. They travel at a good speed. It will only take us about eight hours to get from the harbour where it rests to Venice."

"It sounds exciting," Paolina answered. "At the same time I should enjoy it more if the Duke were not with us."

"I grant you he is a peculiarly unpleasant character," Sir Harvey said.

Paolina looked up at him quickly. She was surprised at his tone of voice. The previous day he had been pressing the charms of the Duke upon her, telling her that perhaps his interest was really serious or at any rate she might be woman enough to make it so.

She looked at him now enquiringly, but she did not say anything until, in almost a shamefaced manner, Sir Harvey explained:

"I hear that His Grace's engagement to the Princesse Violetta d'Este is shortly to be announced."

Paolina could not help smiling. So this accounted for Sir Harvey's change of manner.

"I am sorry if you are disappointed," she said demurely.

"Not really," he answered. "In all my plans for you I have never flown quite as high as a Duke—at any rate, not the Duke of Ferrara."

"And yet you hoped," she smiled.

"Well, dammit all," Sir Harvey snapped. "There are no limits to what a clever woman may attain, no horizons that a beautiful one cannot conquer. And, let me be frank, you are very beautiful, Paolina."

"It is funny that everyone should only just have discovered it!" Paolina smiled. "So it is really true that fine feathers make fine birds. When I was the dowdy, rather miserable daughter who was left at home while her father gambled, practically nobody looked at me."

"There must have been some," Sir Harvey suggested.

Paolina shrugged her shoulders.

"The hangers on at the Casino; gross old men who were really only interested in their wine and the turn of a card; and a few impecunious younger ones who would have been prepared to pass a few hours with me between contriving how to swindle their male acquaintances out of their money and their female ones of their virtue."

"It certainly doesn't sound very prepossessing," Sir Harvey said.

"It wasn't," Paolina said briefly.

"But now you can forget it."

He had walked across the room to her side as he was speaking and now she looked up at him from the low chair in which she was sitting.

"Can I?" she asked.

He looked down into her dark eyes and wondered at the misery he saw in them. Her little oval face was so lovely that it seemed somehow wrong that there should be unhappiness amidst so much beauty.

"What do you mean by that?" Sir Harvey asked.

"I mean," Paolina answered in a low voice, "that if you grow tired of me, if you are no longer amused by trying to find me a husband, then I shall go back to the poverty and sordidness of the life that I knew before. Moreover it will be worse because now I have known a different life—the life you have shown me."

"And if I promise you that I will not tire of you?" Sir Harvey asked.

Her face lightened for a moment.

"I wish I could be sure of it," she said. "The other night when you were incensed with me for not responding to the Duke I was desperately afraid. I am in a very vulnerable position because I am utterly dependent on you. I cannot help wondering what will happen if you cast me away."

Sir Harvey bent down and took her hands in his.

"Paolina, why torture yourself?" he asked. "Can you not enjoy this adventure for what it is—a gay, daring, rather wild escapade? There is humour in the idea that you and I are trying to outwit the brains, the wealth, the pomposity of the most illustrious city in the world. Venetians give themselves great airs, I can promise you that. Well, you and I together will pick their pockets and teach them a trick or two."

"You may do that," Paolina answered. "But I am not clever enough."

"Who wants you to be clever," Sir Harvey asked, "when you are as beautiful as you are at this moment?"

He pulled her suddenly to her feet and with his arm

59

round her shoulders led her across the room to where a gilt mirror hung on the wall.

"Look at yourself," he commanded.

She did as he told her, seeing a complete stranger instead of the familiar reflection that she had known for eighteen years. It was, indeed, hard to recognize the humble, unobtrusive little figure she had been wont to see.

Instead she saw a figure with shining, fashionably dressed hair, with carmined lips, with a low-cut, exquisitely modelled gown which showed every curve of her figure to its best advantage. Her skin was dazzlingly white, the long, dark lashes of her big eyes fell against the pink and white delicacy of her cheeks.

"It is not really me," Paolina said in a soft, almost frightened voice.

"Of course it isn't," Sir Harvey answered. "The girl who went aboard the *Santa Maria Lucia*—wasn't that the name of the accursed vessel?—was lost in the tempest, as were so many other poor souls. This is my sister you see before you—Paolina Drake of London, the toast of St. James's, the woman whose beauty has caused a sensation even in the precincts of His Majesty's Palace."

Paolina could not help laughing.

"To whom have you been telling all that nonsense?" she asked.

"To everybody," Sir Harvey replied.

"And they believed you?"

"But of course! I am the most exceptionally accomplished liar that you are likely to find anywhere in the world."

Paolina put her hands up to her face, but she was laughing.

"It is wrong, wrong," she said, "and yet I cannot be anything but amused. If only these people knew—the *Conte* and *Contessa* who called on us yesterday; the Abbe de Froscani; the Duke himself! Oh, how do you dare to deceive them?"

"I dare because we must," Sir Harvey said.

For once the smile was missing from his lips, and as if he had raised a danger signal in his words Paolina asked quickly:

"Is it as bad as that? How long will your money last?"

"Quite a long time," he replied evasively. "But not so long that we should be heedless of the future. Our clothes should be completed by tomorrow or perhaps the next day.

Then I will try to persuade the Duke to leave for Venice a little earlier than he originally intended."

"You think there is nothing to be gained by staying here?" Paolina asked.

Sir Harvey shrugged his shoulders.

"We are being received; that in itself is a good introduction to Venice. But it does not worry me unduly. When we set up house in the *palazzo* I have rented on the Grand Canal, all Venice will call, I am sure of that."

"A *palazzo* on the Grand Canal!" Paolina breathed. "Are you crazed? How can we possibly afford such a thing?"

"We must!" Sir Harvey answered. "To get money in this world you have to spend money. We have to appear as people of great riches and great importance. Only the right setting will convince them that we are what we say we are."

"But it will cost a fortune," Paolina expostulated.

"No," he contradicted. "That is what you are going to cost. I am putting you in the shop window, my dear, and the window must be the right setting for the jewel it displays."

Paolina turned away. She didn't want Sir Harvey to see how much his words jarred upon her. She could hardly bear it when he spoke to her in that bantering, cynical tone. And yet she knew that it was the truth. She was for sale—for sale to the highest bidder. And because she was helpless and penniless, there was nothing for her to do but to accept the position and be grateful that she had not found herself in worse circumstances.

"Don't do that," Sir Harvey said suddenly, a sharp note in his voice which made Paolina turn towards him, wide-eyed and apprehensive.

"Do what?" she asked.

"Stand with your head drooping, your hands hanging limply at your sides. You look dejected, defeated. There is no grace—nothing in such a stance."

"I am sorry," Paolina said.

"You must be on your guard the whole time against dropping your pose. Beauty is not only of the face, it is an art of the whole body. Now walk across the room, smiling and happy and yet proud, as if the whole world was there for you to walk on."

Paolina obeyed him. He stopped her before she had taken a few steps.

61

"You are not smiling," he said. "You are not radiating that inner joy which comes from being a beautiful woman in a world that has got nothing to do but to admire you. Now try again. . . . Yes, that is better. . . . Now again. . . . And yet again!"

When finally he was satisfied Paolina walked to the table to look at the flowers the Duke had sent her. Somehow she did not even wish to touch them. There was something about the Duke she had hated instinctively from the very first moment of their meeting. She had not yet forgotten the look on his face when she had bade him good-bye the night they had dined there.

All the evening he had besieged her with requests, demands, pleadings that she would be alone with him. She had evaded them all and then finally, as she had said good night, she had felt the caress of his fingers against hers, and the hard insistence of his lips against her skin.

"You are cruel," the Duke had whispered almost beneath his breath.

Her eyes had fluttered beneath the look in his, but not before she had seen the fiery desire which made her afraid. Forgetting all Sir Harvey's admonishments she had almost snatched her hand away.

She had sunk down in a low curtsy. When she rose, she did not look at the Duke again. She knew his eyes were following her and yet she managed to keep her own on the ground, to move from the room with what she hoped was an almost severe dignity as a rebuke to his impetuosity.

Only when she got back to the safety of the inn did she wonder why she had been so afraid. After all, compliments were something which every Italian paid to any woman, old, young, pretty or plain. Flirtation was taken as a matter of course. Why then did she shrink from the Duke? She felt ashamed of being so stupid, so unsophisticated, especially when Sir Harvey told her in no uncertain terms that she was both those things.

"Gauche and ill bred, that is how you appeared," he said scathingly. "You should have responded to the Duke—not too eagerly, of course, but you should have shown that you were pleased and captivated by what he was saying to you. After all, you are not likely to meet many more men of such importance."

Paolina wept when she was alone in her own room. She cried because she wanted so hard to be all that Sir Harvey asked of her, and she knew that tonight at any rate she had failed miserably.

Yet in the morning, when the flowers arrived with a note from the Duke, Sir Harvey was no longer annoyed.

"Perhaps you are right," he said. "Perhaps the way to get him interested is to seem indifferent. He has plenty of women flinging themselves at his head."

It was, to Paolina's relief, Sir Harvey who thought it would be best for her to refuse any invitations which might come from the Castle that day. When the Duke's Major-domo arrived later in the morning to invite them to visit the theatre that night and to supper afterwards, Sir Harvey refused, saying that his sister was still fatigued after their journey and he himself had already made other arrangements for the evening.

"Keep them guessing," he had said when the Major-domo had gone, and Paolina could almost have cried with relief at the respite.

Now, as she looked down at the flowers and the note lying on the table, she gave a little laugh.

"So he is to marry the Princesse d'Este, is he?" she asked. "I thought you said he was a confirmed bachelor."

"There is a rumour in the town that it is a linking of two great fortunes, the amalgamating of two powerful families who have run this part of Italy for five hundred years."

"Well, I hope that she is happy with him," Paolina smiled. "I am not jealous."

"You are being very tiresome about the man," Sir Harvey retorted. "I hope your likes and dislikes will not show themselves so obviously when we get to Venice."

He spoke severely and the mischief died out of Paolina's eyes.

"I will try to like everyone," she promised.

"And now what about a walk in the sunshine," Sir Harvey asked. "We could call for a carriage, but I feel a slow promenade along the main street would show you off to your very best advantage."

"I would love that," Paolina said.

She ran into her own room to drape a scarf around her shoulders and place a straw hat trimmed with lace and ribbons on her head. She could not help thinking as she went back to the sitting-room what a handsome couple they made.

Sir Harvey was wearing one of his new coats, an embroidered waistcoat and a jabot of Venetian lace. He was so handsome that she was not surprised that every woman turned her head towards him whenever he appeared.

A large number of fashionable people were taking the air in the flower-filled gardens in the centre of the town. A fountain was playing and the fragrant perfume of orange blossom seemed to fill the air.

There was no doubt that Sir Harvey and Paolina caused a sensation, which was obviously just what he intended. They strolled along apparently deep in talk until one of the men they had met the first night at the Duke's dinner-party came up to speak to them.

He bowed, raised Paolina's hand to his lips, and asked if they would honour him the following night by dining with him.

"My *palazzo* is only a little way outside the town," he said. "We may perhaps persuade the Duke to come too, but he usually prefers dining in his own Castle."

"Then pray do not ask him!" Paolina exclaimed. "It would be more amusing, my Lord, to meet new people. There appear to be so many charming persons living in Ferrara that I am anxious to encounter them all."

"Then, of course, you shall," the young Italian promised gallantly. "I will give a party for you to make your choice, *Signorina*. Is that agreed?"

"It is agreed," Paolina laughed.

They moved away and when they were out of earshot she said to Sir Harvey:

"What a delightful man. What is his name?"

"The Conte Piero Rossitti," Sir Harvey answered. "Though I cannot imagine why you should think him charming. A more conceited jackanapes it has never been my misfortune to meet."

"But how can you say that?" Paolina asked. "I thought him delightful and look how kind he was in saying he would give a party for us."

"Well, I dislike him intensely," Sir Harvey said. "And I think it is very unlikely that we shall be present at his party."

"Oh, but we cannot let him give it and then not turn up," Paolina said. "It would be too unkind."

"That will be for me to decide," Sir Harvey said in a disagreeable voice.

Paolina sighed but thought it best to say no more. She

64

wondered, as they continued their walk in silence, what could have upset him. But by the time they returned to the inn he appeared to have recovered, and he made her laugh by recounting a holiday he had spent with some friends attempting to climb the Alps and failing to achieve anything but a frost-bitten toe.

Back at the inn they talked and rested until late in the afternoon.

"Tonight we dine with the Conte and Contessa Mauro," Sir Harvey said. "But that is not for some hours. I think I will go for a ride. I am so used to taking a lot of exercise that I find this leisurely life gives me a headache."

"But, of course, I understand," Paolina said. "'A ride will do you good."

"The landlord tells me he has some decent horseflesh. I have said I will try out his best and if it is not good enough he must find me something better. I shall not be long."

"Do not worry about me," Paolina said. "What time shall I be ready for you?"

He told her and when he had gone she went to her bed-chamber and sat down at her dressing-table to think. After some time she realized that her fingers were stroking the pearls that she wore round her neck. She took them off to look at them. They were warm and glowing from contact with her flesh and she wondered what sort of woman had worn them before her.

Perhaps, she thought suddenly, it was someone who had sold her body just to obtain jewels such as these. The thought made her shiver. She put the pearls down on her dressing-table as if for the moment she had no longer any wish to wear them.

Because she was restless, because she was afraid of her own thoughts, she started to undress. It took her a long time to bathe, to sit in a wrapper until the coiffeur came to do her hair in a new style. He arranged a long curl hanging over one shoulder, and at the side of her head he set two pink rosebuds freshly picked from the garden.

The gown she had chosen for that evening was of white satin embroidered with tiny pink flowers. There were pink bows on her sleeves and on the panniers of the dress. She had pink slippers and a fan on which small pink cupids scattered armfuls of roses.

She was ready long before the appointed hour and wondered whether Sir Harvey had yet returned. She was too shy to cross the sitting-room and knock on the door of his bedchamber, and yet she felt suddenly bored with sitting alone in her own room.

She opened the door. The sitting-room was empty. There were only the great bowls of flowers from the bouquets the Duke had sent her, the fragrance of them filling the whole room until it seemed almost like a bower.

There was no sign of Sir Harvey. His hat was not on the chair where he habitually threw it when he came in, and although Paolina listened hard there was no sound or movement from the other bed-chamber.

It was then she heard someone coming up the stairs. She turned expectantly, feeling sure it was Sir Harvey returned from his ride. But when the door opened a flunkey stood there. He wore a dark cloak and a tricorn hat on his powdered wig.

He swept the hat from his head and bowed low.

"I have brought a message, *Signorina,* from His Excellency your brother," he said in a better-educated voice than might have been expected from a servant.

"A message?" Paolina enquired. "Why has he not come himself?"

"His Excellency is detained," the flunkey replied, "and he asks that you will be gracious enough to join him. He has sent a carriage for you."

"Yes, of course, I will come," Paolina answered.

She went back into her room to collect a cape to put round her shoulders. Then as she joined the flunkey she asked:

"Where is my brother?"

"His Excellency is in the house of a friend," the flunkey replied. "He is anxious that you should go to him as quickly as possible."

Paolina suddenly stood still. An idea had come to her, something which made her voice tremulous as she asked:

"There has not been an accident, has there? He has not fallen from his horse?"

"His Excellency is quite well, *Signorina.* If you will come this way."

The flunkey preceded her down the stairs, through a side door of the inn to where, in the courtyard, a carriage was waiting. Paolina just had time to see that it was a closed carriage without the usual coat of arms embellishing the door; then she was inside and the horses started off. Four horses! It struck her as strange that there should be so many if this were a hired carriage that Sir Harvey had sent for her. And yet, if it belonged to one of his friends, why was there no coat of arms?

She wrinkled her brow, puzzling as to the meaning of all this. And if there had been no accident, why had Sir Harvey not returned? It was time for him to change for dinner. He could not dine in his riding clothes.

She began to suspect that whatever the flunkey might have said Sir Harvey must have had a fall. There must be some reason to stop him from returning. She wondered if perhaps she was being taken straight to the Conte Mauro's palace. And yet if that was so, why could not the flunkey have told her that that was her destination?

She began to feel more and more worried as the carriage, travelling swiftly, passed out of the town. They had left the houses behind, and now they were in the open country. Paolina, leaning forward, could see fertile fields and vineyards while tall cypress trees, churches and monasteries occurred only occasionally to break the green of a flat landscape.

On they went, and now she was utterly and completely convinced that Sir Harvey had suffered an accident.

"Dear God, do not let him be hurt," she murmured, praying, because she was anxious for him, with an intensity which seemed to come from her very heart.

She began to think of all the accidents she had ever known that men had experienced out riding. She felt the horror of them coming closer and closer to her, so that it was with difficulty she did not cry out loud and command the coachman to go quicker and yet quicker.

At last, after what seemed to Paolina an aeon of time—although it was, in fact, only about half an hour—the carriage swung off the road, through high, ornamental gates and up a drive bordered with lime trees.

Paolina sat forward to try to get a glimpse of the house that lay ahead. It was an important mansion, as she could tell by its roofs and turrets. Then, almost before she could get a proper look at it, the carriage swung round and pulled up at a porticoed front door.

She stepped quickly out of the coach as soon as the steps were put down. Flunkeys in gold-braided uniforms and powdered hair ran to assist her and she was led into a great marble hall with green marble pillars supporting an exquisitely painted ceiling.

She wanted to ask questions of the Major-domo who

greeted her, but somehow she felt it would only delay matters, only prevent her from hurrying to Sir Harvey's side. Perhaps he was in pain; perhaps he was unconscious. However he might be, the only thing that mattered was that she should get to him.

The Major-domo threw open the door of a room. It was a small *Salon*, as Paolina saw in one quick glance. She had a quick impression of a gleaming chandelier, of brocade hangings, of great bowls of flowers and exquisite pictures; and then she knew that the person she looked for was not there. The sofas and chairs were empty.

"Where is Sir Harvey?"

She heard her own voice ring out loudly because of the fear that was in her heart. She turned as she spoke only to see, to her astonishment, the doors through which she had come close. The servant had gone!

She stood for a moment in bewilderment, and then stepped forward to open the door herself, to find someone, to demand an explanation.

"Can I help you?" a voice asked from the other end of the room.

Paolina whirled round. Coming from between two softly hanging curtains there was a man. She stared at him for a moment as if she could hardly believe her eyes. Then the sudden tenseness of her body told her only too well who it was. It was the Duke!

She walked towards him swiftly with her head held high.

"What are you doing here?" she enquired. "And where is my brother?"

"I am here," the Duke replied suavely, "because this happens to be my house—my hunting lodge, to be exact. May I welcome you to it with all my heart?"

"Where is my brother?" Paolina questioned.

"Your brother!" The Duke made a gesture with his hands. "As far as I know he is in Ferrara."

"You mean he is not here? There has been no accident? Then why did he send for me?"

"Shall we sit down?" the Duke asked.

"I would rather stand," Paolina said. "I want an explanation from Your Grace . . . and then I must go."

"I regret that my coach has been sent away," the Duke answered.

Paolina looked round her.

"If this is your house, what am I doing here?" she asked. "You sent your servants to tell me that my brother needed me." She looked up at the Duke's face and then stamped her foot. "It was a trick," she said accusingly. "A trick to get me here! Your Grace should be ashamed of himself!"

"You are very lovely when you are angry," the Duke smiled. "You are more beautiful than ever I remember you to be. Why would you not see me yesterday? Did you plan to send me mad with longing?"

"Your Grace," Paolina said with a sudden resolution in her voice. "This may be your idea of a joke, but I assure you it is nothing of the sort to me. You have brought me here under false pretences; by a lie which made me worried and perturbed lest my brother should have been badly injured. It is not how I should have expected a gentleman of your birth and breeding to behave. Nevertheless, the joke is now over. I wish to return immediately to Ferrara."

"Come and sit down," the Duke begged, "and let us talk."

"There is nothing to talk about," Paolina replied. "I wish to leave."

"And I will give you anything in the world that you will ask of me," the Duke answered, "except the right to leave me."

Paolina gave an exasperated sigh.

"This is ridiculous," she said. "You cannot keep me here against my will. Already my brother will have returned to the inn. He will wonder what has happened to me. He will be worried and distressed."

"Will he?" the Duke answered. "Or will he perhaps know where you are? Think perhaps you are in very good hands?"

There was something in his voice which made Paolina's eyes widen.

"I do not know what you mean by that, Your Grace," she said. "But I assure you that my brother will worry at my absence. Please command your coach to be brought round immediately." She paused a moment and then, as the Duke did not reply, she added: "Please, do as I ask."

"That is better," the Duke approved. "Now you are pleading with me. A moment or two ago you were giving me orders."

"If you want me to plead, I will plead," Paolina said. "I wish to return to Ferrara. Kindly be gracious enough to have me conveyed there."

"As I have already told you, anything else that you ask of me—but not your freedom."

"This is nonsensical," Paolina exclaimed. "You cannot kidnap me. This is a civilized country. Can you imagine what would be said?"

"That is just the point; will anything be said?" the Duke replied.

"If you imagine my brother is going to find me missing and just sit down and take it as a matter of course, you are very much mistaken," Paolina said hotly.

"I have sent an emissary to deal with your brother. I think perhaps you will find he is not so incensed as you imagine."

There was a sudden pause.

"What do you mean by that?" Paolina asked after a moment.

"I mean, my very sweet and very lovely lady," the Duke answered, "that I have been making enquiries about your brother. He has at the moment apparently quite a lot of money—money obtained from the jewellery that he sold when he arrived here after your adventures in the storm. But from all accounts he is not always possessed of such funds."

He paused, watching her face, then he continued:

"What I am asking myself is, will that money—a great sum though it may be—last for ever? A man who is sometimes on the edge of penury will often talk sound business."

"I do not know what you are saying," Paolina said.

"I think you do," the Duke contradicted. "At any rate, your brother has a head for business. What I am offering him would, to any ordinary business man, be a very sound and very generous proposition."

"Are you inferring that you are offering my brother money for me?" Paolina asked. "That you are trying to buy me?"

"Must we put things so crudely?" the Duke asked. "What I am offering you, my dear, is the devotion of a man who loves you very deeply."

He stepped forward as he spoke and took her hand in his.

"I love you," he repeated, and kissed her fingers.

At the touch of his lips Paolina shivered and would have taken her hand away, but the Duke prevented it.

"Are you really so cold?" he asked. "Have your English chills and grey skies got into your blood that there is no fire in you? If that is so then I must warm you. I cannot

70

believe that your lips are so cold as your words. Shall I try them and see?"

He pulled her towards him, but with a sudden spurt of fear Paolina fought herself free.

"Do not dare touch me," she cried. "You have brought me here against my will. You may be trying to buy me, but I still have a will of my own. I will not belong to you, do you hear? I will never be yours, however much you may pay for me."

"Can you be sure of that?" the Duke asked.

He advanced towards her as he spoke and she saw in his eyes that fiery desire from which she had shrunk the first night they had met.

She retreated from him step by step until she came up against a sofa and could go no further. And then suddenly his arms were round her and he was holding her closely in his arms and seeking her mouth with his lips. She struggled, but it was of no avail. He was so much stronger than she. He held her tightly until she felt as if she was enveloped by some monster from which there was no escape.

She twisted her face from this side to that. She could not escape his lips. He kissed her cheeks, and then eventually he found her mouth. She thought in that moment as if he dragged her down into a hell more horrible than she had ever imagined it could be.

She felt repulsed and nauseated by the closeness of his arms, by the hot hunger of his lips. And then, as his kisses grew fiercer and more possessive, she felt as if she must suffocate from the very disgust and horror at what was happening to her.

Finally he freed her and she fell back against the sofa, panting a little for breath, her hands outstretched piteously as if to hold him from her.

"I love you," he said in a voice deep with passion. "I adore you, and I promise you we shall be very happy together. I am going to take you to a house that I own in Verona. It is high on a hill overlooking the town. The river runs like a silver stream through its gardens. There we will be alone, my love—just you and I—to get to know each other. And you will learn to love me."

"Never! Never!" Paolina managed to gasp.

Her bruised lips were parted, her breath was coming fitfully between them, her eyes were wide with terror as she watched the Duke as a frightened rabbit will watch a stoat.

"Tonight we will stay here," the Duke said. "Then

71

tomorrow we will be away. It is all arranged. All you have to do is to be happy and to realize that I love you."

"This is not love," Paolina cried. "If you love me you would want me to be happy. I swear that I could never be happy with you."

"You will tell me in time that what you are saying now is untrue," the Duke said complacently.

"And what about the Princess?" Paolina asked. "The Princess whom you are to marry?"

"You have heard of that?" the Duke questioned. "It is a marriage of convenience, a marriage that has been arranged because she will be a suitable wife for a man of my position. What you and I are talking about is not marriage, but love."

"We are not talking of anything of the sort," Paolina retorted with a sudden burst of courage. "The love that you are offering me is not love, as I undestand it. It is lust, and something from which every decent girl would shrink in shame and horror. I hate you! Do you understand? I hate you!"

If she thought that her words would affront the Duke, she was mistaken. He bent forward with a rather sinister smile on his lips and a greediness in his eyes which made her more afraid than ever.

"Hate can very often turn to love," he said. "And women who are complacent often become boring. I am sure of one thing; you will never bore me."

It was as if his words snapped her last vestige of self control. Paolina jumped to her feet.

"Let me go! Let me go!" she cried, and ran desperately down the room towards the door, her white gown winging out behind her as if she were a fluttering bird who would escape from its tormentor.

The Duke watched her go. Only as she reached the door did his voice stop her.

"I would hate to humiliate you by commanding my servants to drag you back," he said quickly. "Yet should you attempt to leave this house, that is exactly what they will do."

Paolina stood looking at him. She was still on tiptoe, ready for her effort at escape, and yet she could not but realize the truth of his words. She had seen the army of retainers who were waiting at the door when she arrived—stalwart young men against whose strength she would not have the slightest chance of escape.

"I am beaten," she thought to herself; and then some instinct, or perhaps it was some power which protects us all in the very worst moments of stress, whispered to her: "Play for time."

Her hand went up to her hair. She straightened the laces at the bosom of her dress. Slowly she walked back towards the Duke, going nearer but not too near, watching him warily yet trying to gain control over herself.

"It is past the dinner hour," she said. "Does Your Grace's hospitality extend to offering me something to eat?"

He was watching her with that barely concealed desire, and yet now there was also a glint of admiration in his expression.

"We will dine immediately."

"I wish first to tidy myself."

"My housekeeper will show you to your room," he replied. "She will, of course, be in attendance so that you can ask her for anything that you require."

There was a threat lying beneath the courtesy, as Paolina well knew.

In silence she allowed herself to be escorted up the broad staircase to a magnificent bed-chamber on the first floor. There was a great four-poster bed on a raised dais; there were chandeliers of Venetian glass; there were mirrors framed in silver, pale pink marble tables and rugs which had come across the sea from Persia. But to Paolina they were all the trappings of a prison from which her whole being cried for a method of escape.

The housekeeper brought her warm and scented water, and stood while she washed, holding a linen towel edged with a deep lace border. Automatically Paolina washed her face and tidied her hair. All the time her brain was seeking desperately for some method of escape; all the time she was trying to avoid the fear in her heart—not only of the Duke, but of another deeper fear that had come from the words he had spoken to her.

She could not help the question asking itself—whether Sir Harvey might not be tempted to accept the money which the Duke was offering him in exchange for her.

After all, she told herself, what was she to him but a girl he had befriended two days ago? It was hard to believe that he could feel any affection or any loyalty towards her. Why then should he not accept this windfall and go on his way, as he had originally intended to do, richer in his pocket and unencumbered by someone who meant nothing to him except that he had saved her life?

Over and over again Paolina felt the queston worrying and tormenting her. She moved automatically about the bed-chamber; she looked in the mirror and saw, not herself, but Sir Harvey's handsome, sunburned face.

"I am an adventurer!"

She could hear him saying it, and saw no reason why this adventure should not end with a profit to himself.

She felt suddenly that she must go to the window and cry out for him, believing that by some miracle her voice would carry as far as Ferrara so that he would hear it and come to her rescue. But even if he did, she asked herself, what could he do? The Duke's servants could throw him out; the Duke could even deny all knowledge of her presence. What appeal was there for Sir Harvey? What hope was there in this foreign country, for he was unknown and, even though he might be a nobleman, of little importance.

"Help me! Help me!" She breathed the words beneath her breath, but even so the housekeeper asked:

"M'lady spoke?"

"No, it is nothing," Paolina answered.

She looked at the woman almost for the first time as she spoke, wondering if there was any chance of help here.

The housekeeper was a dark-faced, ageing Italian and, Paolina was certain, owed all her loyalty to the Duke, whose family she had doubtless served all the years of her life.

There was nothing else to delay her. She was ready for dinner and she knew that downstairs the Duke would be waiting. What was Sir Harvey doing? She wondered if he was packing his bags, leaving the inn, going his own way to Venice, delighted with the knowledge that he had enough money to keep himself in comfort for many years.

"Help me! Help me!"

Her heart cried out the words silently, and then with a dignity that was somehow pathetic because of her utter helplessness she went slowly down the great staircase into the marble hall.

5

When Paolina reached the hall, her feeling of bravado had vanished. She knew she was facing the most desperate and dangerous moment of her life. Yet there was nothing she could do to avoid it.

If she were to try to stay upstairs, she felt that the Duke was quite capable of having her dragged into his presence. Besides, the mere fact of having dinner would delay matters and might also give her a chance of finding some way of escape.

There was also at the back of her mind the hope that Sir Harvey would come and save her. She thrust from her the urgings of common sense which said that she could mean nothing to him. She shied away from the idea that he might accept this windfall and ride away.

A footman hurried forward as her foot touched the last step of the staircase.

"His Grace's compliments, and he is waiting for you, Milady."

Paolina merely inclined her head and followed him down a long corridor lit with a hundred tapers, then up another staircase not so elaborate as the one she had just descended, but smaller and obviously leading to a special wing of the house.

She could not help feeling that this was ominous in itself. She guessed that she was being taken to the Duke's private apartments, and she wondered wildly if she could insist on dining in the main Banqueting Hall. Intimacy was the one thing she dreaded, and as the footman ahead of her opened the door she saw that her fears were not unjustified.

The room into which she was shown was beautiful but small. Decorated with paintings depicting various aspects in the life of Venus, it had obviously been designed as a temple of love. The soft sofas and hangings were all covered with a heavy silk brocade embroidered with cupids; there were more cupids rioting around the gilt mirrors and carved on the backs of the chairs.

Linked hearts pierced by feathered arrows were engraved in the crystal wine glasses which stood on the dining-table. The table itself was small and intimate. White orchids were arranged amongst gold ornaments and there were orchids, tuberoses and lilies on every available table and in every corner of the room. They were all white—bridal white—and their sweet fragrance scented the air.

The Duke was standing in front of the fireplace. He had changed his coat, Paolina noticed, for one of white satin embroidered with silver, and there was no doubt that his magnificence had been chosen to match the room.

He came forward as Paolina approached and taking her hand raised it to his lips. The mere touch of his mouth made her shudder, but she managed to say, in a voice which even to herself sounded calm:

"I had hoped we would dine in your Banqueting Hall, Your Grace. I am sure it is very fine."

"I prefer that we should be here," he answered. "This is a very special room and adjoins my own bed-chamber."

There was something significant in his voice. Paolina shivered as she turned away from him, and she saw, even as she did so, that a door in the corner of the room was discreetly ajar—a door which, as His Grace had said, led to his bed-chamber!

She was not, however, prepared to bicker with him while the servants were in the room. At the Duke's request she seated herself at one side of the table and, frightened though she was, she noticed the exquisite lace-edged table-napkins and the thread of gold which ran through the table-cloth, making a pattern of cupids entwined with lovers' knots.

The dishes on which dinner was served were all of gold, and the food was exotic and exciting although Paolina could eat little. Indeed, she felt as if every mouthful she swallowed must stick in her throat and choke her, and it was only because she was desperately anxious that dinner should be prolonged that she took something from every dish and toyed with it on her plate.

76

The golden wines, to fill the engraved glasses, seemed still to hold the sunshine which had ripened the grapes.

"Tell me about yourself," the Duke commanded.

Paolina shook her head.

"Tell me, instead, what you do," she answered. "I know that there have been Dukes in Ferrara since mediaeval days."

"And before that," he answered, but she could see that his thoughts were not on her questions but on herself.

His eyes flickered greedily over her, lingering on her mouth, making her feel that once again his hot lips were fastened on hers. She could not help a blush rising to her cheeks and she wished she had a shawl with which to cover her naked shoulders. His eyes seemed to miss nothing, and after a while Paolina made no further pretence of eating but sat white-faced, as the flunkeys in their colourful liveries proffered dish after dish.

Finally they withdrew, and Paolina realized with a sinking of her heart that dinner had ended. The Duke picked up his glass half filled with brandy, sipped it, then poured out another glass and put it down at Paolina's side.

"Drink this," he said. "It will being the colour back to your cheeks."

"Only you can do that, Your Grace," Paolina replied, "by letting me return to my hotel."

"That is peculiarly ungracious of you," he answered. "I offer you the best of my poor hospitality and you ask only to be rid of me."

"You know full well what I mean," Paolina whispered.

"Let us sit on the sofa and talk about it," the Duke suggested.

Paolina rose from the table, but when she saw the sofa she regretted that she had not remained where she was. It was wide and the soft cushions made it seem more dangerous than the upright chair on which she had been scated during the meal.

She arranged herself on the very edge of it, holding in her hand as if it were a weapon of defence the glass of brandy that the Duke had pressed on her. The Duke threw himself down beside her, and then laughed.

"You are very stiff and very English," he said. "Surely many men must have made love to you before now?"

"No man has kidnapped me and forced his attentions on me unwillingly," Paolina retorted.

"A rather romantic action, do you not think?" the Duke

asked. "Many women have a yearning for adventure such as this."

"Then I am not one of them," Paolina said sharply.

She hesitated for a moment and then added in a different tone:

"Your Grace has had your joke. Will you now be generous and allow me to depart?"

The Duke's eyes narrowed as he watched her.

"You are exquisite," he said. "I thought so that very first afternoon when I called on your brother. When you dined at the Castle I was convinced that you were the most beautiful woman I had ever seen in my whole life. Today has merely confirmed what I already knew—that I love you."

Paolina turned her head aside. She could not bear to look at the fire in his eyes or watch his thick lips speaking the words which she knew only too well were chosen so that they might entice her.

"It is not love you feel for me, Your Grace," she said.

"Then what is it?" he asked. "Have you never felt that your whole being was tingling and afire because someone in particular was near you? Have you not longed to touch him; to feel his lips on yours; to know his heart was beating quicker because you were near?"

As he spoke he put out his hand to touch her. Before he could do so Paolina had sprung to her feet.

"No! No, Your Grace!" she protested. "That is not love."

She put down the untouched glass of brandy on to a table and then turned to him, her little hands clasped together.

"I beg of Your Grace to let me go. Say you are only doing this to frighten me; that you do not mean to keep me here."

"If I let you go, what will happen to you?" the Duke asked softly. "Your brother, by now, is on his way to the coast. Part of the bargain that he made was that my *burchiello* should take him to Venice. Within the space of an hour he should be aboard. Without me, without friends, I think it impossible that you could ever reach him."

"It is not true," Paolina cried. "He cannot have gone; he cannot have left me."

"I assure you that he has," the Duke answered. "I did not doubt for one moment that my offer would fail to tempt him, but while you were upstairs preparing yourself

78

for dinner my Officer-of-Horse, who had been in communication with your brother, returned. He informed me that my offer had been accepted."

"It is not true! It cannot be true!" Paolina said through lips which were suddenly white and stiff.

"My dear, brothers are not always so fortunate as to be rid so easily or so comfortably of their sisters. I had, I can assure you, the greatest difficulty in getting rid of mine."

"But, at least you were rid of them by marriage," Paolina answered. "I cannot believe, my Lord, that you sold them into shame and degradation."

The Duke smiled.

"There was not much chance of that," he answered. "They were, I assure you, all monstrously ugly."

Paolina stamped her foot.

"Do not joke," she said. "What you are suggesting to me is a life of humiliation and shame, as well you know it."

"I cannot offer you marriage," the Duke replied. "That is true enough, I must marry as befits my rank, with a settlement which will bring the utmost advantages to my lands and this Province. But I can offer you comfort, money, luxury and, if you choose it, happiness."

"Happiness would be impossible in such circumstances," Paolina replied.

"Then I must be content with my own happiness," the Duke said. "For I know that to possess you, as I intend to do, will make me very happy."

Paolina looked at him and then suddenly she stepped forward and kneeled beside him.

"Spare me, Your Grace," she pleaded. "There are thousands of women in the world who would be only too thrilled and honoured to be where I am at this moment. Take them all, but let me go."

The Duke looked at her and then bent forward to cup her little chin with his hand.

"You entrance me," he said. "I cannot remember ever before having a woman kneel at my feet. Everything about you is new and exciting. It would be impossible, I feel, for you to bore me or for us to find anything but happiness together."

"And if we did not, what will happen then?" Paolina questioned. "Will you discard me callously as I am convinced you have done to so many others?"

"I will make provision for you, I promise you that," the Duke replied.

79

Paolina rose to her feet.

"We talk a different language," she said in a quiet voice. "You do not understand that I feel degraded, humiliated and besmirched at what you suggest. Does my enmity and my hatred mean nothing to you?"

"It mean merely that you excite me the more," the Duke answered. "I have found complacent women and women who are too willing, infernally tiring after a while. If you could have said anything that would have given a zest to my pursuit of you, you have said it now."

"Then I wish it were unsaid," Paolina sighed. "But it is the truth. I hate you! I have been afraid of you, I think, since the very first moment I saw you. I feel repulsed by you. When you touch me I want to scream."

"Scream then," the Duke answered, rising slowly to his feet, "for I am going to kiss you."

Paolina gave a little cry of sheer fright, and then, as he advanced upon her, ran from him. She fled across the room, her dress rustling behind her, and wrenched at the door through which she had entered and through which the servants had brought their dinner.

It was locked! She struggled with the handle for a moment before she realized that it was barred against her.

The Duke watched her from the fireplace. He had not followed her.

"You cannot escape, little song-bird," he smiled. "The servants have retired. We are now alone in this pretty cage. No-one will hear your screams, no-one will come, however much you shout. That door will not be opened until the morning—and by then you will be mine."

"I would rather die!" Paolina stormed.

The Duke only laughed.

"Nonsense!" he said. "You are very young and very beautiful. Life is pulsating quickly through your veins. You would not lose it because a man loves you! And I promise you one thing—when I awaken your love in response to mine, you will thank me for keeping you alive."

With a sudden panic Paolina turned and beat with her fists on the door.

"Let me out! Let me out! Help!" she cried.

Her voice sounded weak and ineffectual even to her own ears. The beautiful walls seemed to fling it back at her. She felt as if it could not be heard even a few feet away.

With a sense of utter impotency she turned once more to face the Duke.

"Is there no mercy in you?" she asked.

"None," he answered. "All my life I have got what I want, and now I want you more than I have ever wanted anything before."

"I will fight you until it kills me, as I pray it does," Paolina said.

"We will see how effective your strength can be," he answered, and advanced slowly towards her.

She wanted to run away from him again. Yet she felt as if he mesmerized her so that she could only stand with her shoulders pressed against the door, praying that she could escape him, knowing that there was not the slightest chance of her doing so.

Nearer and nearer he came, his dark eyes alight with excitement, his thick lips parted; and then his hands went out to grasp her.

She screamed, but the sound was lost almost immediately as his mouth descended on hers and silenced her voice. She tried to struggle against him, but it was hopeless. His arms completely enfolded her. She heard the lace of her dress tear as she struggled, but his lips held her utterly captive. She could feel her very will failing because her struggle against him was utterly unavailing.

His kiss grew more passionate. She felt his hands caressing her, and she hated him with a hatred which made her feel almost faint with its intensity.

Suddenly he picked her up in his arms. She tried to struggle again, but somehow even her spirit was failing her. She knew where he was carrying her. They moved across the room to the half-open door which led into his bedchamber.

She knew then that she was completely and utterly his captive. There was nothing she could do to save herself, and whatever struggles she might make would only inflame him more. With a sense of desolation she stared up at his face and knew that she was defeated. . . .

There was a sudden crash, the sound of breaking glass. The Duke, still carrying Paolina, swung round and as he did so the curtains over one of the windows parted. Almost unconsciously the Duke's grasp of Paolina loosened, and with a sudden movement she sprang from his arms and on to her feet.

"Harvey!"

She was hardly able to say the word, and then she had

81

run across the room to fling herself against him as he stood there, sword in hand, confronting the Duke.

"Harvey, you have come! You are in time. Oh, thank God!"

The tears were streaming down Paolina's face. She had not cried before in her terror, but now the tears came and with them a relief so overwhelming that she felt as if her whole body dissolved in the ecstasy of it.

"What are you doing here?"

The Duke had managed to speak at last, and in answer Sir Harvey pushed Paolina a little aside and walked towards him.

"I think you know the answer to that."

"I understood that you had accepted my terms," the Duke replied.

"Did you really think I would allow you to ravish a woman who did not want you? You must have queer tastes, Your Grace. I have never forced my attentions on anyone unwillingly. It is something which no decent man does."

"That is my business and not yours," the Duke snarled. "Get out of here or my servants will put you out."

"Your servants have, I think, retired for the night," Sir Harvey answered. "This is a matter we can settle by ourselves. Get your sword."

The Duke looked at the naked sword in Sir Harvey's hand and said:

"And if I refuse to fight you?"

"Then I shall run you through as you stand there," Sir Harvey said. "I am treating you as if you were a gentleman, which, under the circumstances, is, I consider, very decent of me."

Without a word the Duke took up his sword from where it lay, hanging in an embroidered belt, over the back of a chair. Its fine, tempered steel shone in the light of the candles as, without a word of warning, he lunged at Sir Harvey. Only by a quick movement of his whole body did Sir Harvey manage to avoid being killed.

"So, that is the way you fight, is it, you swine?" he said through his teeth.

Watching them, Paolina thought she had never in her life seen such agility or skill, and knew that it was because both men were fighting with all the determination and strength that was in them.

Each meant to kill the other. It was obvious in the tenseness of Sir Harvey's face and the steel grey of his eyes, the grim determination of his chin. It was obvious in the expression on the Duke's face, which was one of violent and irrepressible anger.

But although he may have lost some advantage by his temper, he was the better swordsman of the two. He fought with a violence which Paolina knew only too well would show no mercy to a defeated enemy.

As they fought, small tables, priceless *objets d'art*, chairs with their carved cupids, and even the flower-vases with their exotic contents were spilled over the floor. The sofa they thrust aside; the dining-table was pushed so violently against the wall that the gold-threaded tablecloth was caught by one of the duellists and everything on it was pulled to the floor. The orchids lay trampled amidst the broken crystal glasses and gold ornaments.

"I will kill you for this," the Duke said once, as Sir Harvey kicked aside a table laden with jade and enamel curios and a huge vase of exquisite Venetian glass was shattered.

"Unless I kill you first," Sir Harvey answered. "There is always that possibility you know."

"If you do, my soldiers will throw your corpse to the crows," the Duke answered. "And I doubt if your sister will prefer their love-making to mine."

"She certainly wants none of yours," Sir Harvey answered and with a sudden thrust tore the Duke's satin coat and left a scratch on his arm which began to bleed.

Perhaps it was the sight of blood which made Paolina realize that there could be only one end to this fight. If the Duke was only wounded, he would somehow try to have Sir Harvey and herself apprehended and perhaps imprisoned. Only if the Duke were dead could they be free.

And yet even though she loathed him, she could not bring it on herself to wish the death of another fellow being. She almost cried out to the men to stop fighting. Was she worth such a fight? And yet she knew now that they were so intent on their battle that she, the reason for it, was half forgotten.

As their fighting grew fiercer and still more fierce, they ceased to speak. She could hear their breath coming gaspingly between their lips. It was then that the Duke began to fail. He was the older man of the two, he was heavier of build, and while Paolina had merely pecked at her dinner he had eaten heavily and drunk a considerable amount of wine.

The sweat was running off his forehead and Sir Harvey

saw his advantage. With a tremendous effort, because he himself was beginning to get fatigued, he circled round the Duke and while he was still striving to face the quick-moving Englishman, Sir Harvey made a sudden lunge at him.

The point of his sword passed through the Duke's coat and pierced his left breast. He staggered, dropped his sword, clapped his sword-hand to the wound, and then collapsed slowly on the floor.

Paolina ran forward.

"Is he dead?" she asked.

Blood was beginning to spread over the Duke's white coat. Sir Harvey bent down and pulled it off.

"Get me the table napkins," he said brusquely.

Paolina hurried to do his bidding. Sir Harvey tore off a portion of the Duke's shirt. She saw that the wound, while pouring blood, was not as low as she had at first thought.

"Have you killed him?" she asked again.

Sir Harvey shook his head.

"Heavens, no," he answered. "He's unconscious from shock more than anything."

As he spoke he was making a pad of the napkins, staunching the wound with them and then bandaging the shoulder in a rough-and-ready manner which, at the same time, was singularly effective.

"How do you know how to do that?" Paolina asked.

"I have learned quite a number of things in my life, and this is perhaps one of the most useful," Sir Harvey answered. "Get cushions from the sofa, there's a good girl. We want to prop him up."

The Duke was still unconscious and Sir Harvey piled the cushions behind him so that, though his legs were straight out before him, his body was almost upright. The cushions also supported his injured arm and shoulder so that by the time they had finished he looked comparatively comfortable.

"He is still unconscious," Paolina said, and added doubtfully: "You are quite sure that he is not dead?"

"Not he," Sir Harvey said. "It is really only a flesh wound. Had it been several inches lower, that would have been a different matter."

"We cannot leave him like this," Paolina said. "And anyway, the door is locked."

"We are going out the way I came in," Sir Harvey said briefly. "He will be quite all right until the morning. Cover him up with a rug or something. He will feel cold when he comes to."

To do his bidding Paolina went to open the door which led into the bed-chamber. The room was illuminated by a dozen candles and she saw that it was nearly as beautiful as the little *Salon* in which they had dined.

The bed was of carved wood painted gold, and the furniture was the same, with cupids rioting with dolphins or carrying great bunches of roses to lay at the feet of Venus. Its beauty made her shudder, and after a quick glance round she concentrated on pulling the sable-edged, embroidered coverlet from the vast bed and hurrying back with it.

"That will do," Sir Harvey said with hardly a glance at what Paolina carried.

They covered the Duke's legs and tucked the coverlet round him. Then Sir Harvey sheathed his own sword and glanced round the room as if in search of something.

"What do you want?" Paolina asked.

"Something to keep you warm," he answered. "Look, this will do."

As he spoke, he pulled from a side table, which had not been knocked over, a beautifully embroidered tablecloth. It was edged with lace but otherwise was made of satin, richly embroidered with coloured silks inset with tiny precious stones. The flowers and orchids which were on the table crashed to the floor. Sir Harvey paid not the slighest heed to them.

"Put this round you," he said, draping it over Paolina's shoulders. "You have got a long drive ahead of you."

"A drive?" she queried.

"We cannot waste time in explanations," Sir Harvey answered. "Come along."

With hardly a backward look at the Duke who was begining to moan and regain consciousness, he pulled aside the curtain through which he had entered. Then he drew Paolina out on to the small balcony. They were on the first floor and she saw that on this side of the house it was not very high. Yet, nevertheless, as she looked over the balcony it was quite a drop into the darkness below.

"How are we going to get down?" she asked.

"The same way as I got up," he answered. "You will find a foothold amongst the wistaria."

Paolina looked where he pointed, then she shivered.

"But I cannot do that."

"Come along," he answered. "There is no time for squeamishness."

She would have protested again, but some pride that she had not known she possessed made her feel that she would not stoop to argue with him. Instead, with hands that were trembling and which were suddenly very cold, she grasped hold of the twisted stems of the wistaria and very gingerly tried to raise herself on the edge of the balcony.

Sir Harvey settled the matter by picking her up in his arms and putting her over the edge.

"I have hold of you," he said. "Do not be frightened. Just find a place for your feet."

"Please, do not leave go of me," Paolina begged.

"It is all right," he said soothingly. "Now put your right hand lower than your left and your foot down at the same time."

Trembling so that she could scarcely do as he told her, Paolina somehow managed to obey. He was still holding her tightly round the wasit and then he transferred his grip to her arms, and then, as she went lower, he gradually let go of her. For a moment Paolina was too frightened to move, but with an effort she put her foot down once again, felt a little branch crack and break beneath her weight, and almost panicked.

"You are all right," Sir Harvey said from above. "Keep your head. It is only a few more feet and then you will reach the ground."

His voice seemed to steady her, and a moment later she found her foot was touching the ground and that she was none the worse for her climb save that her hands were roughened and her gown soiled.

She picked up the tablecloth, which had fallen from her shoulders, and wrapped it round herself again. Sir Harvey was coming quickly down the wall. He reached her side and without a word hurried her into the shadow of some trees.

"Come along," he said. "We do not want to be seen and caught at this juncture."

They started running through some shrubberies, moving so swiftly that more than once Paolina caught her foot in the root of a tree and would have fallen headlong if Sir Harvey's arm had not sustained her.

She felt her skirt catch on the brambles. She pulled it loose and hurried on. She was breathless and quite incapable of speech when, after nearly a quarter of an hour, they came through a small wood on to a road. In the moonlight Paolina could see a travelling carriage was waiting.

Sir Harvey hurried forward and opened the door. There was a lighted lantern inside, and to Paolina's astonishment she saw that a man was lying on the seat, gagged and bound. His eyes, turned towards Sir Harvey, were wide and frightened.

"It is all right, my good fellow," Sir Harvey said. "I have done all I had to do and now I have come to release you."

Deftly he undid the ropes which held the man's feet and hands and then took the handkerchief from off his mouth.

"Listen," Sir Harvey said. "I am in a hurry and I have no time to argue with you. Get up on the box and drive me to the coast as you were instructed to do this evening. If you are there within three hours, I will give you a crown; and I will give you another crown for every quarter-of-an-hour you are there before three hours. Is that understood? And now, if you want to make your fortune, hurry."

"And what will His Grace——"

"Never mind what His Grace will say," Sir Harvey answered. "You were told to take me to the coast a short while ago. Well, there has been a small delay, but now we will carry out your orders. Is that understood?"

"*Si, Excellency*," the man said with a sigh, as if he resigned himself to his fate.

He scrambled up to the box and Sir Harvey helped Paolina into the carriage. Then he slammed the door and they were off. The man was obviously determined to make as much money as possible. He whipped the horses into a gallop and the vehicle swayed dangerously from side to side so that Paolina was flung against Sir Harvey time and time again, until, laughingly, he put out his arms and held her close to him.

"There, that is better," he said.

"What are we doing? Where are we going?" Paolina gasped.

"We are going to Venice," Sir Harvey answered. "That was our original destination wasn't it?"

He spoke jokingly, but Paolina put her fingers up to his lips.

"Do not laugh," she begged. "I somehow cannot bear it at the moment. I can think of nothing but that you came in time, that you saved me when I had almost given up hope."

"I should have been there sooner," Sir Harvey answered, "only I had to wait until the servants were dismissed."

Paolina looked at him in surprise.

"How did you find out about that?"

"I caught one of the footmen coming out of the back premises for a breath of air. I half throttled the wretched fellow until he told me what I wanted to know. Then I tied him to a tree. They will find him in the morning."

"So that is how you knew where I was," Paolina exclaimed.

"Exactly," Sir Harvey replied. "I must say when I saw the size of the house it was a bit of a shock. I wondered how the devil I was going to discover which room you were in."

"But how did you know I was there in the first place?"

"Well, fortunately, the Captain-of-Horse gave that away after he had made me a charming little offer of three thousand crowns for you."

"Three thousand crowns!" Paolina ejaculated. "As much as that?"

"Yes, quite a lot of money, is it not? I had no idea that you were so valuable," Sir Harvey said with a little laugh.

"Where did you see the Captain-of-Horse?" Paolina questioned.

"I see you want the story from the beginning," Sir Harvey smiled. "When I left the inn to go for a ride, I passed the Duke within five minutes of leaving the city."

"Was he riding?" Paolina asked.

"No, he was in his coach, as it happened. I took my hat off and he stopped and asked me where I was going. I told him I was in need of exercise and he recommended a certain ride for me to take. I informed him that we were dining out and I did not want to be too long, but he assured me it was well worth my while and I would do it easily in the time."

Sir Harvey laughed without humour.

"I was fool enough to believe him. So I went on, unsuspecting. About half-an-hour later, just as I was turning for home, a company of horsemen came galloping up to me. I recognized the Duke's uniform and the Officer-in-Charge took me out of earshot of the troop and said the Duke wished to make a certain proposition to me."

"Did you guess what it would be?" Paolina asked.

Sir Harvey shook his head.

"No, not for a moment or two. The Officer was quite a decent chap. I think he was really embarrassed at what he had to do."

"I am not surprised," Paolina said.

"Well, he hum'd and ha'd and then came down to brass tacks. I was to receive a certain sum of money if I left for the coast immediately in a carriage which the Duke would provide. His *burchiello* would be waiting and it would take me to Venice. As far as I was concerned my sister, or rather my interest in her, was from that moment to cease to exist."

"Three thousand crowns!" Paolina said. "And you refused it because of me."

There was something more than awe in her voice, something warm and pulsating.

"Refused it!" Sir Harvey ejaculated. "But I did not refuse it. I accepted it."

"Accepted it! What do you mean?" Paolina asked.

"Exactly what I am saying," Sir Harvey answered. "I accepted the offer of three thousand crowns. It was the only thing I could do. Apart from my being only too eager for the money, the Officer-of-Horse insinuated that if the Duke's offer were not appreciated I might have a very regrettable accident while I was out riding. If the horse returned riderless to the stable, there was, of course, every chance of your finding yourself bereaved of your only relative."

"But that was diabolical!" Paolina cried.

"Of course it was," Sir Harvey answered. "It was heads the Duke wins, tails I lose. There was only one thing to be done, and that was to accept his offer and thank him profusely for it."

"But . . . but what happened then?" Paolina asked.

"Well, as soon as the Captain-of-Horse had promised me that the carriage would be at the inn within an hour, I hurried back to find, as I fully expected, that you had left. I had our boxes packed and loaded on the carriage. I paid the landlord and, of course, our debts to the tailor and the seamstress—who, fortunately, had delivered the last of our clothes about twenty minutes earlier. Then I got into the carriage and told the driver to set off towards the coast."

He paused—and chuckled.

"As soon as I was out of the town I forced him to double back. As I have already told you, I managed, by putting an adroit question to the Captain-of-Horse, to find
89

where the Duke had taken you. I did not, somehow, imagine that he would be likely to carry you off to the Castle in the town. When we were near to the hunting lodge I stopped the carriage, tied up the coachman, as you saw, and walked the rest of the way."

"And you came in time!" Paolina exclaimed. "I had given up in despair. The Duke had told me that he had made an offer to you. I somehow felt sure that you would not accept it, and yet when you did not come I began to be afraid."

"Did you really think I was going to abandon you?" Sir Harvey asked.

"Why should you do anything else?" Paolina replied. "And, after all, as the Duke said, what is a sister anyway?"

"Perhaps it is fortunate that you are not my sister," Sir Harvey said. "Three thousand crowns for one might have seemed quite a lot of money."

He was teasing her, Paolina knew that, but her voice was very serious as she said:

"I cannot ever thank you enough for coming when you did, for risking your life. If the Duke had killed you, what would have happened then?"

"You would have had to look after yourself," Sir Harvey answered. "Somehow I feel you are not as helpless as you make out."

"He was very strong," Paolina said.

She felt herself trembling as she remembered the Duke's strength as he had lifted her in his arms and her own feeling of utter and complete despair. Quite suddenly she turned and hid her face against Sir Harvey's shoulder.

"I shall never forget it," she said. "He . . . he kissed me."

Sir Harvey's arms tightened round her.

"Forget him," Sir Harvey admonished. "It was my fault. I should have sensed from the very beginning that he was untrustworthy. But somehow I did not expect him to go to such lengths as this."

"How could he dare?" Paolina murmured, her face still hidden against Sir Harvey's shoulder.

"He was not risking anything very much, if you think about it," Sir Harvey answered. "We are two travellers of no very great importance. We have no servants, no retinue with us. If we disappeared, it would be months and months before the British Consul in Rome learnt of it. By then nothing could be done—not as far as you were concerned at any rate."

"Don't," Paolina said with a sudden sob. "I cannot bear it."

Sir Harvey stroked her hair.

"Just look upon it as an adventure," he said. "You are safe, that is all that matters."

"But are we?" Paolina asked. "What will happen in the morning when the Duke is found? Suppose he does die?"

"He will not die," Sir Harvey asserted. "And by the morning we will be in Venice. The Duke has no jurisdiction there, the city has its own government. I think, however, that when we return home we will not pass through Ferrara. It might be slightly—unhealthy."

"But the money?" Paolina said. "Can he not demand that back?"

"On what count?" Sir Harvey answered. "Even the Duke would not openly admit to having connived at the kidnapping of a young English woman of gentle birth. And he cannot prove, by any possible means, that I sold my sister for three thousand crowns."

"But you cannot keep the money," Paolina said.

"Can I not?" Sir Harvey smiled. "I have told you already, I am an adventurer. If I can outwit His Grace and keep both the money and my charming little sister, then I should be bird-witted not to take advantage of such a windfall."

"I think it is wrong," Paolina said, but her voice was not very convincing.

"I think it is a lesson which the Duke well deserves," Sir Harvey replied.

"I hate him," Paolina whispered. "Even though you have injured him I cannot be sorry."

"There is no reason why you should be," Sir Harvey answered. "But, do as I say and forget about him now. The nightmare is over."

"You are sure about that?" Paolina asked. "He cannot catch up with us? You do not think that even now his soldiers are in pursuit?"

Sir Harvey gave her a little squeeze with the arm that he had around her shoulders.

"Stop being full of fears and apprehensions," he said. "This is an adventure. Enjoy it as I am doing."

"It is different for you," Paolina protested.

"But, why?" Sir Harvey asked. "We are together. We are going to Venice and we possess a much greater fortune than when we woke this morning! What could be better than that?"

Paolina did not answer, but she was thinking that in Venice there would be other men, men who might desire her, as the Duke had done and, above all, a man to whom she must travel in a golden gondola.

6

Paolina opened her eyes and for a moment thought it
must be night and that she was looking at a chandelier
ablaze with a hundred tapers. Then she realized that it was
the sun glittering iridescently on the glass windows of the
burchiello and sending out a thousand facets of light from
the gold fittings with which it was embellished.

She sat up and found it was morning. Outside she could
hear voices. It was Sir Harvey who was talking.

At the thought of him her eyes went quickly to a mirror
attached to the wall of the tiny cabin, and she saw her
face, rosy from sleep, her eyes still a little heavy and
mysterious with her dreams. Her hand went to her hair;
and then, as she rose from the couch on which she had
been sleeping, she looked out of the window and gave an
exclamation of sheer joy.

They were in Venice! She could see the tall *palazzi* on
either side of them, the gondolas moving slowly on the blue
water of the canal, the rounded dome of Santa Maria della
Salute.

She wanted to see it all, to miss nothing.

Hastily she smoothed her hair, then opening the door of
the cabin called to Sir Harvey.

"Why did you not tell me that we were here?" she asked.
"How could you let me sleep for so long?"

He put out his hand and drew her to his side where he
stood on the narrow deck.

"Yes, we are here," he said. "But I had not the heart to
waken you. You were so tired last night."

93

"I can hardly remember coming aboard," Paolina answered. "I believe you carried me."

"I did," he agreed. "But I think you were past walking."

"Ah! Now I remember," Paolina exclaimed. "And I recall too that you had a discussion with the coachman. Did he come with us?"

Sir Harvey nodded.

"He is over there," he said, pointing to the poop where a young man was sitting hugging his knees and gazing around him with obvious delight.

"That was generous of you," Paolina said softly.

Tired though she was when they had reached the coast after their wild dash for fear the Duke's soldiers might be following them, she had roused herself when, at length, Sir Harvey stepped from the coach to find out if the *burchiello* was waiting.

He was away for some little time and she sat alone in the darkness with only her fear for company and her anxiety lest at the very last moment they should not be able to escape.

Sir Harvey returned and she could see by the lights in the lamps that he was smiling.

"All is in readiness," he said. "The men are coming in a moment to carry our baggage aboard."

He put his hand in his pocket and drew out his purse.

"Here are three crowns for you," he said to the coachman. "You have driven well and I am grateful for your service."

The coachman, who was little more than a boy, took them but without the eagerness that might have been expected.

"I thank Your Excellency," he said, "but I dare not return to the Duke."

"You dare not!" Sir Harvey exclaimed. "For what reason?"

"Because, Excellency, my life will be forfeit. His Grace will know that I helped you escape with Milady. And even though I swear to him that you gagged and bound me, he will still say that on your return I should have refused to drive you—or, at least, should have taken you somewhere where you could have been captured by his own men."

Sir Harvey laughed.

"Courage, my man," he said. "It may not be so bad as you think."

"The Duke never forgives anyone who fails to carry out

his instructions," the man said gloomily. There was a pause and then he added: "Take me with you, Excellency."

Sir Harvey looked surprised.

"But how would you serve me?" he asked.

"I could valet Your Excellency. My father worked in an inn at Milano. I learnt his duties when I was only a lad. Take me with you, I pray of you."

"Very well," said Sir Harvey. "I have defrauded the Duke of so much already that one thing more will not matter. But you had best make arrangements about the horses."

"There is an inn not far away where I should have stayed with them anyway," the man said. "Will Your Excellency wait for me if I drive them there?"

"I will give you exactly twenty minutes," Sir Harvey answered.

The Italian's face lit up and with a fervent *"grazie mille"*, he started with a will to help the men who had come up the path from the sea to get down the trunks from the roof of the carriage.

"That was a kind action," Paolina thought. Her eyes closed, and it was what seemed to her a long time later when someone picked her up and carried her on to the *burchiello*.

She could remember murmuring something which must have been an expression of thanks, and then as her head touched a soft pillow she had fallen into a deep sleep from which nothing had aroused her all night.

Now the world seemed almost too beautiful to behold. The Gothic and Lombardesque marble palaces on either side of the Grand Canal were magnificent. It was little wonder, she thought, that she could hear the boatmen reciting their names, telling that each one was the home of some great and noble family.

The gondoliers, waiting in their straw hats and red sashes, were as colourful as the lackeys who stood on the steps waiting to receive the guests visiting their owners. The latter wore liveries of silk and velvet in the most exquisite colours trimmed with gold and silver epaulettes, and their powdered wigs were as snowy white as their gloves and stockings.

Everywhere, it seemed to Paolina, there were evidences of great wealth and luxury. There were flowers decorating the balconies as well as tapestries and wonderfully embroidered cloths thrown over the balustrades. The gondolas tied to the *pali* in front of the palaces were adorned with brilliant coats of arms, while the lamps, screwheads, hooks and brackets were all in gold, some of them even embellished with precious stones.

They passed slowly down the canal until the *burchiello* came to rest outside a magnificent *palazzo* with wide marble steps covered in an exquisitely woven carpet coming down to the water's edge.

"Why are we stopping here?" Paolina whispered.

"This is our house," Sir Harvey answered.

"Ours!" she exclaimed. "But it is too big, too magnificent! How can we possibly afford it?"

She had spoken in English, but he put his finger to her lips.

"Hush," he answered. "In Venice even the walls have ears. Come and inspect your new home. I only hope that you will find it to your liking."

He stepped from the *burchiello* and gave her his hand to assist her alight. Slowly she walked beside him while flunkeys bowed on either side of them and a Major-domo greeted them from the doorway of the *palazzo*.

"Your commands have been obeyed, Excellency," he said. "I am hoping that my poor efforts to engage a staff worthy of your service will receive your approval."

Sir Harvey waved him aside and they went into a large entrance hall and up a wide staircase which led to the first floor. Here magnificent rooms opened off a long, wide gallery which Paolina could see had been designed specially for entertaining.

The decorations were exquisite and in perfect taste. There were wonderful Murano glass candelabra with brackets of silver, and furniture quite unlike anything Paolina had ever seen before. On tables of tarragon and ebony inlaid with ivory there were ornaments of ancient sculpture, bronzes and carved quartz.

But what she noticed more than anything else were the exquisitely painted walls depicting gods and goddesses rioting together in bacchanalian splendour, and the heavy ceilings with wooden beams carved, painted and ornamented in colours that vied with each other in brilliance and splendour.

"Is this really ours?" Paolina asked in an awestruck voice.

"We have rented it for two months," Sir Harvey answered. "At the end of that time we may have to slink away into one of the back canals in search of cheaper lodgings, or you may have moved into an even more splendid *palazzo*. This is but a moderate one."

"To whom does it belong?" Paolina asked.

"To some Prince who has chosen to visit his estates in another part of Italy. He would not have rented it to anyone had he not incurred vast gambling debts the very night before his journey began. In fact, we must thank the goddess of chance that we are able to be here."

"I never expected anything so magnificent," Paolina said.

"Nor I, for that matter," Sir Harvey confessed. "I expect the man I sent to make the negotiations will charge me a pretty penny for his services, but I believe it was worth it."

Paolina had run to the balcony overlooking the canal.

"It is so fascinating," she said. "One could not imagine anything more like a fairy-tale than a city built upon a lagoon. Look how shallow the water is, and yet it transforms everything as if by magic. I cannot believe that it is real."

"It is real enough," Sir Harvey assured her. "And, now, would you like to retire to your bed-chamber? Here is your maid to attend to your wishes."

"Yes, of course. I must change," Paolina said.

She smiled at the young Italian girl, who curtsied and awaited her instructions.

"What I want more than anything else is to bathe and take off my gown. I do not think I can ever bear to look at it again after last night."

"I should throw it away," Sir Harvey said, "and with it your memories of what happened."

"I do not want to forget what you did for me," Paolina said.

"Forget it all," he admonished her. "And now go and make yourself look beautiful. I have no desire for anyone to see you as you are now."

His words were light, but they brought a flush to Paolina's face. She was suddenly conscious that her hair needed the attention of a hairdresser, that her dress—torn from the Duke's attentions and dirtied by her climb down the wistaria—was also creased and crumpled from the journey.

She was not used to thinking of herself over much, but now, at Sir Harvey's words, she felt ashamed and humiliated that he should have been the one to draw attention to her untidiness.

Without a word she turned away from him and following her maid went across the gallery to the bed-chamber which had been allotted to her.

It was a lovely room, but Paolina had eyes only for her own reflection in the mirror. She wished, then, that she had taken longer when she first awoke. Had she thought of it, she could have demanded that her toilet requisites be brought to her from the trunk in which they had been packed.

Her maid was bringing them now and laying out on the bed one of the gowns which had been ordered in Ferrara and which had not even been delivered before she had been spirited away by the Duke's emissary.

She looked at it now and wondered if Sir Harvey would admire her in it. It was of pale green brocade and decorated with bunches of violets tied with velvet ribbon. It was a gown which, to Paolina, seemed so beautiful that she was almost afraid to wear it. And yet, amidst the magnificence that was Venice she knew already that it would not seem in the least sensational but almost ordinary.

Nevertheless, when finally she had bathed herself, had allowed the hairdresser to dress her hair in the very latest fashion and been helped into the green brocade gown, she felt that even Sir Harvey's critical eye could find nothing amiss.

She sent a maid to see if he was ready to receive her. The maid returned to say that Sir Harvey was expecting her to join him in the Banqueting Hall. It was only then that Paolina realized that she had not eaten since her dinner with the Duke the night before. Now she was conscious of feeling hungry and she hurried across the gallery, eager to find Sir Harvey and find out what were his plans for the day.

She entered the Banqueting Hall—a large, square room with a heavy marble fireplace and an ornate ceiling of stucco emblazoned with beautiful scenes in the history of Venice.

Then, as she entered the room eagerly, she stopped. Sir Harvey was not alone. There were two gentlemen with him, and as she entered they rose and bowed politely, waiting for Sir Harvey to effect the introduction.

"My sister," Sir Harvey said briefly. "Paolina, may I present the Marquis Dolioni and Conte Allessandio Calbo?"

Paolina curtsied.

The Marquis raised her hand to his lips. He was a good-looking, rather serious young man of perhaps twenty-six. He was dressed soberly compared with his companion, but everything about him proclaimed wealth and affluence.

"The Marquis has called here," Sir Harvey said, "hoping to find an old friend, Prince Foscolo, to whom this palace belongs. I have been telling him that we have just this morning arrived as strangers to Venice but guests of the Prince in his absence."

"Yes, of course," Paolina said, wondering where this conversation was leading and not quite certain what Sir Harvey wished her to do.

"I have asked the Marquis and his friend to join us in the meal we are about to enjoy," Sir Harvey went on, and turning to his guests, he explained: "It is indeed late for breakfast, but my sister and I have not broken our fast since last night."

"Is that your *burchiello* outside?" the Marquis asked. "My friend and I thought it looked extremely seaworthy."

"We cannot claim the ownership," Sir Harvey replied. "It was lent to us by the Duke of Ferrara, who was host to us while we were in the city."

"Indeed!" the Marquis replied. "I knew the Duke some years ago when I was only a boy. He used to visit my father in the south of Italy."

"I am afraid we left him in ill health," Sir Harvey said with a twinkle in his eye.

"I am sorry to hear that," the young Marquis replied.

While he was talking in rather a grave manner, he was watching Paolina. As if a little uncomfortable beneath his gaze, she moved to the table, for the servants were bringing in steaming hot chocolate, wine, fresh bread and dishes of fish, young lamb and strange sea foods cooked with rice.

Paolina had felt hungry enough to eat anything, but the delicacy of the dishes would have tempted the dullest appetite. She noticed however that while Sir Harvey ate heartily of everything that was provided, their guests only sampled the wine.

"Tell us all the gossip of Society," Sir Harvey entreated them.

"That would take too long," the Marquis replied. "You will have to meet my sister. My *palazzo* is only a very short distance from here and there you will find the *Salon* from which emanates all the chatter and, I vow, all the scandal of Venice."

"Is your sister married?" Sir Harvey enquired.

"She is widowed," the Marquis replied. "The wife of the Conte Aquila Dolfin. She now resides with me. I hope that I may give myself the pleasure of introducing you this very day."

"We shall be honoured," Sir Harvey answered.

The Marquis rose to his feet.

"Thank you for entertaining us," he said. "I shall hope to see you about four o'clock this afternoon. Please give me the pleasure of remembering the invitation."

"We shall certainly do that," Sir Harvey answered.

The gentlemen kissed Paolina's hand and the servants showed them downstairs. As soon as they were gone Sir Harvey turned to Paolina with a smile on his lips.

"That is a piece of good fortune," he exclaimed. "I have heard of the Marquis. He is a member of one of the richest and most powerful families in Venice. To have an invitation to his home within twenty-four hours of our arrival shows that luck is with us—as it has been, I may say, since the very moment of that storm."

"But, if he came here to see the Prince," Paolina said, "how did he manage to enter the house? I should have thought he would have turned away from the door when he heard the Prince had left."

Sir Harvey threw back his head and laughed.

"You miss nothing, do you?" he said. "You are very intelligent. I am glad of it. We shall need all our wits about us at this game. But, you are quite right to ask the question. Fortunately, I saw the Marquis approaching. I recognized his coat of arms on the gondola and hastily sent a message downstairs to say that he was to be brought up here immediately. The Marquis asked for the Prince and the servants feigned stupidity, brought him to where I was waiting and announced him to me."

"How clever of you!" Paolina cried.

"It was little to do with me," Sir Harvey said modestly. "It was sheer good fortune that made the Marquis wish to call upon the Prince this morning of all mornings. Now, all we have to do is make ourselves pleasant and all Venice will accept us."

"Would they not have done so anyway?" Paolina asked.

"Of course, in time. But time is the one thing we cannot afford—though I must admit the Duke's generosity has made things much easier than I anticipated."

"I still feel very guilty about that money," Paolina said.

100

"Forget it," Sir Harvey admonished her. "It is not for you to feel guilty. If anyone has done something wrong, it is I; and I am prepared to account for it if the time comes."

"Do not say that," Paolina said quickly. "It might be unlucky."

"I am thinking that the day I met you was a lucky one," Sir Harvey answered. "I went aboard the *Santa Lucia* with much trepidation. I had meant to visit Venice for some time, but I had been unable to afford it. I won enough at cards the night before the ship sailed to pay my fare. I left the rest on the lap of the gods, and how right I was to do so. Here we are, in luxury, at least for two months."

"It is a gamble," Paolina said.

"Everything is," Sir Harvey answered simply. "But who wants dull security and the boredom of knowing what is going to happen day after day?"

Paolina rose from the table and walked towards the window.

"I am a woman, so I think perhaps I prefer safety," she said. "This sort of life can be frightening."

Sir Harvey joined her.

"Yet it has its compensations!"

He was looking at her gown as he spoke.

"You have been very kind to me," Paolina replied.

"Nonsense!" he answered. "At the moment we are about quits. All that I have spent on you has been returned with interest, only, unfortunately, you had to suffer a somewhat disagreeable hour or so to pay for it."

"Does one pay for everything in life?" Paolina asked suddenly.

"Everything, in one way or another," Sir Harvey answered. "Personally, I am a man who prefers to meet my debts. There is a rather tiresome streak of honesty in me."

There was laughter in his voice and Paolina could not help smiling at him.

"Your ideas of right and wrong are all mixed up," she said. "But, somehow, here in Venice it does not seem to matter. I am quite convinced that this is all a dream from which I shall wake to find myself in the cabin of the *Santa Lucia*. What do you think?"

"I think you are awake," Sir Harvey answered. He looked at her for a moment, then said: "That dress is extremely becoming, but I think you will want more and better gowns within a week. You have got to make an impression, a tremendous impact from the very first moment of your arrival. The Marquis was bowled over. Did you realize that?"

"Was he?" Paolina asked.

"You know damned well he was," Sir Harvey answered. "Well, he will talk—or, rather, that vacant-looking friend of his will. The news will be round Venice by midday, and this afternoon they will all be agog to see you. Whatever happens they must not be disappointed."

"Surely this gown is magnificent enough?" Paolina said. "But I have others, as you well know."

"Wait! I want to think," Sir Harvey answered.

She turned away from him onto the balcony overlooking the canal. A gallant moving past raised his hat and bowed. She drew back a little into the shadow of the window lest he should think that she was deliberately inviting his attention.

She was conscious all the time as she did so of Sir Harvey's eyes upon her. He was watching her, assessing her points, it seemed to her, as if she were a horse or a dog rather than a human being. She walked across the room a little petulantly, standing at the mantelpiece to look up at the carved figures which ornamented it.

It was then that Sir Harvey gave a sudden shout.

"I have it! That gown of silver lamé. Where is it?"

"In my room," Paolina answered.

"Tell your maid to bring it here. I want to look at it."

Paolina ran across the gallery to give the order. A few minutes later her maid, who she had learned was called Thérèse, came into the room carrying in her arms the silver lamé gown which had been made in Ferrara. It shone and glittered in the sunlight, the silver reflecting, almost as if it were a mirror, the brilliant colours of the room and Sir Harvey's own coat of cherry-red velvet.

"It is pretty," Sir Harvey said. "Hold it up against you."

Paolina did as she was bid. She was surprised to find how heavy it was, for in the hand it had almost an ethereal look as if it were made of water. Sir Harvey beckoned Thérèse to stand beside him.

"You see those bows of ribbon," he said, "and the lace on the edges of the sleeves and round the bosom?"

The Italian maid nodded.

"Si, si, Excellenza."

"Take them all off," Sir Harvey commanded. "Remove every one."

"But, Harvey," Paolina expostulated, "it will look so plain."

Sir Harvey ignored her.

"Then go to the market," he said to Thérèse, "and buy camellias—white camellias, dozens of them, as many as you need—and sew them on the gown from where you have taken the lace and the ribbons. You understand? White camellias, without a touch of colour in any of them."

"*Si, si,* I understand," the maid said.

"Real flowers!" Paolina exclaimed as Thérèse left the room carrying the gown. "Will that not look very strange?"

"It will be sensational," Sir Harvey answered. "You will look different from anyone else. You must wear a silver veil over your hair and white camellias to hold it in place."

"It sounds rather theatrical," Paolina said after a moment.

"That is exactly what I mean it to be," Sir Harvey answered. "You have got to be outstanding, a contrast to every other woman who will be at that reception this afternoon. And, though you think you are beautiful, Paolina, make no mistake, this is the city of beautiful women."

"I do not think I am beautiful," Paolina answered. "I have never thought so; but I hope that other people will imagine I am, for your sake."

Sir Harvey put out his hand and laid it on her shoulder.

"I think you are very beautiful," he said. "And I am trying to present you so that everyone will agree with me. You must trust my judgment in these things."

"But I do," she answered.

If Paolina had any doubts as to her appearance when she left the *palazzo* at four o'clock that afternoon, after half-an-hour in the Palazzo Dolioni, she knew that all Venice was ready to acclaim her.

Sir Harvey's unerring sense of the dramatic had made every woman turn and stare at Paolina's gown as she entered the great high *Salon*. The gentlemen present were more concerned with her face and Paolina found it hard to answer the compliments and gallantries which they showered upon her.

The Marquis introduced her to his mother, a distinguished-looking woman with white hair and inquisitive eyes. Then he took her up to his sister, a dark, vivacious and extremely pretty little Venetian who was making half a dozen gallants laugh heartily at the gossip she recounted in a sweet, almost childish voice which somehow made everything she said seem piquant and amusing.

"I am so glad you have come," she said to Paolina in an

effusive manner which had a captivating charm of its own. "My brother has talked of you without ceasing ever since he discovered you this morning. You are even more beautiful than his description."

"You are too kind," Paolina answered, "and this is very exciting for me."

"You have never been to Venice before?" the Countess enquired. "Well, then, we must do our best to make your visit a memorable one. Where shall we take her first, gentlemen?"

She turned to the gallants around her and received a chorus of suggestions which left Paolina's head whirling. But while the gallants vied with each other with invitations and with ideas, she could hear the ladies present talking of her gown.

"Real flowers," one of them said. "Why have none of us worn them before?"

"Because we have not the brains," someone replied with a little laugh.

"Personally, I think it is an affectation," another remarked a little acidly.

"Only because it is a new idea and you did not think of it," the first speaker retorted, and there was laughter at that.

After some time the Marquis drew Paolina a little aside to show her a snuff-box which had been sent to him from England. It was a beautiful little piece of inset enamel and when Paolina had admired it and heard its history she looked up to find the Marquis's eyes fixed upon her.

"Will you come with me tonight to the theatre?" he asked. "I have arranged a theatre party which I feel both you and Sir Harvey would find amusing."

"You must ask my brother," Paolina replied. "As far as I am concerned it sounds delightful."

"You make me very happy," he said in a low voice. "I did not believe, until you entered the room this morning, that beauty such as yours could exist outside a picture."

"You are flattering me," Paolina faltered.

She looked up and saw the sincerity in his eyes.

"You are so beautiful," he insisted, "that I am half afraid you will vanish, or fade as quickly as the flowers you are wearing will fade. Will you promise me that you will stay as you are?"

"You are saying to me what I want to say to Venice,"

Paolina answered. "I feel it is all unreal, a fairy story from which I shall awake."

"Venice is real," the young Marquis replied, "but you have come from some Olympic spot to which we mere mortals could never find our way. What are you—the goddess of youth, of innocence, or perhaps of unawakened love?"

"How magical you make it sound!" Paolina said. "I wish I were all those things, but actually I am a very ordinary, rather simple person. When you know me well, you will perhaps be disappointed."

"All I ask tonight is the privilege of knowing you well," the Marquis replied.

She laughed a little and moved towards an open window where they could look across the lagoon.

"Do all Venetians flatter as glibly as you do?" she asked. "You must remember I am English and am not used to compliments."

"Then Englishmen must be more stupid than even the stories against them relate," the Marquis answered. "No-one could be with you and not pay you what you call compliments. Actually they are but the truth, spoken from the very depths of my heart."

"Thank you," Paolina smiled. "And now I must find my brother."

"Do not go. I cannot bear to lose you," the Marquis pleaded. "Will you come tonight? And may I call on you tomorrow?"

"Again, you must ask my brother," Paolina answered.

"I want to hear you say that you will be pleased to receive me."

"Of course I shall be pleased if my brother permits it."

"You drive me to despair," the Marquis cried.

Paolina gave him a little smile and then moved away to where Sir Harvey was standing talking to some of the older women and making himself, she could see, very agreeable. When she reached his side he turned to her and said:

"Paolina, we must say good-bye and thank our kind hostess for a most enjoyable time."

"It has been wonderful," Paolina replied in all sincerity.

The Marquis's mother smiled.

"You must both come again. My naughty daughter will doubtless be asking you. She can never resist the excitement of new faces and new people. She says that we get into a groove in Venice. Sometimes I begin to think she is right."

"I wonder if you and your sister would honour me by being my guests at the theatre tonight?" the Marquis said to Sir Harvey.

Sir Harvey shook his head.

"It is very kind of you to invite us," he answered, "but we have made other plans."

Paolina looked up at him wide-eyed. She had not heard of any other plans and she was disappointed, not only for herself but for the Marquis. She saw by the expression on his face that he was perturbed.

"Will you meet me afterwards?" the Marquis insisted. "I planned to take you both to meet some of my friends at one of the casinos. There will be dancing for your sister and, of course, a game of cards for yourself."

"I am sorry, my Lord Marquis, but we cannot accept your most kind invitation," Sir Harvey replied formally.

"But, Harvey . . ." Paolina expostulated.

"I have made other arrangements," he said, with a sudden tightening of his lips.

Paolina was silent. She knew he had a reason for what he was saying. The Marquis raised her hand to his lips, holding her fingers over-long, with a little pressure on them before he released them, which told her all too clearly what his feelings might be. And then they moved downstairs and outside to where the gondola was waiting.

They were hardly out of earshot of the *palazzo* before Paolina began to speak the words that were bubbling on her lips:

"Why could we not go? I am longing to visit the theatre and you said the Marquis was one of the right people for us to know. Why did you refuse?"

Sir Harvey did not reply for a moment. And then, as Paolina turned to him almost fiercely and asked again, "Why?" he answered her.

"Because the Marquis is married!"

"Oh!"

Paolina's ejaculation came spontaneously from between her lips.

"Yes, married," Sir Harvey repeated.

"Why did he not say so? Where was his wife? Was she there?"

"No. Apparently she has left him. They are not divorced. The Dolionis would not stand for a scandal of that sort. But he is a married man and, as such, no use to you."

"But he seemed so nice," Paolina said. "I like him."

"That was obvious," Sir Harvey replied. "Unless you wish to become his mistress, there is no point in wasting your time on a man who can offer you nothing else."

"Must you put it so crudely?" Paolina asked. "Must everything be reduced to the question of what we can get out of it? Are we to have no friends, nobody to whom one can talk naturally?"

She spoke angrily, but Sir Harvey did not raise his voice as he replied vehemently:

"The answer to all those things is, no."

"I cannot believe it," Paolina retorted. "Surely we are here to enjoy ourselves as well as——"

She stopped suddenly. She was wondering why she felt so incensed at Sir Harvey's abrupt refusal of the Marquis. Was it that she really liked him, or was it because his quietness and gravity had made him seem safe and secure after the fiery turbulence of the Duke?

"The point is this," Sir Harvey said patiently, as if to a child. "There is no purpose in your wasting your time or your affection on someone like the Marquis. He has served his purpose; he has introduced us to Venetian Society. Tomorrow we shall be overwhelmed with invitations. Tonight we shall sit quietly at home."

"But we might have been to the theatre," Paolina said.

"And you might have been with the Marquis! Exactly!" Sir Harvey snapped.

"Oh, surely you do not think that he could mean anything to me personally?" Paolina questioned. "Really, it is too nonsensical. It is only that he seemed nice and . . . friendly."

"And of course, very interested in you," Sir Harvey finished.

"He paid me compliments," Paolina replied. "But I do not suppose they meant anything serious."

"The question is not what the Marquis meant by them," Sir Harvey said, "but what they meant to you."

He turned to look at her as he spoke and she thought, for the first time, there was something rather hard and cruel in his eyes.

"I understand your meaning," she said stiffly. "I am a performing animal who must only do my tricks to the right audience at the command of my master."

"That is crudely put, but I suppose generally it is a fairly accurate assessment of the situation," Sir Harvey replied.

Paolina suddenly stamped her foot.

"At times I hate you!" she stormed.

"I am afraid that does not disturb me," Sir Harvey answered. "All that I am asking is that you shall do as you are told."

They had arrived at the steps leading up to their own *palazzo*. Paolina jumped out without touching Sir Harvey's hand and flounced to the doorway ahead of him, her head held high, a kind of burning indignation smouldering in her breast.

Somehow he had spoilt everything for her. For one moment in that *Salon*, with the Marquis whispering sweet things, she had begun to think that she really belonged to this sort of life, that she was not so foreign to it as she had seemed in Ferrara or in those first frightening hours when she had set off alone with Sir Harvey on their adventure.

And now, abruptly, he had put her back in the place where she belonged. She was only a girl he had picked up out of the sea, someone of no consequence, not of noble blood, merely a protégée of his own. And she owed him everything, from the very clothes she wore to every mouthful of food she put into her mouth.

"It is intolerable," she told herself as she went up the stairs. And yet, even as she raved, she knew that her real anger was not because he had refused the invitation of the Marquis but because he could keep his mind always on the ultimate aim for which they were working—to dispose of her by marriage to someone rich enough to pay generously for it.

In her own room Paolina pulled off the silver dress and flung herself down on her bed. Even as she did so, the softness of it struck her and made her realize how grateful she should be. Whatever else happened, she had had this experience. It was something to have met luxury at first hand, to be in Venice, to meet people whom she was well aware if she had been with her father she would never have had the slightest chance of ever seeing, save in the distance.

Sir Harvey had brought her all these good things—a maid to wait on her in a *palazzo* in which she could look out on to the almost incredible beauty of the Grand Canal.

"Venice! Venice!"

She said the words over and over to herself as if she

would recreate the magic that it had meant to her a few hours ago. And yet, already, now she was here she knew she was more concerned with personalities than with what she could see with her own eyes.

The Marquis was married, and yet instinctively she liked him. It was the sort of trick that might be expected from Fate—to bring a man into their lives so that he would be useful enough to introduce them to Society, to make him fall at her feet in genuine admiration, and then produce a barrier which must keep them apart, however much they liked each other.

It was infuriating, and yet Paolina knew there was nothing she could do about it. Sir Harvey was right. There was no point in her wasting either her time or her interest on a man who could offer her nothing of importance.

After a time Paolina rose from her bed and slipping a wrapper over her petticoats opened the door of her room softly. She wondered where Sir Harvey was and what plans he had made for the evening. She was ashamed now that she had stalked away from him in anger. She would apologize and beg his forgiveness.

There was no-one in the gallery outside her room. She crossed it, thinking to find Sir Harvey on the balcony or perhaps in the small library. He was in neither and she suddenly felt a sense of panic in case he had gone out without her, angry and bored with her ingratitude.

It was then she saw him. He was lying on one of the sofas with his feet up and his eyes closed. He was asleep. She realized then that he must have been very tired. He had not slept last night, as she had done, and the fight with the Duke must have taken a toll of his strength even though he had emerged from it victorious.

She looked down at him and, for the first time, saw how young he was. Because he put himself in a position of authority over her she had almost thought of him as old—as old, almost as her father.

Now she saw that when he was still and relaxed his face was young and strangely vulnerable. He did not look a schemer, or even a man who lived on his wits. He looked, instead, just a trustworthy English gentleman, a man whom a woman would find gallant and kind, a protector against any adversities the world could produce.

Paolina stood beside the sofa for some time and perhaps it was the intensity in her gaze which disturbed Sir Harvey. He turned his head, his eyes still closed, and in a voice hoarse and hardly above a whisper, he asked:

"Paolina, are you safe?"

She dropped down on her knees beside him.

"Of course I am," she answered. "And I am so sincerely sorry for the way I behaved just now. I did not mean it. I do not know how I could be so ungrateful after all you have done for me. Please forgive me."

He opened his eyes now, to find her face above him. Her fair curls framed her little face like a halo, her big eyes were dark and troubled.

"Of course I forgive you," he answered drowsily. "It is only that I worry about you. You are so beautiful, so absurdly, incredibly beautiful."

He closed his eyes again and she saw that he was almost drugged with sleep. Yet there was something in his voice that left her heart fluttering. But she knew from his soft breathing that he was unconscious again. She rose from her knees and going to her room brought a soft quilt of satin and swansdown and laid it over his legs.

Then she sat down beside him and watched him. She knew that there would be no gaiety this evening, no visit to a theatre, casino or ballroom.

And yet she was strangely content to sit there beside him, as the sun went down and the stars came out in the translucent sky.

7

Paolina was sitting up in bed finishing her morning
chocolate when there was a knock at the door and before
she could speak it opened.

She looked up in surprise. Thérèse, her maid, was tidy-
ing the room and the hairdresser was heating the curling
irons behind the screen. To her astonishment, because he
had never come to her room before, Sir Harvey stood there.

He was half dressed, but instead of a coat he wore a
gay-coloured brocade dressing-gown which somehow contrived to make him look more dashing and debonair than
usual.

Paolina put down her cup of chocolate and almost
instinctively drew the silk sheets more closely around her
as if to cover the transparency of her nightgown. But her
fair hair, flowing over her shoulders and on to the
pillows, was almost a natural covering for her nakedness.

"Good morning, sweet sister," Sir Harvey said, and then
with a flick of his fingers indicated that he wished Thérèse
and the hairdresser to leave the room.

They withdrew and Paolina looked at him in wide-eyed
surprise.

"The news I have for you could not wait," he said. Seat-
ing himself on the end of the bed, he added: "You are in
exceeding good looks this morning."

Paolina blushed.

"And pray do not look so startled at my intrusion," Sir
Harvey admonished. "Remember I am your brother and
there is nothing in the least improper in receiving your
brother while you are still in bed."

111

"I will try to remember," Paolina said slowly. "What is it you wish to tell me?"

"That I have found the ideal husband for you," Sir Harvey replied.

Paolina felt a strange feeling. It was as if a stone had suddenly dropped on her heart. But she said nothing, only her eyes, very big in her small face, were dark with terror, as Sir Harvey went on gaily.

"It was Alberto who put me in mind of him, although, as it happens, we have met before."

"And how do you know that this gentleman will . . . wish to . . . marry me?" Paolina asked in a strangled voice.

"Because, my dear, he has come to Venice in search of a bride," Sir Harvey answered triumphantly. "It has been the talk for many years that this old uncle, who adopted him and brought him up, desired his marriage. But Leopoldo Ricci—for that is his name—has always resisted wedlock because he found life too amusing as a bachelor. Now I have learned this morning that his uncle is dead. Leopoldo has succeeded to the estates—but there is a condition attached to them. He must marry within the twelvemonth."

"Why should he choose me?" Paolina asked.

"How could he fail to choose you once he has seen you?" Sir Harvey asked gallantly. "Besides, Alberto—who knows him well because he stayed last year with the Duke—says that he has sworn that only a fair-haired woman shall be his bride. That, of course, narrows the selection quite considerably."

"Is he . . . nice?" Paolina asked a little hesitantly.

"He is rich, handsome and charming," Sir Harvey said. "What more could you want? His estates in the south of Italy are fabulous. He has a *palazzo* in Rome and another here in Venice. If I had searched all Europe I could not have thought of a better choice of a husband for anyone. You should be grateful to Fate for such a chance."

"I . . . am . . . of course," Paolina murmured.

"You do not sound very excited," Sir Harvey reproved her. "Listen, my dear. The status of unmarried women in this world is not a happy one. Once you are wed you can do as you like and go where you wish. A clever woman can always twist her husband round her fingers. But if through force of circumstances, or simply and solely, shall we put it, because I have no more money, we have to part—what will become of you?"

"I have asked myself that," Paolina answered.

"The answer is a husband," Sir Harvey said a little aggressively as if she had challenged him. "And what could be easier than to effect an introduction to the *Conte* today when the Carnival starts?"

"The Carnival!" Paolina exclaimed. "I have heard so much about it!"

"Not the big Carnival that begins in October and ends at Christmas—but one to celebrate Saint's Day, an historical anniversary, or merely because people are feeling happy. Nobody knows why a Carnival is proclaimed and nobody cares. But it gives a freedom for enjoyment which one could never experience except behind the anonymity of a mask."

"Does everyone wear a mask?" Paolina enquired.

"Everyone," Sir Harvey replied. "From the Doge to the lowest scullery maid. I have sent Alberto out to buy you the most entrancingly shaped mask that Venice can provide. Then we must choose your gown and set our plans."

"Plans for what?" Paolina asked a little nervously.

"For your introduction, of course, to Conte Leopaldo," Sir Harvey said. "Our best chance of meeting him is in the Piazza San Marco. Everyone will be there this morning, and so the sooner you dress the sooner we can be off."

He rose to his feet, and then as he reached the door Paolina's voice stopped him.

"You are . . . sure . . ." she said falteringly, "sure that this . . . Conte Leopaldo is a . . . kind, nice man?"

"He is everything that a woman could possibly desire," Sir Harvey answered. "But do not count your chickens before they are hatched, my dear. You have yet to catch him."

With this parting shot he left the room and a moment later Thérèse and the hairdresser came hurrying back.

Paolina dressed in silence. Thérèse told her that Sir Harvey had commanded that she wear her gown of blue satin with pink roses. She did not argue, she merely acquiesced, putting on the gown that had been ordered and allowing the hairdresser to do her hair as he wished, sitting very still staring at herself in the mirror, seemingly in a reverie from which nothing could awaken her.

Only when he had finished her hair and set two pink roses among the curls and laces did she take the mask from Thérèse and put it over her face. There was no doubt that it transformed her, it gave her a piquancy and an air of co-quetry which had been lacking. There was something en-

113

trancing in seeing her tiny, tip-tilted nose emerge from the darkness of the velvet and her eyes glittering seductively from behind it. It made her skin seem very white, her mouth crimsonly inviting.

It was impossible not to smile at herself in the mirror. Then with a little whirl of her skirts she ran across the gallery to find Sir Harvey.

He, too, was masked, as were the gondoliers and the servants. Everyone who stepped abroad from the privacy of the house wore masks to disguise themselves. The sun was shining and to Paolina the world had a sudden mad enchantment such as she had never known before.

Everywhere, like mushrooms that come up overnight, booths in brilliant colours and containing a thousand strange and amazing curiosities had appeared. As she stepped ashore from the gondola on to the Piazzetta di San Marco it was difficult because of the noise of the crowds, the music and the shouting of the stall-keepers, to know where to look or what to see first.

Here, under the Monolithic columns, bearing a lion and a statue of St. Theodore, there were Irish giants and Croatian women, canaries that could count up to thirty, dogs dressed as children and mummers from the playhouse singing or miming. And between the Doge's Palace and the stately Library people danced or watched the amazing fancy dresses worn by other masqueraders.

There were men on stilts and men astride a wooden horse; there were women in Turkish trousers, dervishes, clowns, every kind of Harlequin, Punchinello and Pierrot that could be imagined.

With difficulty Sir Harvey fought a way through the crowd until they were free of the booths and came into the Piazza San Marco where a greater formality was observed. Here the nobility, who were easy to recognize by their elegant gowns and magnificently embroidered coats, moved around, masked, but keeping very much within the confines of an imaginary circle so that the parvenues did not encroach upon them.

Sir Harvey and Paolina joined the throng. Some people were drinking wine or calling for chocolate outside the cafés. Others were merely perambulating up and down, glancing at each other from the slits of their masks, speculating as to who might be who, taking liberties and making quips which they would not have dared to make without a disguise.

A strange gallant whom she had never seen before came up to Paolina, raised her hand to his lips and pressed a bouquet of flowers upon her.

"To the most beautiful woman in Venice," he whispered, and would have kissed her cheek had she not moved quickly away from him.

He laughed and disappeared into the crowd so that she was left bewildered, staring after him with a bouquet of exquisite and most expensive flowers in her hands.

Sir Harvey laughed at her bewilderment.

"That is a compliment of the Carnival," he said.

They sat down at one of the tables outside a café. Paolina noticed that the *Piazza* was paved with marble and trachyte and remembered that someone had told her once that it came from the Euganean Hills. But Sir Harvey's eyes were only for the people, scrutinizing this person and then that, until finally he bent forward and said to Paolina in a low voice:

"You see the man over there in the green coat? That is the *Conte.*"

"How can you know?" she asked. "He is masked."

"Alberto discovered what he would be wearing today. It cost me a heavy tip, but it was worth it. That is the man we are seeking."

"And what can we do about it?" Paolina asked a little sarcastically.

She could see the man in the green coat walking slowly across the square. He was alone, but it was obvious that he was looking around him as if in search of friends.

"Come with me," Sir Harvey said.

Paolina got to her feet obediently and followed him. They plunged into the crowd perambulating to and fro and, being smaller than most other people, Paolina could not see for a moment what was happening or where they were going. She could only follow Sir Harvey blindly, knowing it was no use to argue and even impossible, under these circumstances, to ask him what he was doing.

They moved on, hearing snatches of amorous conversation, an amused laugh, a whispered word of unmistakable passion. Then in an instant Paolina lost sight of Sir Harvey. She stood irresolute, dismayed, and suddenly felt someone give her a push from behind. She stumbled, almost fell, and found herself holding on, quite involuntarily, to an arm covered by a green coat.

"I . . . am . . . sorry, *Signore*," she managed to stammer, and looked up at a pair of smiling lips above her.

"Really, fellow, you might be more careful," an angry voice beside her ejaculated.

Sir Harvey was speaking to the man in the green coat in a furious tone of voice.

"It may be the Carnival, but this is not a bear garden. My sister was nearly felled."

"Then I must beg your sister a thousand apologies," the man in the green coat said courteously. "But I do not think that I was at fault. The lady stumbled against me."

"Are you calling me a liar?" Sir Harvey enquired angrily, his hand going to the sword.

The man in the green coat laughed.

"I am saying nothing of the sort," he said. "If you wish to fight I am only too ready to oblige you, but I assure you that I am perfectly prepared to offer this charming lady my fullest and most humble apologies. Dammit all, 'tis too early in the morning for temper."

As if such good humour was too much for him Sir Harvey laughed.

"You are right," he said. "But we have just thrust our way through that jostling and battering, *mêlée*, and it has made me irritable. My compliments, Sir."

"Let me apologize again," the man in the green coat said, making Paolina a most elaborate bow.

She sank in a deep curtsy and then wondered if this was the end of their conversation and how Sir Harvey would manage to prolong it. She was not left long in doubt. Even as they turned to leave Sir Harvey said:

"But, surely, you are Conte Leopaldo Ricci?"

"That is my name," the man in the green coat said. "But I thought during Carnival we were all incognito."

"We hope we are," Sir Harvey said. "Yet as it happens I was looking for you. The Duke of Ferrara, with whom my sister and I are well acquainted, told me particularly to look you up when we arrived at Venice."

"You know the Duke?" the Conte exclaimed.

"Very well, indeed," Sir Harvey answered. "He lent us his *burchiello* to convey us here and he gave me some messages to convey to you."

"Then I must certainly hear them," the *Conte* said with a smile. "Can we not repair to a wine shop and sit down? I would be honoured if you will join me in a glass of wine."

"We shall be delighted," Sir Harvey said.

"Then lead the way," the *Conte* said.

Sir Harvey put his hand on Paolina's arm to guide her in the direction of the wine shop. She felt his fingers pinch her a little as if in amusement at having brought off exactly what he had intended. And she could not help smiling at his audacity.

They reached the shop, wine was brought and Paolina felt slight pressure on her foot beneath the table as if Sir Harvey reminded her that this was her cue to make herself pleasant.

"I have seen your *palazzo* from the outside, my Lord," she said a little nervously. "It is very magnificent."

"My uncle spent a great deal of money on it," the *Conte* replied. "And where are you staying?"

Sir Harvey told him and then, looking at Paolina, the *Conte* said:

"May I be privileged to call upon you, and perhaps you will do me the inexpressible pleasure of dining with me one evening?"

"An invitation I accept without reserve," Sir Harvey smiled. "But I do not know whether my sister is engaged."

"We must choose a night when she is free," the *Conte* interposed before Paolina could answer. "I should like so much to show her the sculptures and the paintings in my *palazzo*. As a collection they are unique."

"I should enjoy that very much," Paolina said.

Sir Harvey got to his feet.

"Forgive me one moment. I see a friend over there with whom I must have a word. Would you take care of my sister until I return?"

"I am honoured by the charge," the *Conte* answered. "She will, I promise you, be safe in my keeping."

Sir Harvey walked away to speak to the friend, who Paolina was convinced existed only in his imagination. The knowledge of what he was contriving made her feel shy. For a moment everything that she might say disappeared out of her head. She could only sit staring down at her bouquet of flowers, feeling tongue-tied and rather stupid.

"Your flowers are beautiful," the *Conte* said gently.

"A stranger gave them to me just now," Paolina answered. "He kissed my hand and then presented me with this bouquet."

"Saying, of course, they were for the most beautiful woman in Venice," the *Conte* smiled.

"But, how did you know?" Paolina enquired.

"It is the usual compliment that is paid in the Carnival to anyone as beautiful as yourself," he said, his eyes eloquent as his voice.

Paolina looked down, thankful that her mask could hide a little of her embarrassment.

The *Conte* bent forward, his arms on the table.

"Tell me about yourself," he said. "You are not Italian?"

"No, I am English."

"I was sure of it. There is something about you, and your hair is so golden, I felt that you could not possibly be one of my countrywomen. And yet your Italian is almost perfect."

"I——" Paolina began, and then stopped quickly. She had been about to say that she had lived in Italy for some years, then she was not certain, as Sir Harvey's sister, how long she was supposed to have been here. So, rather lamely, she substituted: "I have studied the language."

"And you have become word perfect," the *Conte* exclaimed. "But do not let us talk of pedantry. I want to look into your eyes. How strange they are not blue, as one might expect."

"No, they are dark," Paolina answered.

"A combination which could only have been thought of by the gods! One glance could raise a man to heaven or send him down to hell," he murmured in a low voice, his face very near to hers.

Instinctively Paolina's long eyelashes veiled her eyes and she lowered her head to hide the colour which suffused her cheeks.

The *Conte* glanced across the *Piazza*, saw that Sir Harvey was returning, and said quickly: "When can I see you again? Do not torture me by making me wait. Dine with me tonight."

"I do not know what my brother has arranged," Paolina answered.

"In Carnival time all invitations are elastic, they can be amended, altered or forgotten. Nobody minds, there are no reproaches, no recriminations. Promise me you will come."

His insistence was almost mesmeric and yet Paolina was reluctant to say yes. She had somehow a feeling that she was committing herself, and before she could reply Sir Harvey had reached their table.

"I just caught him," he said cheerily.

118

"I am trying to persuade your sister to agree that you will both dine with me tonight," the *Conte* explained. "I have already invited a few friends and we might go on afterwards to the Ball at the Palazzo Gritti. The Princess has begged me to bring a party. Won't you honour me by coming as my guests?"

"I have already said," Paolina interposed quickly to Sir Harvey, "that I thought you had another engagement."

She felt somehow it was shaming to seem so eager.

"If we had an engagement, I have already forgotten it," Sir Harvey said. "What could be more enjoyable than your company, *Conte*? Your *palazzo* is irresistible to someone like myself who is a lover of beautiful things."

"I, also, love things that are beautiful," the *Conte* said softly. He looked at Paolina as he spoke and then, rising to his feet, took her hand and pressed it. "I pray you will not fail me," he said urgently. "I shall count the hours until this evening."

"Thank you," Paolina answered, and Sir Harvey, bowing to him as he left, added:

"I can then give you my messages from the Duke."

"I shall be impatient to hear them," the *Conte* replied.

He moved away and when he was out of earshot Sir Harvey looked at Paolina, his eyes dancing with mischief.

"It came off!" he exclaimed.

"I do not know how you could dare do it," Paolina answered. "I was ready to swoon with embarrassment! Besides, he might have seen you push me against him."

"But he didn't," Sir Harvey answered. "Whenever I do things there is always the chance that they may go wrong, but they seldom do. We are in luck, little sister. What do you think of your future husband?"

"Don't say it," Paolina begged. "I think it is unlucky."

"Fiddlesticks!" Sir Harvey retorted briskly. "The only luck that matters is the luck you attract to yourself by being determined, by knowing what you want in the world. If it's a question of good luck, what could have been better than running into him like this?"

"Did you know he was going to be here?" Paolina asked.

Sir Harvey smiled.

"His valet did tell Alberto that the *Conte* had an appointment to meet the French Ambassador at noon today, and the French Ambassador is known always to drink a glass of wine at one particular coffee-house in the *Piazza*."

"So it was not luck at all but just forethought," Paolina said.

"That is the secret of most good fortune," Sir Harvey answered. "Forethought, careful planning and a gambler's instinct for 'taking a chance'."

Paolina sighed.

"I only wish," she said in a low voice, "that you were not gambling with me."

"With you I am on a certainty," Sir Harvey said reassuringly. "Anyway, that is a very charming young man. I feel sure you will be happy with him."

Paolina shivered.

"Please do not speak as if everything was already arranged," she pleaded. "It frightens me."

She got quickly to her feet.

"Let us go back to the booths. I do not know what else you are plotting, but I feel safer there."

Sir Harvey laughed, but he let her lead the way back towards the noise and gaiety of the merrymakers. A gypsy in a mask but wearing the traditional red skirt and embroidered velvet jacket of her race stopped Paolina.

"Let me tell your fortune, pretty *Signorina*," she begged. "Cross my palm with silver and I will reveal what the future holds for you."

"That is something I should really like to know," Paolina said without thinking.

She was only joking, but Sir Harvey took her seriously, and drawing some coins from his pocket gave them to the gypsy.

"Tell us what you see," he said.

"I do not think I really want to know," Paolina hesitated.

"Too late," he answered, while the gypsy, taking Paolina's small white hand in her dark fingers, said:

"Do not be afraid, little lady. You have a lucky hand. No harm will come to you although there is danger around you and at times the shadows make you afraid."

"That is true enough," Paolina agreed, thinking of the Duke and those moments of sheer terror before Sir Harvey had arrived to save her.

"What do you foresee in the future?" Sir Harvey asked.

"I see the pretty lady walking reluctantly down a path which has been planned for her. I see shining jewels and vast riches and between them and her a broken heart."

The gypsy spoke in a low, almost hissing voice.

"A broken heart," she repeated. "But it will be mended. Yes, it will be mended, but only by violence and the shedding of blood."

Paolina snatched her hand away.

"Oh, do not tell me any more," she begged. "I do not want to hear. It is horrible."

"Do not be afraid," the gypsy said. "You are lucky. The circle in which you stand is a charmed one. You will be safe."

"With all that happening?" Paolina said sharply. "I very much doubt it." She caught hold of Sir Harvey's arm. "Take me away," she pleaded. "I wish we had not listened to the woman."

"It is all nonsense," Sir Harvey exclaimed. "You need not believe a word of it. She says the same thing to everyone."

They moved away quickly, but Paolina could not help looking back at the gypsy. The gypsy looked like a witch, she thought. She was old and wrinkled, her skin almost black from the sun, and there was no doubt that her Romany voice had a kind of clairvoyance about it. There was something eerie in the way she had spoken and everything she had said had somehow a ring of truth about it.

"Are you sure it was nonsense?" she asked Sir Harvey.

"Quite convinced that the whole thing is a pack of lies," he answered. "If six other women go and have their hands told after you, she will foretell an almost identical future for them."

"She sounded so . . . truthful," Paolina faltered.

"Forget it," he commanded.

They plunged into the crowd, stopping to look at a booth selling the most exquisite lace, moving out of the way of a crowd of ballet dancers who, as they threw roses to the crowd, were followed by a collection of gallants declaiming the sonnets that they had written in praise of the prima ballerina.

"It is all quite mad, isn't it?" Paolina said.

"It is like a children's party," Sir Harvey answered. "But that is what the Venetians are—children who want to play all the time—which is why they are losing their trade and their prestige."

He spoke seriously and Paolina looked at him in surprise.

"If I were the Doge, I should forbid the Carnival, except perhaps for one week of the year, and I would make people

121

work. Their greatness and their glory is already declining; in a few years it will be gone beyond recall."

"It could never be anything but the most beautiful place in the world," Paolina said.

Sir Harvey looked out over the blue lagoon.

"I wonder what it will be like in the future?" he said. "They do not seem to realize that it is their ships and their trading which have made them rich and which have paid for all this beauty."

He shook himself and hailed their gondola.

"Do not let us be serious," he said. "This is Carnival. Let us laugh with the rest and prepare ourselves for tonight."

It seemed to Paolina that all through the long, warm day the thought of the night hung over her like a little black cloud. They ate delicious meals, they went in the gondola down the Grand Canal, looking at the *palazzi*, making the acquaintance of several people who had called on them, and finding that everyone was only too ready to be charming, friendly and hospitable.

But all the time Paolina was thinking of what would happen that evening. The *Conte* had fallen so easily into the trap that Sir Harvey had set for him. Would it be as easy to trap him further?

The question seemed to haunt her and she could not help remembering the gypsy's words. She was indeed walking down a path which had been prepared for her. And she was certainly reluctant to do so. Yet, at the same time, she could not help realizing how wonderful it was to be here, to see the great *palazzi*, to meet the people who owned them, to feel the warm sunshine on her head as she stepped into the gondola, to be carried swiftly into the labyrinth of small mysterious canals winding through the fabulous city.

Sir Harvey was particularly lighthearted, talking nonsense, paying compliments, contriving to be as gallant as any of the Venetian noblemen with their exquisite manners and their quick turn of wit.

Paolina began to feel as if she were acting in a strange masque in which everyone had a script they had learnt previously and from which they recited their lines. It was all so unreal, so artificial, and yet so utterly delightful.

They felt a little tired when they left their last call—a *palazzo* on the Grand Canal—and started for home.

"You must rest before dinner," Sir Harvey said as they

lay back against the soft satin cushions of the gondola. "Tonight you must be incomparable."

"Must we go?" Paolina asked suddenly. "Could we not for once forget all our schemes and just enjoy ourselves?"

"If you could choose what would you do?" Sir Harvey asked.

"I think I would dine in the *palazzo*," Paolina answered dreamily. "Just you and I. Then I would like to go out in the gondola under the stars, to move through the little canals which are very quiet, and then perhaps to drift near San Marco and hear the music, the laughter, the crowds; to be near and yet not part of it. And then later to go out on to the Lagoon. It must be very beautiful when the moon comes up."

"Do you think you would be quite content to be there also with me?" Sir Harvey asked almost harshly. "You could not expect me to whisper sweet nothings to my sister."

"I think I am a little tired of compliments," Paolina replied petulantly. "There are too many of them. They are spoken so easily that one can hardly credit that they mean anything to the person who says them or to the person who receives them."

"Shall I pay you a compliment that I really mean?" Sir Harvey asked.

"Oh . . . yes," Paolina answered, suddenly for no reason a little breathless.

"I thought this afternoon when I was watching you that you had the natural and gracious manners of noble breeding. Whoever your mother might be, however your father might have misspent his life, they could only have been aristocrats. Only someone of great sensibility could have surmounted the obstacles which have been put in your way these last few days. I know full well it has not been easy for you to act the part I have asked of you, and yet you have done it supremely well."

Paolina felt a warm glow of satisfaction within her at his words. Her eyes were shining as she said:

"Oh, how can I thank you for saying that? I have been so afraid that I should fail . . . you."

"My dear, I am not worthy of having the faith and confidence you have in me. You have trusted me. It is I who should be afraid of failing you."

"I do not think you could ever do that," Paolina replied. "You pretend to be so many things that you are not. You

123

pretend to be tough and hard and an adventurer, but really you are kind and gentle and understanding. I have not said so before, but I have thought how generous it was of you to bring poor Alberto with us when he was so afraid. You did not really want him, but you made a place for him."

Paolina gave a little sigh that was almost a sob and went on in a low voice:

"And you have been kind to me when I have been tiresome and fearful. I have not missed those things even though I find it difficult to tell you how much I appreciate them."

"Then pray do not do so," Sir Harvey said with a brusqueness which told her he was deeply embarrassed by her words. "Perhaps the Italians are right. We English are bad at receiving compliments."

"I like some compliments," Paolina said. "The sort you pay me; the sort that someone really means."

He put his hand over hers and squeezed it. Then his mood changed, and she felt as if mentally he stiffened himself.

"We have got to look on this adventure as a business proposition," he said. "So tonight we cannot afford to indulge ourselves. Remember, at the outside, we have only two months in which to achieve our goal."

"It seems a long time," Paolina sighed.

"Time and money run through the fingers like water," Sir Harvey quoted.

They were getting nearer to the *palazzo*. Paolina said no more, but as they stepped out and she gave him her hand she felt the warm strength of his and was happy with a kind of inner radiance because he was pleased with her.

It did not seem to matter after that what lay ahead. Sir Harvey had praised her, and everything else seemed of little importance because of it.

That evening she wore a dress of white satin and lace which Sir Harvey had decided should be trimmed with real pink roses that were just turning from bud to bloom. There were pink slippers for her feet and a wreath of flowers for her hair. Paolina found that he had planned the gown before they left the *palazzo* after their midday meal, and she knew that he had chosen roses so that her hair would look the fairer and she would remind the Count that she was a simple English rose.

"Let me look at you," Sir Harvey said a little sharply as she came from her bed-chamber into the gallery. She turned round and round so that he could see the gown both back and front.

"*Bellissima! Bellissima!*" Thérèse exclaimed as if prompting Sir Harvey to approve her handiwork.

"The roses could have been a shade deeper in colour," Sir Harvey said critically. "And there is a hook undone at the back of the *Signorina's* gown."

"Oh, *scusi!*" Thérèse said, hastening to do it up.

Like Thérèse, Paolina was waiting for the word of approval. For some reason he did not seem inclined to give it.

"Are you ready?" he said. "If we do not leave at once, we shall be late."

"I am ready," Paolina answered, and ignoring the hurt expression on Thérèse's face, Sir Harvey hustled her away.

The Palazzo Ricci was nearly twice the size of those on either side of it. There were footmen in purple and gold livery to assist them to alight from the gondola; the chandeliers which hung in the entrance hall with its lapis floor were of solid gold. Paolina's eyes were growing used to magnificence, but the Palazzo Ricci left her almost breathless as she was hurried through rooms and corridors to where, in a huge, brilliantly lit *Salon*, the Count was waiting.

There were nearly twenty other guests with him and as Paolina curtsied she saw the women eyeing her a little maliciously, while the men accompanying them were all too anxious to be introduced.

The Contessa Dolfin was present, her eyes sparkling, her red lips parted animatedly and her gown a dream of gold-threaded brocade trimmed with crimson ribbons. She ran at once to Sir Harvey's side and holding on to his arm looked up at him flirtatiously and started to compliment him in a soft, warm, almost girlish voice which had an irresistible charm of its own.

Paolina felt herself stiffen. She found it difficult to concentrate on what the *Conte* was saying to her. It was only after a few minutes that she realized she had looked at him for the first time without a mask and that his face had made no impression on her.

He was good-looking, there was no mistaking that. He had clear-cut features, a square forehead, deep-set, twinkling eyes, and an engaging smile which made it impossible for anyone not to like him.

125

"I was half afraid you would not come," he said to Paolina in a low voice.

"How could we be so rude?" she asked.

"I thought afterwards I should have sent you a more formal invitation. I was fearful that when you got home you would say to yourself: 'Who is this fellow whom we have picked up in San Marco? We really cannot be bothered with him. There are a dozen better invitations than his awaiting us.'"

Paolina laughed.

"I do not believe you are as modest as that," she said. "Not living in a palace such as this."

"You forget it is a very new acquisition," he replied. "I am really a very humble person."

"I cannot believe that either," she answered.

"Then I must try and convince you," he replied, "that where you are concerned, I am abject in my humility."

She suddenly realized that she, too, was flirting. It was all so easy, this little exchange of conversation, the look in the eyes which said so much more than the words, the way a man's head would come down as if to watch the very curvature of her lips, the lilt she herself could put into her sentences which made them sound amusing even when in themselves they were quite ordinary.

Then she glanced across the room and saw that Sir Harvey was laughing, and wondered what the *Contessa* had said that amused him so much.

"She is not really pretty," Paolina thought, almost spitefully. "But I suppose she has a rather obvious attraction."

She saw the *Contessa* standing on tiptoe to whisper something in Sir Harvey's ear, and felt a sudden pain within her and to her astonishment realized what it was.

"I am jealous," she told herself. "I suppose that I want Sir Harvey to be preoccupied with me. How despicable, and yet it is true."

She found the *Conte* had been talking to her and she had not heard a word of what he said.

"I . . . I am sorry," she stammered. "I was thinking of something else."

"And not of me," the *Conte* said. "How cruel you are! I was merely saying that after dinner the Ball at the Palazzo Gritti promises to eclipse in splendour any dance that has ever been given in Venice. Thousands of hostesses vie with each other, you know, in providing something different, more elaborate than has ever been seen before. The place is full of rumours as to what will happen tonight."

Paolina forced herself to seem interested.

"It must cost an awful lot of money!"

The *Conte* looked surprised.

"I do not think anyone ever worries about money in Venice," he said. "And, after all, what is money except to be spent?"

Paolina longed to answer, "It is very inconvenient if one does not have it," but she felt that would be indiscreet and merely murmured:

"What, indeed?"

The *Contessa* was really audacious, she thought. It might be the Carnival, but there was no reason for her to touch Sir Harvey's coat with her thin, bejewelled fingers, to smile up at him so enticingly with her red lips that somehow looked like ripe cherries.

"Where is the Conte Dolfin? Is he here?" Paolina asked in a rather stiff voice, forgetting that the Marquis had said that his sister was a widow.

"Goodness, no!" the *Conte* replied. "He has been dead these past three years. He was a very boring man and I do not think Zanetta ever cared for him."

"Zanetta! Is that her name?" Paolina asked.

"It is charming, is it not?" the *Conte* answered. "And she is one of my favourite people. I see your brother finds her very attractive, too."

"Yes, obviously," Paolina said coldly.

There was no doubt at all that Sir Harvey was enjoying himself.

"Why can I not make him laugh like that?" Paolina asked herself savagely. Then, because she was piqued, she forced herself to turn her attentions to the *Conte*.

Somehow she no longer wanted to flirt, no longer found the words for the quick exchange. Instead she listened, through dinner, to the *Conte* telling her about himself, and half the time her mind was wandering across the table to where Zanetta and Sir Harvey were obviously very engrossed in their almost whispered conversation.

It seemed to Paolina that never had a meal taken longer to be served and eaten. Hours seemed to drag by before, at length, the ladies retired from the table and went into one of the elaborate bed-chambers to tidy themselves and put on their masks.

"Your brother is so charming," the *Contessa* said to

127

Paolina. "He and I had so much to say to each other at dinner."

"So I observed," Paolina replied stiffly.

"We made a great many plans," the *Contessa* smiled, "for the lovely, gay, wild things we will do. He is so witty, such a—how do you say it in English?—man of the world. I have always loved Englishmen, but, alas, far too few of them come to Venice."

She turned and looked at herself in the mirror and tidied her dark hair.

"Your brother has big estates in England?" she enquired, too artlessly for the question to be disinterested.

Paolina felt her heart turn over. So the *Contessa* was really interested in Sir Harvey. Perhaps he was not only planning for her, but also for himself. The *Contessa* would undoubtedly be rich. She would not only have the money which was her own as sister of the Marquis, she would doubtless have great wealth left her by her deceased husband.

Was Sir Harvey contemplating marriage? Did he feel that what was sauce for the goose could also be sauce for the gander?

With no effort Paolina forced herself to answer cautiously.

"You must ask my brother all about them," she said. "I am sure he will want to tell you himself."

If the *Contessa* was disappointed she made no sign of it.

"Your pearls are very lovely," she said, looking at the necklace round Paolina's neck.

"My brother gave them to me," Paolina replied, and she saw the sudden glint in the other woman's eyes and knew exactly what she was thinking.

Money! Money! That was what everyone was seeking, everybody was angling for. However rich the *Contessa* might be, she did not want a penniless husband or one who could not bring her prestige, lands and power.

As Paolina put her hands up to her hair, she realized that they were trembling. This was something she had never anticipated, never imagined could happen. Somehow Sir Harvey had seemed immune from the foibles of other men, concerned only with promoting her marriage. She had not thought for a moment that he might be concerned with planning, at the same time, his own future.

"If he marries the *Contessa*," Paolina thought, "then there will be no reason for him to concern himself with me.

He can throw me away, leave me, let me disappear into oblivion. He will have what he wants without me."

She had a sudden wild desire to call out the truth, to tell the *Contessa* that they were nothing but penniless adventurers and warn her against them both; to see the horror and shock in her eyes when she realized that they were not even brother and sister—a man and woman united only in their desire to defraud people richer than themselves.

The words almost trembled on Paolina's lips, then she bit them back. "How can I be so stupid as to mind what he does?" she asked herself. But she knew there was a sudden pain in her breast that had not been there before, a choking feeling in her throat, a dryness of her lips.

Masked, the ladies went back into the *Salon* and the men came from the Banqueting Hall. The *Conte* hurried eagerly to Paolina's side, but she was watching Sir Harvey. He caught her eyes and gave her a smile of encouragement which seemed to ease a little of her pain and unhappiness.

Perhaps she was merely imagining it. Perhaps he was no more serious about the attractive Zanetta than she might be about him.

The *Conte* drew her on one side.

"I want you to see this picture," he said aloud, and when they were a little apart from the others he whispered in her ear:

"Must we go to the Ball? I would like to go out on the Canal alone with you, I want to float beside you under the stars. Can we not do that, my little English rose?"

"No! No!" Paolina answered, and heard in her own voice a cry of sheer unadulterated pain.

8

The Ballroom was more fantastic than anything Paolina could possibly have imagined. It was, indeed, so lovely that it took her breath away.

The huge room, with its windows overlooking the Canal, had been transformed literally into a forest of flowers. In Venice of all places, where there were no woods or greenery, the sight of the massed fragrant blossoms was so unexpected that they were a more effective decoration than anything else could have been.

The whole ceiling was covered with camellias, wistaria, orange and cherry blossoms, magnolias and many other perfumed flowers which occasionally dropped a tiny petal like a snowflake down on the moving throng beneath them. And the walls were concealed with trunks and entwined stems, with green leaves glittering like emeralds and arranged so realistically that every now and then one discovered, as if by chance, a tiny bird's nest filled with eggs.

There was a fountain playing at the far end of the room, but instead of water it distilled an exotic Eastern perfume which the men declared had a magic property which made every woman who wore it irresistible.

There was a bouquet for each woman guest when she arrived—posies of flowers which were chosen so that each matched the dress of the owner. Paolina was given a tiny nosegay of pink rosebuds that had not yet begun to open.

"They are like you," the *Conte* whispered. "Unsophisticated, unaware of the world, and yet so exquisite that one wants them to remain just as they are."

"Do I seem like that to you?" Paolina asked curiously.

"There is an innocence about you that is almost fright-

130

ening," he replied. "Here, where every woman is a so-phisticated coquette from the moment she is born, you are like a sleeping princess. Shall I be the one to awaken you? The question tortures me."

She turned her head away from him with a little smile, but the smile vanished as she saw that the Contessa Zanetta was slipping a flower from her bouquet surreptitiously into Sir Harvey's pocket.

"Sleep on it," she whispered, "and perhaps you will dream of me."

"I need no flower to make me do that," he answered gallantly.

Petulantly Paolina accepted an invitation to dance and was swept into a gay throng who were all masked and yet dressed with that fabulous extravagance which proclaimed all too obviously to what society they belonged.

"Later we must go to the Piazza San Marco," the *Conte* said. "There will be great revelry there tonight and we shall be free to enjoy ourselves."

"Are we not free now?" Paolina asked.

"With all this crowd around us?" he smiled. "You do not imagine for a moment that our masks are a disguise here. Everybody knows who we are and is ready to gossip about everything we do, and to repeat, if they overhear it, every-thing we say."

"Then why be masked?" Paolina asked.

"It is a pretence that gives us more licence for enjoy-ment," he answered. "Unmasked I might be afraid to make love to you; but now, protected by a strip of velvet, I can tell you that you entrance me. I think you must be a witch who has escaped from being burned at the stake."

"I think it is Venice that has bewitched you," Paolina answered, "just as it has bewitched me."

"You like it?" he asked. "You would be happy to live here?"

"How can I answer that question after so short an ac-quaintance?" Paolina parried.

At the same time she felt her fingers, which were held tightly in his hand, tremble a little. Was it coming so quickly? This invitation to marriage which Sir Harvey had anticipated and which he had brought her here to receive.

She was, however, prevented from saying more for at that moment a masked Harlequin swept in amongst the dancers and, seizing Paolina in his arms, whirled her away.

"The licence of the Carnival," he said. "One can steal

131

whom one fancies from any man who is not clever enough to hold her."

Paolina thought she recognized the grave, rather slow voice of the Marquis, and a moment later found she was not mistaken. He danced with her until they came to an open window, then drew her out on to the carved stone balcony which overlooked the Canal.

"Why did you not answer my letter?" he asked.

"Your letter?" Paolina questioned in surprise.

"I wrote a letter with the flowers I sent you asking you to see me."

"But I never received it," Paolina said. "Nor the flowers."

She was puzzled for a moment and then she realized, with something almost approaching anger, that Sir Harvey must have intercepted both the letter and the gift.

He was nothing if not thorough, she thought, and having made up his mind that the Marquis could not be of any use to them, he was ready to ensure by any method, however autocratic, that she should forget him.

"Pray forgive me if I seem rude," she said. "There must have been some mistake. Perhaps the servants put the flowers on the table and I did not see them."

It was a lame explanation and the Marquis brushed it aside for what it was worth.

"Your brother is a most efficient chaperon," he said. "Who shall blame him for that? If my sister were as beautiful, I should be just as severe a watchdog."

"But your sister is beautiful," Paolina answered. "She is obviously very attractive."

"She will be glad that you think so," the Marquis answered. "But she would be still more pleased if she heard that your brother admired her too. She is already infatuated, did you know that?"

Paolina caught hold of the cool stone of the balustrade.

"I guessed it," she said.

"When Zanetta makes up her mind she likes someone, nothing can change her. Not, indeed, that I would wish to do so. It is hard, though, while your brother can take what he wants, I must be denied even the happiness of seeing you."

"I think you know the reason," Paolina replied.

"That I am married?" the Marquis enquired. "I guessed that was why your brother refused my invitations. But must you be so harsh?"

"You have a wife, my Lord," Paolina said gently. "It would be best if you paid attention to her rather than to me."

"I see you have only heard half the truth," the Marquis answered. "I have a wife, but I suppose no-one troubled to tell you we were married when we were only children. I was fourteen, she was twelve. Our fathers decided to amalgamate our estates. It was an excellent idea from their point of view, but from mine it was disastrous."

"Why?" Paolina asked.

"Our marriage was but a mere formality," the Marquis explained. "Immediately the ceremony was over, my child-bride was taken back to her father's house and within a week something happened which changed the whole course of our lives. She had a fall from the stairs in the courtyard. Nobody knows quite what happened, but it is thought that she caught her heel in the hem of her gown—something as simple as that. But she fell, breaking her leg and hitting her head against a piece of heavy statuary which stood at the bottom of the staircase. When she was picked up she was unconscious. Though she recovered consciousness some time later, she never regained her full senses."

"What do you mean?" Paolina asked in horror.

"I mean, to put it bluntly, that she is mad," the Marquis answered. "She lives in her father's house, and while I have grown older she has remained a child. Every physician of note in the whole of Europe has prescribed for her. Her father has even sent to Egypt and to Persia for apothecaries and priests learned in the art of medicine and herbs, but nothing is of any avail. She does not even recognize me and I think that her family are only known to her because she sees them so frequently, not because she has any real idea of their relationship."

"It is the saddest story I have ever heard," Paolina said in a low voice.

"It is not something I speak of to many people," the Marquis told her. "But I wanted you to know the truth."

"Thank you for telling me," Paolina answered. She paused a moment and then added: "It seems so inadequate to say I am sorry."

"I do not want your sympathy," he replied, "only your understanding and perhaps the promise that you will be a little kinder to me. I am a very lonely person. I suppose by nature I was never intended to be a rake or someone who only went from party to party seeking amusement with a

133

different woman every night. I want a home of my own. I would like to settle down and have children. What hope is there for me?"

He sighed and impulsively Paolina put her hand on his arm.

"Is there no way of your becoming free?" she asked.

"There is nothing I can do," he answered. "And so I must remain as I am until her death brings me a merciful release."

There was nothing Paolina could say. Instead she moved to lean over the balcony to look at the water below. The Marquis stood beside her, his eyes on her face. After a long pause she said:

"I am deeply sorry for you, but you must not let it embitter you. Everyone has troubles, everyone has secrets which must be hidden from the world with a brave face."

"And what are your secrets?" he asked in an amused voice.

"I assure you that I have some," Paolina answered.

"Will you not confide in me?" the Marquis enquired. "I have been honest with you. Tell me what you are hiding behind that exquisite little face and in the darkness of those purple eyes."

"Who said they are purple?" Paolina enquired.

"I do," he answered. "When you are worried or troubled, it is like looking into the heart of a violet. But when you are happy there is a kind of shimmering radiance about them which makes me think I am staring at a star."

"The compliments Venetians pay me are beginning to turn my head," Paolina said with a little laugh. "Fortunately I do not take them seriously."

"Yet I want you to take me seriously," the Marquis insisted.

"How can I?" Paolina enquired. "Although my brother has not forbidden me to see you, I think you know that he would put every obstacle in the way of our meeting or becoming friends."

"Then what can I do?" the Marquis asked passionately. "I want to see you, I want to be with you more than I have ever wanted to be with any woman before. Yet, what can I offer you? Only the heart of a man who would love you better than his life or his hope of Heaven."

Paolina made a little gesture of helplessness.

"There is nothing I can answer to that," she said. "I am

134

honoured that you should feel that way about me, but you know that we can be nothing to each other and therefore it is best not to make it harder by talking of what might be."

She was trying to be kind and thinking only of the Marquis, but he took it that she was also interested in him. Raising her hand to his lips he covered it with kisses.

"I love you!" he said. "I have loved you wildly, passionately, eternally, from the very first moment I saw you. Do you mean that you could care for me a little?"

"She means nothing of the sort," a severe voice said behind them.

They both started guiltily to see Sir Harvey standing in the doorway.

"I found out," he said, "who was the Harlequin who had invaded this party and carried off my sister from her host at dinner. I do not wish to fight with you, my Lord Marquis, but my sister's good name is one that I shall not hesitate to defend if the necessity arises."

"Your sister is safe with me," the Marquis answered.

"The reputation of an unmarried woman, when she is constantly in the company of a married man, is bound to suffer," Sir Harvey said.

"Very well, I will be honest," the Marquis confessed, "and admit that I came here tonight only because I hoped to see your sister. Now I will go back to the revels which of course make those who take part in them extremely happy."

He spoke bitterly and instinctively Paolina's hand went out towards him.

"Do not speak like that," she pleaded. "I want your happiness—we all do. It is only that neither of us can help each other at the moment. I must do as my brother wishes and not see you. But, I promise you one thing, I shall remember you in my prayers."

He took both her hands in his, bent his head and kissed them. Then, without another word, he was gone.

"Must you be such a fool as to waste your time with him?" Sir Harvey asked angrily.

The tone of his voice brought the blood to Paolina's cheeks.

"He is unhappy and I have a right to speak with whom I please," she retorted. "I also think it insufferable that you should have prevented me from receiving his letter."

"I could see that you liked him," Sir Harvey replied.

"And what was the point of getting yourself involved with a man who could offer you nothing save the position of his mistress?"

He spoke brutally, but instead of feeling shy and embarrassed Paolina only felt angry.

"I do not expect to get something out of every man with whom I speak," she said. "I do not debase myself as far as that, however much I may pretend to be what I am not. I am sorry for the Marquis. He is in a pitiable position from which no one can rescue him. At the same time, I am proud that he has honoured me by telling me that he loves me."

"So that is what he has been saying to you, is it?" Sir Harvey asked. "Oh, well, it is easy enough to say if one has not to complete the sentence with a wedding ring. If the Marquis was free I dare say he would pipe a very different tune."

"That sort of sneer is unworthy of you," Paolina cried.

"Is it?" Sir Harvey asked. "Well, then, let me be blunt and say I do not believe in these quick infatuations. If a man is going to propose marriage, he thinks it over seriously and doesn't rush bald-headed into it with a woman he has only seen for a few hours and of whom he knows nothing save that she has a pretty face."

"Unless, of course, she is also rich as well," Paolina said.

"What do you mean by that?" Sir Harvey asked angrily.

"I mean," Paolina answered, "that the Contessa Zanetta——"

She was interrupted by a gay voice:

"Who is talking about me? Oh! I do hope you are saying something nice."

The *Contessa* came running through the window on to the balcony.

"I have been looking for you everywhere. Oh, Sir Harvey, how could you neglect me so? I have been feeling very sad because you vanished."

"I was only looking after my rather tiresome little sister," Sir Harvey answered. "Now that I have found her, let us collect the *Conte* and go down to supper."

"I saw Leopaldo a few minutes ago," the *Contessa* answered. "He was searching for your sister. I have never known him so attentive."

She gave Paolina a little mischievous smile and added:

"All the women in Venice are longing to scratch your

136

eyes out. Perhaps it is fortunate that you are wearing a mask."

"I think they are exaggerating the politeness of a host to his most insignificant guest," Paolina said a little stiffly.

The *Contessa* laughed.

"Oh, you English are so funny!" she said. "You hate anyone to say nice things. You always have to disparage it or turn it aside. When I told your brother just now that he was the most attractive man I had ever seen, he blushed beneath his tan. It made me feel as if I had been too bold."

"I am not surprised," Paolina said in a low voice.

The *Contessa* turned to Sir Harvey, hanging on his arm, her red lips turned invitingly up to his.

"The English are so tall besides being so handsome," she said. "That is what we women like, to walk beside a tall man. It makes us feel as if we are fragile and in need of protection."

"I think it is I who needs protection, not you," Sir Harvey laughed.

"From me?" the *Contessa* answered. "But, there you are very right. I think you are so charming that if I do not make it plain to the world that you are my *beau* someone else will try to snatch your first."

"Come along down to supper," Sir Harvey said, looking towards Paolina with an embarrassment in his eyes as if he tried to explain to her that he could not help the extravagances of the *Contessa*.

But Paolina was not looking at him. Instead she was holding herself very stiff and straight as in a cold voice she said:

"I think I can see the *Conte* in the Ballroom looking for us. I will go and tell him we are here."

She swept away before Sir Harvey could protest, slipping through the crowd and quickly reaching the *Conte's* side.

"Ah, there you are, Miss Drake," he exclaimed in relief. "I wondered what had happened to you. You vanished with that impudent Harlequin and I was afraid he had carried you off."

"We were only on the balcony getting a little air after the heat of the room," Paolina answered. "The Contessa Dolfin is there now with my brother."

"That does not surprise me," the *Conte* smiled.

"They have suggested that we all go down to supper together," Paolina answered.

137

"Then let us go right away," the *Conte* suggested, offering Paolina his arm. "While Zanetta is engrossed with Sir Harvey, Heaven knows how long it will be before they follow us."

"Perhaps we had better wait for them," Paolina answered in a troubled voice.

"No need at all," the *Conte* said. "They will find us in the Supper Room. Come, it is over here. I think you will agree that the decorations are as beautiful as those in the Ballroom."

The great Banqueting Hall of the *palazzo* had been transformed into a grotto. Stalactites dropped from the roof, the walls sparkled as if with diamonds and everywhere there was the drip of water, showing behind miniature waterfalls, faintly lit pools, deep caverns and dark caves in which nymphs and mermaids seemed to lurk.

Much of it was an optical illusion contrived with mirrors, and yet the effect was startling and, at the same time, very beautiful.

There was every form of delicacy to be eaten, and wines which were drunk out of huge goblets of gold inset with precious stones.

"The treasure of the Grittis is unbelievable," the Count said. "And yet the family lives quite quietly as a general rule. It is only when there is a party like this that we see their magnificent gold ornaments which must be worth a king's ransom."

Paolina found it hard to attend to him. Her eyes were wandering towards the door, wondering where Sir Harvey was, wondering why he had not joined them.

She thought suddenly that she hated the *Contessa* with her enticing, baby ways and her exaggerated compliments, which would put any decent reserved Englishwoman to shame.

Still Sir Harvey did not come, and she was wondering desperately if she should suggest that they should go and look for him when he appeared. He was alone and he came quickly to their table with a muttered apology at having been so long.

"Where is Zanetta?" the *Conte* asked.

"She was called away," Sir Harvey replied. "I think there is some trouble at home. A servant arrived who wished to speak with her and when she had heard what he had to say she went off with him immediately."

"I wonder what it can be," the *Conte* said with a puzzled frown.

"I imagine it is of little consequence," Sir Harvey answered.

As he as only starting his supper while Paolina and the *Conte* had nearly finished theirs, the *Conte* pressed upon him many delicacies, some of which had been brought hundreds of miles for this special occasion.

Sir Harvey was just finishing a dish of caviare when a man, rising from another table to go back to the Ballroom, stopped suddenly and gave a loud exclamation.

Paolina, who was seated with her back to him, turned her head. She saw that he was obviously a middle-aged man, slightly corpulent, wearing a narrow mask, which showed beneath it a wide, rather disagreeable mouth.

"Tell me, *Madame*," he said, in a rough voice, addressing himself to Paolina, "where did you get that necklace of pearls?"

"My necklace!" Paolina answered in surprise, putting her fingers up to the pearls which lay, warm and glowing, at the base of her throat.

"Yes! Where did you get them?" the man repeated.

Sir Harvey half rose from the table.

"May I ask, Sir," he enquired, "why you think you are entitled to address my sister, without introduction, in such terms?"

"So she is your sister is she?" the man retorted. "Well, perhaps you can answer the question better than she can. Where did that necklace come from?"

"What the devil has it got to do with you?" Sir Harvey asked.

"A good deal, I fancy," the man replied. "Because it belongs to me—or, rather, to the lady to whom I gave it!"

"I think you must be foxed," Sir Harvey remarked. "Take yourself off and cease to bother us."

"I shall do nothing of the sort," the man replied aggressively. "I tell you that necklace, which this woman is wearing, is not hers. If you have stolen it, as I imagine you must have, I shall force you to return it to me."

Paolina sat rigid with surprise and fright. Sir Harvey gave a short laugh.

"You are indeed in your cups," he said. "Maybe this is your idea of a joke during Carnival time, but I find it rather tiresome. Run away and find someone else to play with."

The man moved forward to the table and brought his fist crashing down amongst the plates and goblets.

"You shall not laugh it off like that," he said. "That is the necklace that I gave to Contratina only last Christmas. It was of three rows, but I would recognize that clasp anywhere. I had it specially designed for me by one of the finest jewellers in all Naples."

"This is past a joke," Sir Harvey answered coolly. "But to be rid of you I will tell you what you wish to know. I bought that necklace for my sister less than a week ago in Ferrara. We were shipwrecked; all our clothes and a number of our jewels were lost in the tempest. She needed something to adorn her neck and so I purchased it for her. I can give you the name of the jeweller if you are interested."

The man's eyes narrowed.

"Are you telling the truth?" he enquired.

"I swear it," Sir Harvey answered blithely. "My sister will confirm what I say."

He looked at Paolina who made an inarticulate murmur which might have meant anything. She was kneading her hands together under the table—afraid of what would happen, afraid that the necklace, of all silly things, would give away all they had built up with so much care.

"I tell you," the man was saying, "that I had that clasp especially designed for Contratina. You have heard of her, I presume?"

"The singer?" Sir Harvey asked. "Who has not heard of the 'Nightingale of Naples'?"

"Contratina honoured me with her friendship," the middle-aged man said a little heavily. "My name, Sir, is Bondi."

The *Conte* spoke for the first time.

"Signor Bondi is a very important ship-owner," he announced.

"I thank you for your recognition," Signor Bondi remarked, with a little bow in the *Conte's* directon.

"In which case the *Signor* has doubltess heard of the loss of the *Santa Lucia*," Sir Harvey said, "the packet boat carrying passengers between Naples and Venice which was wrecked on the rocks off the coast of Ferrara."

"The *Santa Lucia* wrecked! I do not believe it!"

Signor Bondi stared at him wildly, and then, as no one said anything, he went on:

"I only arrived today from Constantinople. I have been there in one of my own ships. I enquired if Contratina had

140

arrived and was told that although accommodation had been reserved for her for the last five days she has not turned up. There was a letter for me saying she was arriving on the *Santa Lucia*. You are quite certain it was wrecked?"

"Not only wrecked, but everyone, except my sister and myself, was drowned," Sir Harvey said quietly.

The middle-aged man put his hands to his face. He was obviously stricken.

"And Contratina?" he asked.

"No one else was saved," Sir Harvey replied.

"I cannot believe it. I must make enquiries," Signor Bondi blustered. And then in a quieter voice: "You saw her on board?"

He spoke to Paolina but it was Sir Harvey who answered.

"I saw her the night before the storm. She was looking forward to arriving in Venice. She retired to bed early because she was a bad sailor."

"She hated the sea," Signor Bondi said in a voice choked with emotion.

He turned away from the table and Paolina could see he was very near to tears.

"I will go and make enquiries," he muttered. "I cannot believe that there is no hope—no possiblity of her being saved."

His voice broke on the last word and he staggered away.

"Poor man," Paolina said. "I do not think I noticed the lady on board, but then I was in my——" She stopped suddenly. She was going to say "my father's cabin," and realized that the *Conte* was listening.

"You were not well yourself," Sir Harvey interposed quickly, filling in the gap. "As you say, you were in your own cabin most of the time. But I saw Contratina. She was attractive, but getting on a little in years."

"The necklace!" the *Conte* said curiously. "How does it happen that your sister has her necklace?"

"It is extraordinary, to say the least of it," Sir Harvey replied. "I presume one of the fishermen who were collecting everything they could from the wreck must have found it and sold it in Ferrara. The day after we got ashore they were going out all the time with their boats to salvage every single thing they could."

The *Conte* smiled.

"They are like hawks, aren't they? I have seen them at it myself. Well, it must have been a good haul for the lucky fellow who found Contratina's jewels. They were famous, of course. She had received them from Emperors, Kings, Oriental potentates, and all sorts of people. I imagine Bondi must have contributed quite a few. He was certainly very infatuated, to judge by his sorrow at the lady's death."

"I do not know what to say," Paolina said in a low voice. "I was so thrilled with these pearls. Now I feel as if they do not belong to me any more."

"You must not feel like that," the *Conte* answered. "All jewels have a history. The ones in my family, for instance, have been passed down from generation to generation. Hundreds of women have worn them, and yet that does not detract from their beauty for the woman who wears them last."

"And yet Contratina died in the storm," Paolina faltered.

"She was unlucky," Sir Harvey said. "And she did not suffer. The water came into the cabins so quickly that it drowned those who were trapped below before they realized what was happening."

Paolina gave a little shudder.

"If I had not come up on deck at that particular moment," she whispered.

"Do not think about it," Sir Harvey admonished.

He put out his hand and laid it on hers, and she felt the command in his fingers, the insistence by which he told her to pull herself together.

"I think I would like to go home," she said.

"That is impossible," the *Conte* expostulated. "Besides, why be unhappy? We all have to die some time. Personally, I would rather die when I was young and enjoying life than disintegrate slowly in old age, finding all pleasures denied to me, all excitements past."

"That is exactly how I feel," Sir Harvey agreed. "Death is but a little thing so long as it comes swiftly. It is life which is far more difficult."

"I suppose you are right," Paolina said. Nevertheless, she reached up her arms and undid the clasp of her pearls. "Keep them for me," she begged Sir Harvey, and slipped them into his hand.

"I want to give you a necklace to put round your neck," the *Conte* whispered as they moved away from the Supper Room and back into the Ballroom.

"I think I am content to wear nothing, at the moment," Paolina answered.

"I would like to see you wearing my family emeralds," he went on as if she had not spoken. "They would show up the whiteness of your skin and the gold of your hair. Yet perhaps the sapphires would be better still. There is a depth in them which reminds me of your eyes."

There was no need for Paolina to answer him. A crowd in the Ballroom precluded conversation. More revellers in fancy dress had surged in with those who were more conventionally garbed. They were laughing and teasing the masked dancers and forming a crocodile to thread their way through the throng, making everyone join in, and gradually turning the whole Ballroom into the noisy jubilance of a fair.

Paolina found herself whisked away from the *Conte's* side by a tall pierrot who forced her, by steering her with his hands on her waist, to become part of the crocodile which was threading its way through the Ballroom and into the Palace.

Round the reception rooms they went, through the hall and out of a side door into the narrow, paved street which wound behind the *palazzo* to the Piazza San Marco.

Paolina tried to escape, to prevent herself from accompanying the merrymakers, but the pierrot was too strong for her and propelled her along. Although she called out that she wished to stay, her voice was lost in the general noise and laughter.

There was music playing all the way along the narrow streets, and then suddenly they were in the brightness of the Piazza San Marco. The café doors were open, the chairs outside were crowded with men and women drinking wine, singing, or merely staring at their fellow creatures. There was dancing in the *Piazza* and it was almost impossible to make oneself heard above the general hubbub.

"Please, let me go," Paolina cried, but her voice was inaudible until at last the dancing crocodile came to a stop.

She turned to face her captor.

"I must go back," she said a little breathlessly.

"Not yet, Pretty Lady," he answered in a laughing voice. "There is so much to see here. Why not enjoy yourself? It is the Carnival, you know."

"It is certainly an excuse for every sort of madness," Paolina answered. "But my brother will be worried about me."

143

"He will know that no one could harm such a sweet creature at Carnival time, or at any other time for that matter," the stranger replied.

"I wish I could be sure of that," she answered. "But all the same, I should like to go home."

"Where is home, Pretty Lady?" he questioned.

She did not answer that, feeling perhaps it would be indiscreet to give her address to someone she had never met before.

"I was a guest at the Palazzo Gritti, as you saw," she answered. "My friends will be waiting there. Will you please take me back?"

"Why must you be in such a hurry?" he asked. "If we walk a little way we can take a gondola. That will be easier—and far more romantic."

There was something in his voice which told Paolina that that at least would be a very unwise thing to do.

"Thank you, Sir, but I must return," she answereed.

She turned to run but he caught her by the hand.

"Not so fast, Pretty Lady," he cried. "You are too pretty to lose just when I have found you. Come and dance with me over there by the band. Or shall we go and look at the stalls and I will buy you something that you can keep by which to remember this evening?"

"No, thank you," Paolina answered.

She tried to struggle against him but he was too strong for her.

"Come along, now," he said. "You are being tiresome. Shyness is all very well in its place, but you do not want to be shy with me. There are lots of amusing things to do. I hate doing them alone. First of all we will have a glass of wine. It might warm the cockles of your cold little heart."

"I have told you that I must go back," Paolina said.

She was feeling desperate now; afraid of this unknown man, and afraid, too, of the crowd milling around, many of them obviously out for any sort of mischief which would make them laugh!

"Let me go."

She twisted her arm in his hold with a swiftness that took him by surprise, and then she was running away from San Marco, down the twisting, narrow roadway through which they had come.

She could hear him pounding behind her and only the fact that she was smaller and quicker on her feet than he was kept her ahead. He let out a hunting cry and she felt that she might, in truth, be a wild boar or a stag escaping from pounding horses and baying dogs.

He seemed to be drawing nearer and though she twisted in and out of the passers-by she knew that her breath was failing and that it was inevitable that within a few seconds he must catch up with her.

It was then she saw coming towards her a man wearing a blue coat embroidered with pearls that she recognized. She gave a little sobbing cry and spurred herself forward, reached him and flung her arms round his neck. Her relief at seeing Sir Harvey was so intense that even if she had not been breathless she would have been unable to speak.

He put his arm round her and held her close just as the pierrot came running up.

"She is mine!" the pierrot ejaculated.

"You leave her alone or I will spike you through the heart, you dog," Sir Harvey snarled at him.

The pierrot, defeated, smiled disarmingly.

"Sorry, old fellow. I didn't know she was your particular pigeon," he answered. "Take care of her, she's a pretty piece of goods."

He strolled away without another word and Paolina, with her face hidden in Sir Harvey's shoulder, could not help laughing.

"I was . . . frightened," she said, her breath still coming with difficulty. "It was . . . silly of me, but . . . I was . . . frightened."

"You are more trouble to look after than a stable of race horses!" Sir Harvey ejaculated. "Come on, let us take a gondola and get home. I have had enough for tonight, and so, I should think, have you."

Paolina raised her head from his shoulder.

"I have never been so glad to see anybody as I am to see . . . you," she said. "It was stupid to be so frightened, and I do not think he meant me much ill. At the same time, I am not used to it."

"Used to what?" Sir Harvey enquired.

"All this attention, men snatching at me, paying me compliments. I do not know what to think of it all."

"You should not be so pretty," Sir Harvey said unsympathetically.

He was leading her, as he spoke, to a little side canal where a number of gondolas were waiting for hire. He helped Paolina in and sat down beside her. She put up her hands and tidied her hair, and as she did so remembered the necklace.

"Signor Bondi," she whispered. "What are you going to say to him?"

"Why should I say anything to him?" Sir Harvey enquired as the gondola nosed its way slowly, almost silently over the dark water.

"Do you think he believes you bought the necklace?" Paolina asked.

"What does it matter?" Sir Harvey answered. "He cannot prove I didn't."

"You took it from her," Paolina said accusingly.

"Yes, I took it from her," Sir Harvey replied firmly.

There was a long silence and then, as if by not speaking Paolina forced him into an explanation, he said defiantly:

"What does it matter? She could no longer enjoy them and I knew where they were. That was why I went back to the ship. If the fishermen had got there first, then there would have been no hope of our having any of the pickings. And we should not be here, for one thing."

"It seems so awful when she was dead," Paolina murmured.

"She did not suffer," Sir Harvey answered. "And, besides, if I had not gone when I did, no one would have had the jewels. They would have gone to the bottom of the sea, and what good would they have done there?"

He paused, but as Paolina did not answer his question he went on:

"Contratina was not a bad woman. She gave a great deal of pleasure, both by her singing and her charms. Many people loved her. I do not believe that her jewels would bring evil or disaster to anyone."

"She would not have wanted us to have them," Paolina said.

"No, she was not like that," Sir Harvey answered. "I became friendly with her on the ship and she was a very generous, warm-hearted woman. She gave as easily as she took. Had she known what was going to happen, she would, I believe, have wanted me to have her jewels rather than that they should have rotted at the bottom of the ocean or been pawed over by some avaricous fisherman."

"She would have wanted you to have them," Paolina repeated slowly. She turned to look at him in the star-

146

strewn darkness, her eyes searching his face. "You made love to her on the ship."

"Why not?" Sir Harvey enquired. "She found old Bondi very generous, but he was not the only recipient of her favours."

"I wish I had known," Paolina said. "I would never have taken the necklace."

"I do not begin to understand women," Sir Harvey remarked in an exasperated tone. "You are making all this fuss about a necklace which belonged to Contratina, who was a charming woman who would never have hurt anyone in her life if she could have helped it; and yet you go into a shop and buy a ring or a bracelet which may have belonged to anyone. You would have no idea who had worn it. It might be accursed or filled with the bitterness and evil of its previous owner. But you would wear it without a qualm."

"I suppose you are right," Paolina said slowly. "And yet there is something horrible in thinking you loved Contratina, that she died, and you gave her necklace to me."

"I did not love her and it was not my fault she died," Sir Harvey answered. "I gave you the necklace merely as a façade, part of the masquerade which you and I are presenting to the world. It was not as if it were an expression of my affection, or anything like that."

"No, of course it was not. I . . . I had forgotten," Paolina said.

She half turned away from him, looking out into the darkness of the open Lagoon, for by this time they had come into the Grand Canal. Then impulsively she turned towards him again.

"Forgive me for being so stupid."

"There is nothing to forgive," Sir Harvey answered. "I just do not understand why you are making all this fuss."

"I am not. It was foolish of me to mind, if only for a moment," Paolina said.

"Let us forget it," Sir Harvey answered. "You need not wear the necklace again if you do not want to—in fact, it would be better if you didn't. When Bondi has recovered from the shock of Contratina's death, he will doubtless start fussing about it again. It was unfortunate that he should have recognized the clasp. It shows what a fool I was not to have sold the pearls with everything else."

"There were a great many other things, were there?" Paolina asked.

"Quite a number," Sir Harvey admitted.

There was another long pause and then Paolina asked in a very low voice:

"Was she nice? Did you love her very much?"

Sir Harvey laughed.

"I have told you, I did not love her at all. She was an amusing companion for a short voyage. She had more to talk about than most of the people on that ship. And I suppose, both being adventurers of a sort, we automatically gravitated towards each other."

"I see."

Paolina's voice was still low, and then they sat in silence until they reached their *palazzo*.

She went upstairs into her bed-chamber. But when she got there she did not undress. Instead she sat for some time staring at her reflection in the mirror. Then on an impulse she opened the door again and went into the gallery to look for Sir Harvey. She somehow felt he would not have gone to bed.

She found him leaning at the open window, looking out, yet seeming to see nothing—neither the lights on the gondolas below nor the stars above.

He was deep in thought and for a moment he did not even hear her. She came close and stood beside him.

"What are you thinking about?" she asked at length.

He started, and seemed surprised to see her.

"I did not hear you," he answered. "I thought you had retired."

"I wanted to say good night first," Paolina said. "And also to say I am sorry I was stupid. I will wear the necklace if you like."

He put his hand under her chin and turned her face up to his.

"What a nonsensical little child you are," he said. "Forget about the necklace. It was a senselesss action on my part in asking you to wear it in the first place. Now it has brought us a certain amount of trouble. Forget it; forget Contratina, too, if that is worrying you."

"Were you thinking about her?" Paolina asked.

Sir Harvey shook his head.

"No, I was thinking about England," he replied. "I was suddenly feeling homesick for the green fields and trees, for the lawns, smooth as velvet, sloping down to a slow, winding stream where the trout lie in the shallows. There is something quiet and safe about it all, something very different from this hectic, insatiable search for gaiety."

"And would you like to be home in England?" Paolina asked.

"Sometimes I think I would sell my immortal soul for a chance to return," Sir Harvey answered, in a serious voice she had never heard from him before. And then he added: "But it is too late to talk about it now. Some day I will tell you why I am here, but now I want you to get your beauty sleep."

"Are you afraid I will decrease in value if I do not?" Paolina asked.

She spoke with a smile on her lips, but there was a slight sting behind the words.

"But, of course," he answered. "Could you imagine that my concern for you was anything but commercial?"

His voice was bitter, but their eyes met. For a moment something strange and magnetic seemed to pass between them. It seemed to hold them both spellbound. Paolina felt as if she could not breathe, as if something overwhelming, irresistible and inevitable was happening.

Then, with a little inarticulate murmur, she turned from him and ran towards her bed-chamber.

9

Paolina awoke with an uneasy feeling that something was wrong. For the first time since she had come to Venice the beauty of her bed-chamber, with its painted ceiling and carved stucco designs over the doors and windows, failed to give her any pleasure.

She had the impression that something was bearing down upon her, and although her head did not ache it was as if something nagged behind her mind, giving her a feeling of apprehension and anxiety which had no foundation in fact.

She hardly sipped the chocolate which her maid brought her and was indifferent to the enthusiasm of the hairdresser who had come with new ideas for dressing her hair.

"Today is a very special day, Milady," Thérèse told her. "There will be a Regatta and the competitors will pass under this very window. The gondolas will be decorated in different ways and the most beautiful and the fastest will receive a purse of money from the hands of the Doge himself, while the last gets a live porker to mock him for being so slow!"

Paolina tried to feel excited, but it was only a pretence. She hurried over her dressing because she wanted to see Sir Harvey. She felt that he, if no one else, could disperse her gloom.

She remembered how last night he had said that one day he would tell her his story. Perhaps today she would hear it, and she thought how little she knew about him—this man to whom she had trusted herself. Although she was with him every day, although they discussed so many things that concerned them both, where his personal life

150

was concerned she was as ignorant as the first day they had met.

She thought a little resentfully how much she had told him about herself. Of those long, dark days with her father, dunned on all sides by their creditors, forced at times to go without food because they had no money to pay for it. And yet she had contrived by some method entirely her own to keep herself unhurt and unsullied by the disreputable people with whom her father was forced to associate.

Sir Harvey knew all this and perhaps a great deal more than she had managed to put into words. But he had never talked of himself. She just knew that he was English and his native reserve hid not only his past but what he was thinking and feeling behind the impenetrable barrier of those steel-grey eyes.

When she was dressed, in a rather more simple gown than usual because somehow she did not feel like being *en fête* today, even though it was the Carnival, she pulled open the door of her bed-chamber and hurried into the Gallery.

Sir Harvey was at the far end of it, talking with a man whom she did not recognize. Because she felt it would be impolite to interrupt them, she went into the little Library which was decorated almost entirely with books save for a magnificent ceiling which showed Neptune rising from the waves amidst a bevy of voluptuous goddesses.

Paolina sat down beneath them and wondered miserably why, when they were surrounded by so much pictured beauty, any Venetian bothered to look at a living woman. She compared her slim, not yet mature figure with the enticing, sensuous curves of Venus and Juno and felt that she stood at a great disadvantage.

She had no idea how lovely she looked, with her eyes dark with foreboding and her mouth drooping a little wistfully, as Sir Harvey came in through the door. She did not see him for a moment because she was so lost in her thoughts, and he stood looking at her, noticing the thin delicacy of her fingers, the slender grace of her arms and the soft, rounded column of her throat, bare of any ornamentation save for the fine laces of her bodice.

"You wanted me?"

His voice was unexpectedly harsh. She started and turned towards him eagerly.

"Oh, yes, I wanted to—see you."

"Why?"

"I do not know. I felt there was something we ought to discuss. Something, perhaps, that you had to tell me."

He walked across the room to the writing-desk which was laden with his papers.

"You must have had a presentiment," he said, "unless you have heard what has happened before it was told to me."

"What has happened!" Paolina repeated. "I had no idea that anything actually had happened. I just felt uneasy."

"You were right to do so," he replied. "I have just been brought news that last night the Marquis killed himself."

Paolina jumped to her feet.

"The Marquis!" she ejaculated. "But it cannot be true. Who told you?"

"One of his servants. The *Contessa* has asked me to come to her. I was just deciding whether I should obey or refuse."

"But, of course you must go to her," Paolina said. "She must be in the depths of despair. It is tragic—unbelievable! Why should the Marquis do such a thing?"

"I think you know the answer to that," Sir Harvey answered coldly.

"I! Why should I know anything about it?"

"It was because of you that he killed himself."

"No! No!" Paolina cried. "It is not true! It cannot be true!"

"But that is unfortunately the fact," Sir Harvey retorted.

"I cannot believe it!" Paolna insisted. "Oh, the poor, poor Marquis! I knew he was unhappy, but not that his life was so intolerable that he would wish to . . . die."

The tears welled into her eyes and she could hardly enunciate the last word.

"What did he say to you out on the balcony?" Sir Harvey enquired.

"He told me that he . . . loved me," Paolina answered in a broken voice. "He told me, too, that he had been . . . married when he was only fourteen and his wife was . . . mad and yet . . . alive. Because of her there was no chance of his . . . offering me marriage."

She paused for a moment amidst her sobs and then she said:

"I was wondering . . . during the night why he could not get an . . . annulment of his marriage."

"It would be impossible for him," Sir Harvey said sharply. "The grand families of Venice would not stoop to such a thing. It is only the parvenues, and very modern-thinking ones at that, who would deign to discuss their private and intimate matrimonial affairs in public."

"Then he was tied for life," Paolina sighed.

"He must have loved you very deeply."

"He . . . said so, but I did not . . . understand."

"And did you love him?"

The words seemed to be fired at her like a pistol shot, and through her tears she looked at Sir Harvey wonderingly.

"I . . . liked him," she answered hesitatingly. "He was quiet and . . . serious and did not frighten me as . . . some of the other men do here. But . . . I did not . . . love him."

"You must have said too much or, perhaps, too little," Sir Harvey insisted. "A tragedy like this cannot be explained away by just a few words on the balcony."

He seemed angry. At the same time there was something else in his voice, something raw and almost brutal which made her blush and stammer.

"N. . . no! You must not . . . think that of me. I . . . liked him. That was all. He seemed . . . kind and understanding."

"He is certainly not kind in what he has done to you now," Sir Harvey answered.

"To me?" Paolina enquired.

"To you," he replied grimly. "Can you imagine how the tongues of Venice will wag? They will not believe it was just an innocent friendship which ended in tragedy. They will put a far more serious implication on it."

"But it isn't true," Paolina cried. "You know how few times I have seen the Marquis. You know that we have never been alone, save for last night when we went on the balcony."

"Blast these hot-headed Latins!" Sir Harvey ejaculated. "The whole place will be in an uproar by this evening. Well, I suppose I had better go to the *Contessa* and see what I can do."

"Why should she send for you?" Paolina asked, suddenly suspicious. "There must be relatives and friends, all sorts of people they have known all their life. The *Contessa* cannot need a stranger's consolation nor a stranger's company at this moment."

"The *Contessa* has her own idea of what part I should play in her life," Sir Harvey said with a little sneering twist of his lips.

Paolina was silent and then, as he walked towards the door, she said:

"And are you going to play the part she requires of you?"

She could not help asking the question. It came to her lips almost spontaneously.

"I do not know about that," Sir Harvey answered. "What I am most concerned about at the moment is getting you out of this mess. For, make no mistake, if Venetian Society should turn against you, we are finished."

"But it is not my fault," Paolina said. "How could I know that he would behave like this? Why, I could almost say that I hardly knew him."

"And yet he has killed himself because of you."

"How do they know that?"

"He must have left a note or something," Sir Harvey answered. "And even if he has not, the whole of Venice will know the truth by midday. Already they may be gossiping in the coffee shops. The old roués from the Casinos will have their ideas of what has happened. The Doge and the Senate will have to be informed. I am only wondering whether I can persuade the family to hush it up—at least as far as the ordinary public is concerned."

"You are concerned only with what is being said," Paolina said accusingly. "I am thinking of the Marquis. He was young and handsome. Why should he do this? Why? Why?"

"Love is a strange thing," Sir Harvey answered. "At times it makes the most sane man mad."

"Then this deed was madness," Paolina whispered.

She wiped her eyes with her handkerchief. Sir Harvey still stood there looking at her, so she asked:

"You are not angry with me, are you?"

It was a very small, pitiful voice in which she spoke; the voice of a child who has already been punished and yet is still afraid of more.

"Yes, I am angry," Sir Harvey replied. "Angry because everything was going so well and now this has to happen. Last night Venice was at your feet, you were by far the most beautiful woman in the whole city and everyone was prepared to acknowledge it. Even the women were paying you compliments amongst themselves and you had the *Conte* literally eating out of your hand."

"The *Conte*! I had forgotten him! What will he say to this?" Paolina ejaculated.

"That remains to be seen," Sir Harvey answered. "If he does not call today and there is no sign from him, then we shall know that this has frightened him off—not a very clever situation just when I thought we could really see our goal in sight."

"I . . . am sorry," Paolina stammered.

Sir Harvey looked at her and there was no relaxation of the grimness in his face. His eyes were as cold as ice.

"Perhaps you are too beautiful," he said harshly. "Perhaps that is what is wrong."

He turned and walked from the room, and Paolina collapsed on the sofa in tears. She cried for a long time, thinking of the Marquis and thinking, too, of the hardness of Sir Harvey's face as he went from the room.

He had gone to see the *Contessa*. She thought of the gay widow with her warm, glowing face and passionate, dark eyes, her flirtatious lips. She recalled the exciting, sensuous movements of her body which never seemed to be still for a moment.

Perhaps that was the sort of beauty that Sir Harvey admired, Paolina thought bitterly; and if the *Conte* failed her, why should Sir Harvey worry? He could marry the *Contessa* and live happily ever afterwards. She would have to go away and leave them. Go to Rome, Naples, France, or even England—anywhere, what would it matter, because she would be alone with no one to look after her, no one to care.

She cried again at the thought and then, with an effort, roused herself to go to her chamber and bathe her swollen eyes. She did not dare go out. She did not even dare go to the window for fear that someone might see her. She could only wander restlessly about the sumptuously furnished Gallery or the small Library and feel that even they were repulsing her.

She did not belong here. She was only a pretender, a playactor, with nothing beneath the surface but hollowness and an emptiness which she could recognize in herself.

She found herself longing for a home, for somewhere that she could call her own. She would not mind how humble, how poor it might be, if only she could be sure of it, if only she could find security.

She thought of all the long succession of shabby hotel rooms and disreputable lodgings she had passed through. Somehow they had not mattered because they had been so utterly impersonal—a few months in a back street, a week in a palace by the sea, a hasty escape to a tiny, dirty room up a broken stairway, a little hut that had been lent them by a lake, and then back again to the towns.

Oh, those towns! All looking the same and all to her father had meant only one thing—a Casino, green baize tables, the clink of money, the shuffle of the cards.

She wondered, now, how she had managed to carry on for so long. At first it had been different because there had been money coming regularly from England. She did not know whether it was a pension, she thought it must be, or a remittance from her father's family.

She only knew it arrived regularly and they had looked forward to it, anticipating it, and prayed for it. It had been there, the one security, the one thing which saved them from the worst predicaments and most desperate moments of need.

And then, one night in a wild, drunken moment, her father had gambled away their monthly cheque. She could still see the man who had got it—a dark, swarthy individual who was clever enough to tie up the legal side of it, to make certain that the money came to him and there was no possibility for her father evading his debt.

After that they had just drifted, sinking lower and lower, moving always into worse rooms in lodging-houses which no decent woman would have deigned to enter. Perhaps it was because she was so different from them, and perhaps because they seldom saw her, that the men in those low, cut-throat districts left her alone.

Sometimes she would be accosted in the market, sometimes a man, seeing her hurrying along the street, would speak to her or shout after her. Otherwise she passed unmolested. After every such experience she would run hastily to her room, lock the door and lie, panting with fear, on the bed.

It was then that she would pray for her father to return, to come home early for once, to be with her, to keep her safe at least from her fears of being attacked. But her prayers were never answered. It was always dawn before he came staggering in, bleary-eyed and usually despondent because his luck had been bad.

They had sold everything there was to sell. She even suspected at times that her father stole. And yet, somehow, he carried on. There was always just enough money to get to the Casino, just enough for one stake, or perhaps two, just enough to be certain that she was alone again without him, from late in the afternoon until the early morning.

"After suffering all that why am I not happier now that I am free?" Paolina asked herself, and knew that the answer lay in the fact that she was still afraid—afraid of being alone, afraid of losing even this transitory, rootless security which Sir Harvey had offered her for just as long as he could afford it.

She tried to reckon up in her head what this *palazzo* must be costing them in servants, in wine, in food; and she knew that however much he had obtained from the sale of the jewels and from the three thousand crowns which the Duke had offered for her it would not last very long at the rate they were spending it.

The day of reckoning was round the corner and the only thing that could save them was if she became engaged to the *Conte*.

Paolina glanced at the clock on the mantelpiece. Already it was past noon. She wondered if he had said anything last night about calling or if she might have expected a letter from him. She found she could remember nothing that was said during the whole evening. It was all indistinct, and the only thing she could recall vividly was that moment when she had seen Sir Harvey's blue coat coming towards her and had run desperately to hide her face against his shoulder.

How broad and strong he had seemed, and how easily all her fears had vanished away just because he was there! He always had that effect on her, she thought. With him she felt safe.

She remembered that overwhelming relief when he had come bursting through the window into the Duke's room when she had almost given up hope of rescue. How strong he was! How handsome! Everything a woman would want to protect her against the world.

She moved restlessly down the Gallery to where she could see the wide, carpeted staircase which led down to the entrance hall. Why had he not come back? What was happening? Had he, perhaps, decided to have no more to do with her, to cast her from him?

She felt herself shiver at the thought and her hands grow cold. He had been gone a long time by now. And then, as she waited there, standing shivering at the top of the stairs, she heard his footfalls on the marble floor below.

She would have known his walk anywhere. That strong,

157

decisive tread of a man who is sure of himself, a man who walks as if the world was put there for him to stand on it.

He started up the staircase and she waited apprehensively without moving until, at the turn of the stairs, she could see his face. He looked up then and saw her, her hair like sunshine against the dark pictures on the walls, her skin as white as, if not whiter than, the camellias that he held in his hands.

He came slowly up the stairs in silence and then as he reached Paolina she could contain herself no longer.

"What has happened?"

Her voice seemed to come from the very depths of her being, and yet it was hardly above a whisper. He put the camellias in her hands.

"The *Contessa* sent you these. She is broken-hearted at her brother's loss, and yet she understands it was not your fault."

Paolina felt as if the relief was almost too much. She swayed a little and Sir Harvey's arm went out to support her.

"It is all right," he said kindly. "They wish to keep everything a secret except from the most intimate members of the family."

"How did he . . . die?"

"He shot himself! With a duelling pistol! It was found beside him on the floor."

"Then how did they know it was . . . because of . . me?"

"He left a note asking that his heart should be embalmed and sent to you in an alabaster urn."

"No! No!"

Paolina almost shrieked the words.

"I will not take it. They cannot . . . make me."

"Be calm now," Sir Harvey admonished.

He helped Paolina to a sofa and then walked across the room to pour out two glasses of wine.

"Drink this," he said. "You need it—in fact, I think we both need it after what we have been through this morning."

She was trembling so much that she could hardly take the glass from him. In the end he helped her raise it to her lips. She took a long draught and the wine coursing down her throat put an end to her trembling and stopped the hysteria which seemed to rise within her.

"How could we have done . . . such a thing?" Paolina managed to gasp after a moment.

"We are dealing with Latins, remember," Sir Harvey replied. "They do not think the same way as we do. Also, love means far more in their lives than in an Englishman's."

"I will not take it," Paolina said a little hysterically.

"Leave that to me," Sir Harvey answered. "You need not see it, you need not do anything about it. But the fact remains: because his letter constitutes a will, the family will carry out his wishes."

"It was cruel, cruel. . . ."

"I agree with you. I have no stomach or sympathy with suicides. There is his mother sobbing her heart out, his sister stricken and the whole house in tears. If ever a young man was selfish, heartless, without thought of those who were dependent on him, it was the young Marquis. I am only sorry that he is not alive and that I cannot teach him a lesson."

"Don't!" Paolina begged. "It is unlucky to speak of the dead in such a way."

"I am not concerned with that sort of luck," Sir Harvey answered sharply. "If you ask my opinion, it was a cowardly act on the part of a coward who had not got the guts to face life as it is. It only shows where the greed for money will carry people."

"The greed for money! What has that got to do with it?" Paolina asked.

Sir Harvey smiled grimly.

"I discovered quite a lot of things this morning. The Marquis had no fortune. He lived in great wealth, he enjoyed all the splendour and the trappings that his position could possibly give him and practically every *sequin* belonged to his poor, mad wife."

"So that is why he did not get an annulment!" Paolina ejaculated.

"The main reason, of course," Sir Harvey answered. "Although the family is as proud as the devil."

"Then the *Contessa* has no money either?"

Paolina could not help it, but there was a sudden light in her eyes and a lilt in her voice.

"No. I never imagined she had any," Sir Harvey answered.

"But I . . . I thought that . . . perhaps she wanted to . . .

159

marry you and that you would . . . consider it," Paolina stammered.

Sir Harvey threw back his head and laughed. The sound seemed somehow to break the gloom which had hung over the room the whole morning.

"So that was what you were imagining," he said. "You were quite wrong. The *Contessa* did not want anything so permanent as marriage from me—although she might have considered it if I could have convinced her I was wealthy enough. No, what she desired was that I should be her *cavaliere*. Every Venetian lady has one, you know—a young man who attends her from first thing in the morning till last thing at night, who looks after her, who obeys her slightest request and who fulfils all the obligations that her husband is disinclined to do. He is, in fact, far more important than her husband."

"I have noticed that every Venetian lady has a gentleman beside her," Paolina said. "But I thought that most of them must be their husbands."

"No true Venetian troubles herself with her husband," Sir Harvey said. "It is the *cavaliere* whom you will find always at her side. Yet somehow I do not think I am cut out to be a boudoir gallant."

He grinned as he spoke and Paolina suddenly found that the world was full of sunshine.

"So that was what she wanted!" she exclaimed.

"I must say I am surprised at the Dolfins' circumstances now that I have learned about them," Sir Harvey said reflectively. "The family's main concern is whether they can go on enjoying the mad girl's money now that the Marquis is dead. If they cannot, it will mean good-bye to the *palazzo* and a great many other of their amusements."

Somehow it did not seem to matter any more. Paolina was sorry about the Marquis, sad that he should have been so foolish as to kill himself while he was still young and strong; everything was less depressing now she knew that Sir Harvey was not really interested in the *Contessa*.

She looked at him and then rising to her feet said:

"I am glad, so glad. I was afraid that you would marry the *Contessa* and then be rid of me."

He put his hand on her shoulder in an affectionate, easy gesture which a brother might have used to his younger sister.

"What a child you are!" he smiled, "with your

imaginings and your fears. The only thing that really concerns me at the moment is to get you married."

She felt herself stiffen beneath his hand. She had almost forgotten, in her relief, there was still the *Conte* to be considered.

"But won't all Venice know about this?" she asked.

"Some of it will get out," Sir Harvey said indifferently. "There is nothing you can keep a secret from the gossiping tongues of those evil old women and those effeminate old men. But it will not be a scandal. We can always deny it, and I think that the *Contessa* and her mother will deny it too. They will not want the Marquise's family to think that her husband was in love—and especially they will not want them to know that he killed himself because of his affection for another woman."

Paolina put her hands to her face.

"It sounds so terrible," she said. "I cannot bear to think of it. Last night he was alive, talking to me, telling me how much he loved me. Today he is dead!"

"Forget him," Sir Harvey said briefly. "There are men at this moment dying on the battlefields, men being drowned at sea; there are men struggling to improve the world in all sorts of different ways and losing their lives during the process. We cannot distress ourselves unduly about a young fool who rated his life so lightly that he was prepared to chuck it away for a whim. Forget him."

"I will try," Paolina said. "But it will not be easy."

She picked up the camellias which had fallen to the ground.

"It was kind of the *Contessa* to send me these. In the same circumstances I might not have been so generous."

"Yes, it was nice of her," Sir Harvey agreed in a tone of voice which made Paolina look at him suspiciously.

"You suggested it," she said accusingly. "You suggested it to make me feel happier."

He laughed, but a little uneasily.

"You must accept things at their face value," he replied evasively.

"You thought of it to save me too much suffering," Paolina said softly. "Thank you. It was kind of you. I shall not forget it."

He laughed again and shrugged his shoulders, and she knew that he was embarrassed by her thanks and said no more.

"We will now decide what to do today," Sir Harvey commanded in a very different tone of voice. "The Carnival is still in full swing. We can see the Regatta from the window and perhaps it would be a good idea to ask some friends here. We must not appear to be apprehensive of our reception—in fact, as the Marquis means nothing to us, we need not even be downcast by his untimely demise."

"It seems so heartless," Paolina murmured.

"We are heartless," Sir Harvey retorted. "We cannot afford to be anything else. In this, as in everything else, your head has got to rule your heart."

He spoke severely and Paolina's eyes dropped before his.

"Yes, I know."

"Do not forget that," he admonished. "Once your heart gets the upper hand, then there is no knowing into what foolishness it may lead you. As for me—I have no heart!"

"Are you sure of that?" Paolina enquired.

"Quite sure," he answered. "Do you remember the words of the old song—'I care for nobody, no, not I, and nobody cares for me'?"

"I think if that were true one might be very lonely."

"That does not worry me."

He spoke with what seemed to her deliberate indifference. She had a sudden desire to run across the room to him, to hold on to him, then beg him to care for her, if only a little so that she would not be so alone, so utterly bereft.

And then she knew that such a demonstration would only annoy him. With a tremendous effort she managed to choke back her feelings and hold her chin high.

"We will have something to eat," Sir Harvey said abruptly, "take our *siesta* afterwards, if we have not heard from the *Conte*, we will call his Aunt."

"Do you think that is wise?" Paolina asked.

"It is forcing things a little," Sir Harvey said, "But we cannot afford to play about any longer. This last episode with the Marquis has told me that I must get your future signed and sealed at the first possible moment.

"The *Conte* remarked only last night that his widowed Aunt was arriving in Venice in time for the Regatta. We will ask her to dinner tomorrow night. That will be our excuse for calling. It will be a breach of etiquette on our part, but they will excuse it because they will think that the mad English know no better."

He paused, looked at Paolina and added almost crossly:

"Put on your prettiest gown and for heaven's sake smile at the *Conte*. We have got to make him declare himself."

"And supposing he does not?" Paolina asked miserably.

"He will," Sir Harvey said confidently.

The servants were present during their midday meal and so they talked of other things. Paolina found, as she had done before, that Sir Harvey was a mine of information on many subjects on which she had never expected him to have any special knowledge.

He had studied the antiquities of Greece, the poets and the philosophers; he had read so much about the Italian masters that it seemed to Paolina that he taught her more about pictures in the course of half-an-hour than previously she had learned in her whole life.

They talked, too, about astronomy, in which Sir Harvey was apparently very interested.

"I first learned about it when I was at sea," he said. "When you have to steer by the stars, you soon begin to know them with an affection. The nights they are not there you feel as if you have lost a friend."

There were many other things he could tell her—of strange parts of Africa where few white men had ever travelled; of the Caribbean, with its wonderful butterflies and beautifully feathered birds; of China with its silks and ivories and strange customs that only the traveller who has been there knows and understands.

It was all too quickly that their meal came to an end.

"Go and have your *siesta*," Sir Harvey commanded. "You have got to look beautiful this afternoon and, to tell the truth, you are a little pale."

"We can soon remedy that," Paolina said with a smile.

"Rouge will not hide the lines under your eyes," he replied severely. "You must bathe them with rose water to erase the effects of your tears."

"How do you know that rose water will take away tears?" Paolina teased. "Have you made so many women cry? Do you have to carry a remedy with you?"

"Perhaps," he answered.

Because he did not deny the accusation she felt suddenly jealous of all those women who had been in his life before and to whom he had ministered so knowledgeably, perhaps, as he was ministering to her.

As if he guessed her thought, he added:

"Go to bed and stop worrying. Leave me to do that, it is my speciality."

She laughed a little at that and he put his hand under her chin and raised her face up to his.

"You are lovely," he said. "So lovely that at times I wonder——"

He stopped suddenly and she waited, looking up at him with her dark purple eyes.

"Go on," she whispered. "What were you going to say?"

"Nothing," he answered sharply, and releasing her turned away towards his own chamber.

He went without looking back, but only when the door had closed behind him did Paolina go to her own bed-chamber, to throw herself down against the soft pillows. Not to sleep; instead she found herself thinking of Sir Harvey. What had he been gong to say? she wondered.

She thought that she could still feel his fingers under her chin—hard, strong fingers and sunburned too. So unlike the effete, useless white hands of the Venetians who did nothing but walk about behind their ladies, write a verse or two, or maybe a love letter.

"He is a man!" Paolina said aloud, and thought how skillful he had been in fighting with the Duke.

She wondered, as she had wondered before, what would have happened if the fight had gone the other way; if the Duke had won and it had been Sir Harvey who had been left bleeding on the floor.

She felt herself shudder as she remembered the Duke's thick lips. And then, remembering those kisses, she thought of the Marquis and knew that even though she had liked him she had not wished him to touch her or to hold her close.

She tired to imagine kissing the *Conte,* and her thoughts shied away from the idea. He was young, he was good-looking, but somehow she did not want him to touch her. It was one thing to be paid compliments in words—quite another to know that a man's arms would go round you, his lips must seek yours.

She was still lying wakeful when Thérèse came in to pull back the blinds.

"The Regatta will be starting soon, Milady," she said. "Already the gondolas are gathering in the Grand Canal. Look out of the window. It is a pretty sight. Everyone is wearing their best."

"Oh, I must look!" Paolina exclaimed.

She put on her wrapper and ran across the Gallery to

the long balcony overlooking the Canal. The servants had arranged embroidered hangings with long, gold fringes over the balustrade. There were garlands of flowers draped along the front of the *palazzo* and down below torchlights were being tied to iron posts to be lit when it was night.

Paolina bent over the balcony. Below her there were gondolas of every shape and size. Those belonging to the great families were decorated in the most elaborate fashion, with flowers, cloth of gold and all sorts of elaborate ornamentation. The gondoliers, too, in private service, wore their gala uniforms—silk jackets, short breeches, silk stockings and red sashes.

The course was kept along the Canal by boats of eight or more oars fantastically adorned; and behind them there was much joking and laughing and singing amongst the sightseers. Wine was being passed from hand to hand, and the more ordinary gondolas were filled with so many people that they were almost in danger of sinking.

Everyone was masked and it gave them the opportunity of shouting ribald remarks to each other, making jokes that were usually capped by a witty repartee which evoked a roar of laughter.

"The Regatta will come in from the sea," Thérèse told Paolina. "It comes past the Doge's Palace, right down the Grand Canal. There will be fifty or sixty gondolas taking part and there will be boats, too, to follow them. It is a fine sight, Milady, I can promise you."

"If it is not going to start yet," Paolina said, "I think perhaps I had better go and get dressed."

Thérèse peered up the Canal.

"They are sure to be late," she said. "They always are. Here is a *burchiello* coming, but I do not think it is part of the Regatta."

"It is very fine all the same—" Paolina started to say and then stopped.

She was certain, almost certain, she had seen that *burchiello* before. The gold carving on top of the central cabin, the glittering ornamentation along the narrow deck, the beautiful carved figure on the prow. Yes, she was certain she had seen it before.

She stood watching it approach. It was coming up the very centre of the Canal, the men pulling at the oars. And the officer giving the instructions had, she was sure, a face that she recognized.

She waited, instinctively gripping the embroidered hangings with both hands, digging her finger-nails into the rich satin without realizing that she was doing it.

The *burchiello* drew nearer and now it was almost level with the *palazzo*, and as the balcony was not very high, Paolina could see every detail of what was happening aboard. In the stern of the ship someone was sitting in a comfortable, cushioned chair. He was wearing a tricorn hat pulled low on his head, and yet Paolina could see enough of his face for her heart to suddenly start beating almost suffocatingly.

His coat was magnificently embroidered and his arm, in a sling of black satin, was dark against the gold and silver thread. The *burchiello* drew level, the man in the stern looked up. His eyes met Paolina's. For a moment they stared at each other and then, deliberately, insolently, the man's lips curved in an unmistakable sneer.

Paolina fell back from the balcony and put both her hands to her heart. It was beating so violently that she felt as if it might jump out of her breasts. The blood must have left her cheeks, for Thérèse said solicitously:

"Are you ill, Milady? What is the matter?"

"It is all right," Paolina managed to ejaculate.

She dragged herself back into the Gallery and crossed it towards Sir Harvey's chamber. She did not knock on the door, but opened it and stood there trembling as he turned round to stare at her in surprise. Wearing only a silk shirt and satin breeches he was standing in front of the mirror tying his lace cravat.

"What is the matter?"

There was no need for her to tell him something was wrong, he could see it in her face.

"The Duke!" Paolina managed to gasp. "The Duke! He has come to Venice!"

10

"The Duke is here?" Sir Harvey repeated questioningly. "What Duke?"

And then, as Paolina stared at him, the realization slowly grew in his eyes. But before he could speak she had run across the room to confront him, her hands reached out towards him, her eyes, tragic in their fear, raised to his.

"We must go away," she said. "We must go away quickly. Do you not understand? He will kill you, or imprison you, for what you have done to him. Quickly! Leave while you are still free."

As she spoke, her agitation grew until at the end she was almost shrieking the words, until suddenly she lost control of herself and with her clenched fists beat against his chest.

"Go! Go!" she cried. "He will kill you and I cannot bear it."

Her voice broke and as Sir Harvey appeared to come to life from the stunned silence in which he had listened to her first appeal, he grasped her wrists and held her hands against his chest.

As if his touch brought her a sudden realization of what she was doing there, she was still, only staring up at him tragically, the terror of what might happen written very clearly on her small, expressive face.

He looked down at her, holding tightly to her wrists, staring into her eyes as if he was seeing her for the first time. With a swift, unexpected movement, he caught her in his arms.

Just for a moment he held her, and then he bent his head and his lips met hers in a long, passionate, wild kiss which seemed to join them both inexorably to one another.

167

To Paolina it was as if a sudden flame shot through her; her terror, anxiety and fear fell away; and instead, a wild rapture, such as she had never known in all her life, made her feel as if she was being taken on wings into the very heart of the sun.

And the flame that had flickered through her became a fire and she felt as if it consumed them both so that they were indivisible, one person. . . .

Then as suddenly as he had taken her she was free, and he had turned away with his back towards her. She stood where he had left her, for a moment as dazed as if she had fallen from the very heights of Heaven down to earth. Only her fingers went up to touch the lips he had kissed.

"I am sorry," Sir Harvey said in a voice hoarse with emotion.

"So you do . . . love me . . . a little."

Paolina's voice seemed to come from a very long distance. It was low and soft, the innocent, wondering voice of a child who awakes to an almost incredible wonder.

"Forget what has happened," Sir Harvey said with his back to her.

"Why should I?" she asked. "I understand now what I have been . . . feeling, what I should have known . . . for a long time . . . I love . . . you."

He turned to her then, his eyes dark with agony, his lips twisted as if with pain.

"Do not say it," he said harshly. "It is untrue."

"No, it is true," she answered in that far-away voice, her eyes shining in her face, transformed by an expression of such unbelievable beauty that he could only stare at her.

"It is true," she insisted. "It has been true for a long time—ever since we first met, I think. And yet I did not understand. I was only hurt and jealous and unhappy because I was afraid I did not please you. And I do please you; tell me that I do."

She put out her hands towards him. As if he was drawn to her irresistibly against his will Sir Harvey came back to her side. He took her in his arms slowly, almost reluctantly, until his control broke.

"Oh, my God! My God!" he ejaculated and kissed her again.

This time his kisses were wild, passionate and possessive. He kissed her mouth, her eyes, her cheeks, and the pulse beating at the base of her white throat.

"I love you!" he said at length, in a voice deep and vibrant with passion. "I have fought against it. I have tried to deny it. But it is too strong for me. I love you!"

It seemed to Paolina as if the whole world whirled around her and then stood still. This was what she had waited for all her life, what she had been seeking, what she had dreamed about, unconsciously and with ignorance, but it had been there, beckoning her towards some unknown horizon to which she must journey unknowingly and yet irresistibly.

This was the fulfilment of everything she had ever desired, the one thing which could make her life complete, could give her happiness such as she had never realized existed in the whole world.

"I love you!"

She could only lay her cheek againt his shoulder in a contentment that was beyond physical feeling and was something of the spirit.

"I love you!"

The words seemed to be whispered between them even when they were not speaking.

Sir Harvey was kissing her again and now he drew the pins from her golden hair and let it fall over her shoulders so that he could bury his face in it.

"I have wanted to do this—so often," he whispered, and kissed her again.

For a long time they remembered nothing except the wild feelings which coursed through their veins and which made them thrill at the very touch or look of each other.

Then after a while, as if their knees could no longer hold them, they sat down on the edge of Sir Harvey's bed and there he kissed each finger of Paolina's hands, the soft, pink palms and the little veins at her wrists.

"I love them all," he said, "because they are a part of you, because they are perfect, just as you are perfect."

It was long time later that Paolina said suddenly:

"The Duke! We had forgotten the Duke." Again there was panic in her voice.

Sir Harvey gave a deep sigh as if he, too, had forgotten the Duke. In that little room they had been in an ecstasy of happiness and the world outside had been non-existent. Now the world was encroaching again.

"We must go," Paolina cried. "Oh, my darling, I could not let him hurt you now."

"He will not hurt me," Sir Harvey replied almost automatically, yet as he spoke he rose to his feet.

"We are crazed," he said harshly. "You know this is impossible. How could I have been so mad as to tell you that I love you when we both know it can be, for both of us, nothing but an idle dream?"

"But, why? Why?" Paolina asked.

"Because you know me for what I am," Sir Harvey replied. "I am not the right husband for you—nor for any woman for that matter."

"But I love you," she said a little piteously.

"And I love you," he echoed. "I have fought against it, I think, from the very beginning. I must have known that very first day when we sat on the cliffs and the sky itself was like a halo round your little head. I thought I had never seen a face that was not only so beautiful but so sweet."

"That very first day when you were so kind to me," Paolina murmured in a soft voice.

"If I had been sensible I should have run a mile rather than have saddled myself with you," Sir Harvey said. "I might have known not only that your beauty would hold me captive but that you would twine yourself about my heart."

He walked across the room, but his eyes were still on her.

"I have watched you very carefully, Paolina. You are made of the stuff that all men dream will come to them in the shape of a woman. You are good and gentle, kind and tender, and all the things which other women forget to be because they think it is only beauty that counts. At the same time, you are so beautiful that your face is always with me, wherever I may be, even when I am asleep."

"When you speak to me like that you make me want to cry," Paolina replied, her eyes like stars. "And yet I am proud, so terribly proud."

"God knows, you have nothing of which to be proud," Sir Harvey answered, his voice raw and rasping. "See me for what I am—a man who lives on his wits, a man who calls himself an adventurer; but that is often but a high-flown phrase for a common thief. I was born a gentleman—through necessity I have failed the standards of my own class.

"Do not think I am ignorant of my faults. But I have no other way of earning my living or even of keeping alive. I am not worthy of you, Paolina, and I have at least the decency to admit it."

"I love you all the more because you are honest," Paolina said. "It is not what you do that makes me love you, but what you are. You may decry yourself, but I have never known you to do a mean or dishonourable thing to someone weaker than yourself.

"You took me with you because you knew I was homeless and friendless, because you are you; I believe you would have done the same thing for someone who was not pretty and who did not attract you in the least."

She gave a little laugh that was half a sob.

"And you brought poor Alberto with us because you thought he would be punished. I have seen you always ready to give a kind or encouraging word to the servants and to those who could never repay you except by affection and loyalty. That is what counts more than any of the other things you do which you think are so reprehensible."

"I wish I could believe you, my darling," he answered. "But I am only speaking the truth when I tell you that my love is really an insult. I have loved many women in my life and I am not worthy so much as to touch the hem of your gown."

He put his hands on her shoulders.

"Forget me. Forget me as quickly as you can. But the memory of you will always be enshrined in my heart, and when everything else in life fails me I shall remember that you once said, in your sweetness and your innocence, that you loved me."

"You talk as if you were leaving me," Paolina whispered, looking up at him. "Wherever you go I am going with you."

Sir Harvey shook his head.

"You are staying here," he said. "In fact, we both are until you marry the *Conte*."

Paolina gave a little cry almost like an animal that had been wounded.

"I cannot marry him. You know it is you whom I love."

Sir Harvey sat down beside her, and took her hand in his.

"Listen, my litle love," he said gently. "I will tell you about myself. I was born in England and my father was Sir Courtney Drake of Watton Park in Worchestershire. He was very proud and a very obstinate old man. He was also

171

rather a tyrant in his own way, and like all boys, I rebelled against his dictation and wanted to think for myself and be my own master.

"I went to London and became one of a very gay set of young rakes who spent their time racing, cock-fighting and gambling, and who were much frowned upon by the more sober courtiers around His Majesty George II."

"You must have had a great deal of fun," Paolina murmued with a little smile.

"We enjoyed ourselves enormously," Sir Harvey conceded. "Though I dare say we made a confounded nuisance of ourselves as well. Youth is always intolerant of other people's feelings."

"Not you," she said quickly.

"Yes, me," he answered with a smile. "And my father, at that time influenced, I suppose, by his more sedate County friends, made a will leaving my Uncle—his younger brother—my guardian until such time as he should think fit for me to take over my estates.

"I had no idea, of course, that this will had been executed until my father died after a long illness about six years ago. I was then twenty-three years of age and considered myself perfectly capable of managing my own affairs. Yet my Uncle, whom I have always disliked and who apparently disliked me, refused to sanction the handing over of the house and the estate. He said he was my guardian and would continue to be so. You can imagine my fury at being landed with a kind of chaperon and tutor when my only desire was to be master of my own establishment."

"But, surely your Uncle did not mean to stay in that position for ever?" Paolina asked.

"That is just what he did intend," Sir Harvey replied. "Unbeknown to my father he had lost a lot of money. He saw an opportunity of living comfortably for the rest of his life. The only trouble, of course, was that I was likely to oppose him. He moved in to Watton Park and I told him that I should take the whole matter immediately to the King. It was then that he proved himself very clever."

"What did he do?" Paolina asked.

"He accused me of theft."

"Of theft!" Paolina echoed.

"Yes," Sir Harvey answered, and she saw by the grim lines of his mouth how bitterly this accusation had struck

172

home. "It was, of course, utterly without foundation. He accused me of stealing from him some bonds which had been placed for safe keeping in my father's safe, and to which, after my father's death, I was the only person who had the key.

"It was, as I say, utterly false, and I think that the bonds themselves were an entire fabrication on his part. But, anyway, he forestalled my appeal to the King by going to London himself. He saw His Majesty, persuaded him that a scandal within high circles would not be at all desirable, and that the best thing possible would be for me to leave the country. In other words, be exiled at His Majesty's pleasure."

"But I cannot believe it!" Paolina exclaimed. "How could such an injustice be done?"

"My reputation was bad," Sir Harvey replied. "I had annoyed a large number of His Majesty's most distinguished Ministers. They had all been fond of my father; they were all prepared to believe anything that my uncle—a man of their own age—was prepared to tell them.

"I was told what had been decided and therefore, because I lost my temper, I stalked away, ready to shake the dust of England off my feet without trying to fight my own case or even troubling to provide myself with enough money to live on. It seems stupid now when I have had time to think about it, but at the time I was so incensed at the whole thing that I could not think clearly."

"I can understand that," Paolina murmured.

"I came abroad determined to show them that I could manage without money, without influence and, if necessary, without honour. I have managed to live somehow. I cannot say that I think my attitude of defiance has hurt anybody except myself.

"A little time ago I humbled myself to write to His Majesty, reopening the whole story and begging him to allow me to return home and look after my own estates. It went against the grain to eat the dust and yet, when I think of my uncle living in my house and administering my lands, I can hardly bear it. Nevertheless such a sacrifice of pride was in vain. His Majesty did not deign to answer."

"Oh, how cruel!" Paolina exclaimed. "I am so desperately sorry for you."

"You would be," he answered gently. "But you do realize, do you not, why I cannot ask you to share my life?

I have no money, nothing except the pickings which come to me as I travel round the world with only my brain and my sword to sustain me."

"I would ask nothing more," Paolina murmured.

He smiled a little wistfully.

"They cannot always be sure of providing a roof over my head or food to eat."

"I do not mind any of that as long as I can be with you," Paolina said passionately.

He put his hand under her chin and raised her face to his.

"Do not say such things, my darling," he begged. "It makes it too hard for me."

"Do you not understand that I must say them?" she enquired. "You cannot send me away now. You cannot make me marry the *Conte*. How can I when I love you? I do not mind if we have to live in a tiny cottage or walk the roads bare-footed. I mind nothing as long as I am with you."

"Oh, you child," he said softly. "You do not realize what you are asking. You do not realize what life is like. You might bear it at first, but I could not stand seeing you become disillusioned. I could not watch your beauty disappear because of the hardships that I must make you endure. I could not stand by and watch you suffer."

"But it would not be suffering if I was with you," Paolina argued. "We should be happy—blissfully, crazily happy—because of our love."

"You tempt me," Sir Harvey said. "But for your sake I must not give in. Do you think it is easy for me, loving you as I do, to say you must go to another man? But it has got to be done. We have a little money at the moment. Soon it will disappear. We are living at a prodigious rate simply because we are gambling on the fact that you will make a rich marriage. But I will tell you one thing."

"What is that?" Paolina asked.

"That when you marry I will not touch a penny of your fortune."

"'But, you must," Paolina said. "That is the whole idea."

"It *was* the whole idea," he contradicted, his eyes dark with pain. "But now everything has changed. The day you marry I shall go away and you will never see me again."

"No! No! I cannot let you do that. I cannot bear it," Paolina pleaded.

With tears in her eyes she tried to hold on to him. But he rose to his feet and walked away from her.

"Let me stay with you. Please, please let me stay with you."

It was the broken, frightened voice of a child in the dark that reached him as he stood at the window, looking out with unseeing eyes. And then there was the sound of tears, of a woman sobbing bitterly as if her heart would break.

He turned at that and in three quick strides was beside her, lifting her arms, holding her closely, his lips against her hair.

"Do not cry. Oh, my beloved, do not cry," he pleaded. And then in the voice of someone who is tried beyond endurance he added: "I will see what we can do. I will think about it. Is that what you want me to say?"

"Oh, yes, yes."

Her tears were checked and a sudden smile, like a rainbow breaking through an April sky, parted her lips. As he looked down at her he could see the tears on her cheeks and on the end of her long lashes and thought they were like dewdrops glittering in the grass in the early dawn.

She was so young, so innocent of what the world could be, he thought in a sudden agony. And then, with a prayer more intense than he had ever prayed in his life before, he beseeched Heaven that he would not fail her.

"We will be together, that is all I ask," Paolina was saying. "Together—you and I."

She was silent a moment and then, in a very soft voice hardly more than a whisper, she said:

"I do not even ask that you should marry me if you would rather not. I will go with you; I will be to you anything you ask of me. But you shall be free, if that is what you prefer."

He drew her even closer to him, holding her so fiercely that she gave a little cry of pain.

"Must you make me feel such an utter cad?" he asked fiercely. "Oh, my sweet, my lovely one, as if I would offer you anything but marriage! And yet, what can marriage to me be but a tragedy for you? With your beauty you could marry anyone, and yet you choose a ne'er-do-well like myself, a man who can offer you nothing but his love."

"But that is all I want," Paolina whispered. "Your love for ever."

He kissed her at that and their kiss, soft and gentle, was

175

almost in the nature of a vow. They felt suddenly as if they were standing in front of some dimly lit altar where, in an atmosphere of faith and sanctity, they pledged themselves to each other for all eternity. . . .

Sir Harvey broke the spell.

"We must go out," he said briskly.

"Out?" Paolina questioned. "But, why? We must go away."

"We are not running away," Sir Harvey replied grimly. "The Duke knows we are here and I would not turn my back on him as if I were a coward."

"But he might . . . kill you," Paolina faltered.

Sir Harvey shook his head.

"He will do nothing of the sort. You must remember that he, as well as ourselves, must be obedient in Venice to the laws of the Senate and the Doge. If the Duke makes a move against us, he will not dare to make it here. Besides, I would not give him the satisfaction of telling everyone we had run from him and then sending his soldiers after us."

"He could not touch us if we were to go to Austria," Paolina pleaded.

"All in good time," Sir Harvey said. "I am not prepared to sacrifice our stay in Venice at a second's notice. And whatever happens we must fulfil our engagements for today."

"And after that?"

"We will make plans tonight," Sir Harvey answered. He glanced at the clock. "We are already overdue at the *Conte's palazzo*. He sent a note while you were resting, inviting us to watch the Regatta from his balconies. I accepted and he will think it strange if we do not turn up. Tonight there is another Ball to which we are invited. We will leave early; we will come back here and talk about ourselves. Will that please you?"

"Above all things," Paolina said. "But oh, my darling, in the meantime you will be careful?"

"I will be careful," Sir Harvey promised. "I will not let you out of my sight for one instant."

Paolina shivered as she remembered the Duke's thick lips and the terror she had felt in trying to escape from him.

"Thank goodness he still has his arm in a sling," she said. "You should have struck deeper."

"So bloodthirsty," Sir Harvey teased. "That is very unlike you."

"Yes, I know," Paolina said. "But I am afraid of him. I have a feeling that somehow he threatens us. We may be safe while we are in Venice, but he will get even with us sooner or later. He is the type of person who will be very revengeful."

"He is harmless as long as we remain here and then move quickly into Austria," Sir Harvey said protectively. "Stop worrying. You will give yourself lines on your forehead and then no one will think you are beautiful any longer."

"Will that make you stop loving me?" she asked.

"I shall love you when you are covered with wrinkles, when your hair has turned grey and your eyes no longer shine as they are shining now," he said. "Do you not understand that it is you I love? Every scrap and bit of you, and most of all that funny little thing you have given into my keeping which you call your heart."

"If only I was sure you had given me yours," Paolina retorted.

"You can be sure of it," he answered. "Because I love you as I never thought it possible to love anyone. Does that satisfy you?"

She stood up on tiptoe to kiss his cheek.

"For the moment," she whispered a little mischievously, and then as his arms moved out to hold her she had slipped away from him to run to her own bed-chamber.

The Regatta took an immeasurably long time, even though they arrived when several races had already passed the *Conte's palazzo*. There was a large company of ladies and gentlemen watching from the balconies, and it seemed to Paolina that they were genuinely pleased to see her and Sir Harvey. She could not help wondering how long their friendship would last if they knew the truth.

"You grow more beautiful every day," the *Conte* said. "I think I remember exactly what you look like and yet, when you appear, I find I am quite wrong and your face is far more entrancing than my memory of it."

"You pay me the most beautiful compliments," Paolina smiled, then she curtsied deeply to the *Conte's* Aunt—an austere old lady whose white hair was piled high under a black lace veil which barely concealed magnificent diamond earrings that matched a huge corsage of the same stones.

"We are so honoured to meet you, Ma'am," Paolina said.

The Dowager bent forward and patted her with her fan.

177

"You are a good child," she said. "I have been hearing about you from my nephew, and what I have heard pleases me."

Paolina curtsied her thanks and when someone else claimed his Aunt's attention the *Conte* drew her to one side and said:

"You have made a conquest of my Aunt. I have never known her so taken with anyone. Usually she dislikes young women and makes the most disparaging remarks about them."

"I am flattered," Paolina said.

"I think perhaps you captivate everyone," he went on in a low voice. "There is something about you which makes them absolutely certain that you are gold through and through. There could not be an unkind or false thought in your mind."

Paolina turned her head away from him.

"You must not say things like that for we are, most of us, not exactly what we seem."

"I know what you are," he said positively.

He would have said more had not his voice been drowned, at that moment, by the cheers and cries of the gondolier race, which shot by below them, the leading gondola being only half a length ahead of its other rivals.

When the excitement was over for at least a little while, the company withdrew into one of the great rooms where there were refreshments of wine and special cakes that were baked only on festive occasions.

"We have many special dishes," the *Conte* explained to Paolina. "Although I must admit they are mostly of French extraction. We Venetians got tired of the heavy, rather uninteresting cooking which had served us for many centuries, and French chefs were introduced; and now we have devised some delicacies which are specialities of our own."

"Nothing could be more delicious than this," Paolina exclaimed.

But she found it hard to eat even a mouthful. She was too excited, too thrilled with this new and glowing wonder within herself to need the earthly sustenance of food.

It was hard not to keep looking at Sir Harvey, or to concentrate on what anyone else was saying. She was conscious of him standing talking to various gallants and ladies. He would have been outstanding anywhere, she thought; but his coat of steel grey satin somehow made all the other men's more gaudy coats seem over elaborate and in slightly bad taste.

As if he knew what she was thinking, Sir Harvey turned and met her eyes and she, almost involuntarily as if she could not prevent herself, moved across the room towards him.

"Are you tired?" he asked solicitously. "Perhaps we had better return so that you will have a chance to lie down before we attend the Ball tonight."

"You have promised to dine with me," the *Conte* answered.

"But we dined with you last night," Paolina protested. "I thought we had other plans."

"The *Conte* has made me cancel them," Sir Harvey said with a smile. "He is very anxious that we should dine *en famille* without a large party."

"My Aunt is so anxious to further your acquaintance that it would be unkind to refuse," the *Conte* said.

"Of course, I am agreeable to anything my brother decides," Paolina smiled.

"You are very dutiful."

"Of course."

She looked at Sir Harvey as she spoke, under her eyelashes; then realizing that people in love always give themselves away, she severely kept her glance in other directions.

And yet, going back in their gondola from the *Conte's palazzo* to their own, she could not forebear to slip her fingers into Sir Harvey's hand. She hoped the gondoliers did not see, but somehow it was imperative that she should touch him and know the comfort of his strong fingers and the warmth of his clasp.

"I love you."

She heard him whisper it. Though it was hardly audible above the soft swish of their passage through the water, she heard and her lips moved in response.

"I love you, too."

She had hoped that they would be alone when they arrived back at the *palazzo*, but they found an elaborate gondola waiting outside and recognized it as belonging to the *Contessa*.

"What can she want?" Paolina asked.

Sir Harvey shook his head.

"I have no idea. Do not be afraid. She is being very pleasant over all this."

"I do not want to see her," Paolina said. "Surely it is

strange for her to come here when she is in deep mourning?"

"I do not understand it myself," Sir Harvey agreed. "Let us go upstairs and face the worst."

He took her hand in his and led her up the stairs. The *Contessa*, wearing black, was seated on a sofa at the far end of the Gallery. She looked very unhappy, small and pathetic, and instantly Paolina's kind heart made her run towards her.

"I am so, so sorry for you," she said, and then the women were kissing each other, and the *Contessa*, in tears, drew Paolina down beside her on the sofa.

"I had to come and see you," she sobbed. "You are the only people with whom I can talk about my brother without pretence."

"What have you told the world?" Sir Harvey asked.

"The doctors have written a certificate to say that it was a sudden heart attack brought on by too much exercise and that he was suffering from an obscure complaint which noone knew he had contracted. We are trying to make our cousins, and the more distant relatives, believe it too. But I felt suddenly suffocated by such lies and thought I would come here to see you."

"I am glad you did," Paolina said in all sincerity. "Harvey, will you fetch the *Contessa* a glass of wine?"

"Please call me Zanetta," the *Contessa* pleaded. "Do not let us be formal with each other now."

"No, of course not," Paolina agreed comfortingly. "And you do know how desperately grieved my brother and I are for you? It was kind of you to send me those flowers today. They helped me a great deal."

"You see, what is so worrying," the *Contessa* said with a strange glance at Sir Harvey, "is the question of what I am to do with myself now that my brother is dead. I lived with him because he was unmarried. Now, my whole life is upset."

She paused for a moment and then added hesitatingly:

"I . . . rather wondered . . . if you were going to . . . London, whether you would . . . take me with you."

"Take you with us!" Paolina ejaculated.

"It was just an idea," the *Contessa* replied. "I want to get away from Venice, from my brother's memory and from all the ghosts which hang about the *palazzo*. I am also told," she continued naively, "that Venetian women have a great success at St. James's."

"You mean pretty Venetian women," Sir Harvey said.

She smiled at him with a fleeting echo of her usual flirtatiousness. Paolina looked helplessly at Sir Harvey.

"We would enjoy it above all things," he said, "But, actually we are not returning to England for some time. When we leave here we are thinking of going to Austria and then to Switzerland. My sister was not well last winter and we thought it would be good for her lungs. We would ask you to accompany us, but unfortunately we are staying with an old friend in not very affluent circumstances, and would impose on his generosity to ask him to welcome another guest."

"Oh, but of course I understand," the Contessa said. "And, perhaps, when you do return to England you will think of me."

"But of course we will," Paolina said. "My brother is, I know, sorry we can arrange nothing at this moment, but you can understand our difficulties too."

"Of course," the Contessa answered. "I just hoped that it might be possible."

She looked at Sir Harvey as she spoke and Paolina knew that she was really in love with him. She felt a sudden throb of pity for this woman, knowing only too well what it was to love—the jealousy, the ache, the empty feeling of wanting something that was out of reach.

Instinctively Paolina put out her hands.

"You are our friend," she said. "Whenever it is possible, we will do all we can for you. Will you believe that?"

There was a throb of sincerity in her voice. The Contessa looked at her gratefully.

"You are so sweet," she said. "So unlike most women, who are ready to tear one to pieces."

"I do not think that is true of you," Paolina protested. "I think everyone must love you."

"You have no idea how lonely I am," the Contessa answered. She gave a little sigh and then added: "Oh, I forgot. I brought you something. I somehow felt you would like to have it."

She opened her reticule and took out a man's signet ring with a carved emerald set in gold and gave it to Paolina.

"But, I cannot take this," she protested.

"Please do," the Contessa pleaded. "He loved you. It was the ring he always wore. He would want you to have it."

She gave a little sob and rose to her feet. Paolina sat looking at the ring as Sir Harvey gave the Contessa his arm and took her downstairs to the gondola. She let them go alone. She somehow felt that that was the kindest thing she could do.

Poor Zanetta, who loved Sir Harvey and had no idea that he could never at any time love her in return. Perhaps she had hoped, when she came there this afternoon, that he would declare himself, that he would suggest her coming to England, not only as their companion but as his bride.

It had been the desperate throw of a desperate woman, and quite suddenly Paolina wondered how many other tragedies were being enacted behind the façade of these beautiful, elaborate *palazzi*. Did their marble fronts and sumptuous luxury hide many heart-breaks, many broken lives?

The thought seemed to take some of the joy from her own happiness. She slipped into her bed-chamber before Sir Harvey returned, and found her maid and the hair-dresser waiting to dress her for the dinner-party.

Owing to the *Contessa's* visit they were nearly late. There was no time to talk to Sir Harvey before they hurried away in their gondola to the *Conte's palazzo*. There they were taken to very different rooms from the ones that had been used in the afternoon. They were smaller, but magnificently furnished, with a fine collection of pictures by the great masters which even surpassed those in the Grand Salons.

When they sat down to dinner there were a dozen people in all, but the conversation seemed to centre round the *Conte's* Aunt, who was quite obviously an extremely dominating personality. She was witty and amusing, too, and Paolina began to see the truth of the saying—"Venice was built by men, but ruled by women."

The *Conte* sat at the other end of the table, but it seemed as if his Aunt was the host, not he. As they finished the first course, he whispered to Paolina:

"My Aunt always prefers to dine in the old-fashioned way. We now move to another room for the next course."

"But what an extraordinary idea!" Paolina ejaculated.

"It is always done by the best Venetian families," he answered.

"Here we have enjoyed the soup and the fish; in the next room there will be the game and roasts, and in the third the sweets, *sorbet* and dessert which finish the meal."

Paolina wanted to laugh, but the other guests took it as

quite the natural course of things and they all rose solemnly from the table and filed into another room where they sat down at a table equally beautifully decorated with gold ornaments and exotic flowers.

In this manner dinner took rather longer than usual, and as they withdrew from the third and last room Paolina whispered to Sir Harvey:

"My head aches lamentably. Can we return home and not attend the Ball?"

He looked at her gown. It was a very elaborate one of French brocade with a gold petticoat, ornamented with brilliants and flowers embroidered and lacquered in the Venetian manner. It had been made for her since she came to Venice, and he asked:

"Do you not wish to show off your finery?"

It was a mechanical question to which he saw the answer in her eyes.

"Very well," he said softly. "Leave it to me."

She walked away from him into the *Salon,* smoothing her gown and knowing that because he admired her in it, what anyone else thought was not of the least consequence.

There was much protestation, especially from the *Conte,* when Sir Harvey said they must return home.

"All day my sister has been afflicted with a headache," he said. "I think there must be thunder in the air. You will, I hope, forgive us."

"I do not want to lose you," the *Conte* said to Paolina, drawing her a little aside so no one else would hear. "Let us attend the Ball, if only for a short while. There is something in particular I want to say to you."

Because of the look in his eyes she knew what it was.

"No, I cannot face . . . the crowds," she said in a sudden panic. "I am deeply sensible of your kindness, but tonight I . . . I am too ill."

"But you will see me tomorrow?" he insisted. "Promise me."

"Yes, yes, tomorrow," she answered, feeling it might never come.

"I shall keep you to that promise," he said, and raised her hand to his lips.

"I cannot bear it any more," Paolina said when she and Sir Harvey were in the gondola. "We must go away. It is all so false, so unreal. I want to be alone with you."

She spoke in English, but he put his finger to her lips.

183

"Be careful what you say in front of the gondoliers," he said in a low voice. "Many of them speak more languages than they admit."

Paolina gave a little sigh. She thought that she could no longer tolerate this pretence and this play-acting. All she wanted was to be with Sir Harvey, hear him say that he loved her, to tell him what he meant to her.

They reached their own *palazzo*. She jumped out quickly and ran up the steps into the entrance hall. There were only two footmen about. The others had gone to bed.

"Buono notte," Paolina said to them, and then hurried up the stairs.

Sir Harvey came behind her. She could hear his steps and thought that when they reached the top he would take her in his arms.

This was the moment for which she had been waiting, this was what her body had been aching for, her mind anticipating the whole evening. She hurried a little faster and then, just before she reached the last two steps, she saw that Alberto was waiting there.

She looked up at him impatiently, then the words of dismissal died on her lips.

"What is the matter? What is it, Alberto?"

She was hardly able to ask the question before Sir Harvey's voice, stronger and louder, said from behind her:

"What has happened?"

The question was sharp, but Alberto did not answer. He waited until they reached the top of the stairs.

"It is the Duke, Excellency," he whispered.

The sound seemed almost as if it had dried up in his throat.

"I know His Grace is here," Sir Harvey said curtly. "We saw him arrive today. I imagine he is staying with the Doge. Do not let it perturb you. He can do you no harm here in Venice."

"It is not that, Excellency," Alberto managed to gasp. "It is his man. He has been here. I saw him as he disappeared over the balcony ouside your bed-chamber window."

"His man! What do you mean?" Sir Harvey enquired.

"I guessed what had happened," Alberto said. "You did not tell me, but I guessed."

"What are you talking about?" Paolina enquired.

But as if Sir Harvey understood clearly what Alberto was trying to say, he was already running down the Gallery.

He pulled open the door of his bed-chamber and then stood just inside looking across the room.

Paolina followed him. She did not comprehend what it was all about, but she hurried after him and stood beside him. She saw what he was looking at. There was a small panel open on the opposite wall.

It was painted like the rest of the room, and Paolina, although she had never seen it before, guessed that it must be a secret hiding-place. Now it was no longer a secret and it was empty!

"How did he know about it?" Sir Harvey asked harshly, and both he and Alberto knew to whom he was referring.

"It would not be hard, Excellency, to discover that, if not from the owner of the *palazzo*, then from someone intimate in his employment."

"Of course," Sir Harvey replied. His mouth tightened and he turned to look at Paolina.

"What has happened?" she asked. "Has something been stolen?"

"Yes," Sir Harvey answered. "Our money. Every crown of it. The Duke has been clever—damned clever!"

11

"What are we to do? What are we to do?"

Paolina found herself saying the words beneath her breath until finally they seemed to burst from her lips and be spoken aloud.

"It was not my fault, Excellency," Alberto was crying passionately, his hands gesticulating with every word he uttered. "I had locked everything up. I went downstairs to have supper and it was only when the meal was finished that I thought I heard a strange sound in the courtyard outside. I looked out and saw a man clambering down from your window and over the wall into the alley. Look, there are his marks on the ledge."

Alberto pointed dramatically, then went on:

"I ran out. It was too late to stop him. But as he swung his leg over the top of the wall he turned and looked down at me. He was not masked and I recognized him. It was Giolamo, the Duke's private clerk!"

"What did you do then?" Paolina asked.

Alberto spread wide his hands.

"What could I do, Milady? I did not know then that he had stolen anything. I shouted, but he was gone and there was no point in giving chase. The courtyard wall, as Your Excellencies know, gives on to a narrow alleyway. By the time we had mustered ourselves to open the courtyard door he would have been away—especially as he would have had a gondola waiting for him."

"Did you think that he had come to steal?" Sir Harvey asked.

Alberto shook his head.

"No, Excellency. I thought he had been sent to spy out

186

the land. The Duke has often used him in such a way. He has spied for His Grace on many occasions—listening at doors, reading letters when the guests were downstairs, ferreting out secrets which they would keep from His Grace. Giolamo was always clever enough to get what his master required."

"So it appears," Sir Harvey said drily.

"It was not until some time later that I came upstairs," Alberto went on. "By Our Lady, I was not to know that Giolamo and His Grace would stoop to being common thieves. I went to your bed-chamber, Excellency, to lay out your nightshirt. It was then I saw the open panel."

"And you guessed what it had contained?" Sir Harvey asked with a sharp look.

"*Ascoltimi,* Excellency," Alberto said. "In every nobleman's house, in every nobleman's bed-chamber there is a secret panel behind which he hides his valuables. I did not know exactly where it was in the room; but when at night you shut me out, I was quite certain that you locked your money away in just such a place as that."

He pointed to the empty darkness behind the painted panel. Sir Harvey walked across the room and slammed the panel to, as if the very action relieved some of his pent-up feelings.

Paolina stared. It was impossible to see where the opening had been. The painted panel blended perfectly into the wall; there was no sign of a join or hinge. Closed, it was exactly the same as the other panels, and she knew that no-one could have found it unless they had a previous knowledge of where it might be.

"I was a fool," Sir Harvey said heavily. "I should have found another hiding-place."

"You could not know the Duke would stoop to such perfidy," Paolina said soothingly.

"I will take our revenge, Excellency!" Alberto vowed. "I will find Giolamo in a dark alley. He is a coward if faced with cold steel."

"No," Sir Harvey said abruptly.

"But, Excellency, you cannot let this go unpunished," Alberto expostulated. "I dare not tackle Giolamo in the daytime, for he always carries a dagger. But at night—that would be different."

"Leave him alone, I say," Sir Harvey commanded. "He was but carrying out his orders. And go to bed, Alberto. There is nothing more you can do tonight."

"Please, Excellency," Alberto begged.

"Do as I say," Sir Harvey commanded. And then, as the man turned towards the door, he changed his mind. "Wait! Tell the gondoliers I want them again."

"Yes, Excellency."

"And you can let us out."

"May I come with you?"

Sir Harvey shook his head.

"No, for we will be going to the Ball."

"To the Ball!"

Paolina's astonishment made her echo the words. And then as Alberto left the room closing the door behind him, she added:

"What do you mean? Why should we go back to the Ball at this time of night?"

Sir Harvey did not answer and after a moment she said:

"Is that really the truth or are you going to challenge the Duke? You must do nothing of the sort. He is stronger than you and he has great influence. If you confront him with this crime, he will find some way to dispose of you. Please darling, do not be rash."

Sir Harvey still did not answer. He seemed to be deep in thought. Then suddenly he turned round to put his hands on Paolina's shoulders, to stare at her hungrily, as a man might stare at his last hope of salvation.

"I love you," he said gently at length. "You know that, don't you? I love you more than I believed it possible to love. I worship you. You are perfect, and more beautiful than any women I have ever seen."

"Why are you speaking like this?" Paolina whispered.

There was something sad in his voice and in his words—something that told her they were not just the rhapsodies of a man in love.

"I am saying this because, my little sweet, we are going back to the Ball so that you can persuade the *Conte* to offer you marriage."

"No! No! Not that!" Paolina cried. "You promised me."

He released her and stood back as if he was afraid to touch her.

"You tried to persuade me to do something against my better judgment," he said. "I admit I wavered because I want you so badly, because I love you so desperately that it is as if all the fires of hell were torturing me and only you could bring relief."

His hands clenched themselves until the knuckles showed white as he went on:

"But when we talked of this this afternoon I had a certain amount of money. All through dinner tonight I have been planning how we could make it go further, how we could use it to get more, how, somehow, we could contrive to live together and feel that our love was enough. But now ..." he looked towards the closed panel, "now we have ... nothing."

"Nothing at all?" Paolina asked.

"Only one thing," he said.

He put his hand in the pocket of his coat and drew out the pearl necklace.

"So that has not gone!" Paolina exclaimed.

"I left it in my pocket after you gave it to me the other night," Sir Harvey said. "I meant to put it away in what I imagined was the safeness of the panel, but I forgot. My pocket is deep and it was only a few moments ago, when I thrust my hand down into it, that I realized that the necklace was there."

"Then we are saved," Paolina cried.

"For the moment," he answered. "But not for long. I had not worried you before, but I learned this morning that Signor Bondi has sent an advocate to Ferrara to discover which jeweller sold me this necklace. Once he is there he will learn that I was not the buyer of the necklace, as I told him, but was, in fact, the seller of a large amount of valuable gems. As he gave many of them to Contratina himself, he will undoubtedly recognize them again."

"But, what can he do to you?"

"That, of course, is a point of law," Sir Harvey said. "But I imagine Signor Bondi will do his best to make it very uncomfortable for me in that, as one of the two survivors of the ship, I salvaged jewellery and not lives. I can give a truthful explanation, of course, of what happened. It is a question of whether people will believe me or Signor Bondi."

"Then let us go away," Paolina begged. "Things are closing in on us, I can feel it. Soon there will be no chance of escape. We must go now, while we have the chance."

"To live only on this?" Sir Harvey asked.

He held out the necklace as he spoke, the light from the candles glittering on the iridescent beauty of each pearl. They seemed to shimmer as if they were alive, and yet Paolina looked at them with positive distaste.

"They are very . . . valuable," she said a little hesitantly.

"Very," Sir Harvey agreed. "But I cannot afford to pick and choose my moment to sell. I must take the best offer I can get. And when this *palazzo* is paid for, and the servants' wages, the food, your dressmaker, hairdresser, and the hundred and one little things which have been purchased in the last few days, there will not be a great deal left."

"Enough to pay our journey to Austria?" Paolina asked.

"Yes," he replied. "And what will happen after that? Do you think I can stand by and watch you starve?"

"We will not starve," Paolina said. "We will find something to do. I can sew and you will be fortunate, perhaps, at . . . at the tables."

"The life you found so intolerable with your father?" Sir Harvey questioned bitterly. "No, I will not allow you to stoop to that. You will marry the *Conte,* and soon—far sooner than you imagine—you will forget me."

"Never! Never!" Paolina cried. "I love you. You do not believe me, but I love you with all my heart."

"You will forget me," Sir Harvey repeated.

There was something about his face and in his voice which told her that she was pleading against an inexorable determination which nothing would alter. She gave a little sob and held out her hands to him. He did not move or touch her.

"It is decided," he said. "We will go back now to the Ball. I shall tell the *Conte* our plans are altered, that we are leaving Venice almost at once. That, I am sure, will bring him to the point."

"He told me tonight that he had something of import to say to me," Paolina said dully. "I thought how lucky it was that I would not have to hear it, because I believed that you wanted my love, and it could mean something in your life."

"You were wrong," Sir Harvey answered.

His face was a mask. But he did not look at her. She went a step nearer to him.

"My darling," she said softly, "I am yours. Does that mean nothing to you?"

"You are going to marry the *Conte,*" he replied sternly. "Come, we must be on our way."

"I will not go," Paolina said stubbornly. "I want you. I want to be with you. How could I bear another man to touch me? How could you bear it?"

She saw by the flicker of his eyes and the sudden tightening of his jaw that her shaft had struck home. It was as if she had stabbed him. And then, with a formal courtesy, he opened the door and bowed to her.

"The gondola is waiting," he said.

"Do not make me go," she begged despairingly. "And, if I must, will you not kiss me? Kiss me once before we leave."

Sir Harvey turned on his heel.

"No," he said harshly, and walked away from her down the Gallery towards the staircase.

She hesitated for a moment, and then, because there seemed nothing else to do, she followed him. The sound of her heels moving across the wooden floor seemed to echo the slow, agonizing beats of her heart. It was as if he led her to the scaffold; but he did not look back.

They sat in silence as the gondola carried them swiftly to the Palazzo Gondini where the Ball was being held. The whole place was bright with lights and there were crowds of gondolas still emptying their laughing, masked occupants on the steps, which were covered with a rich carpet.

Inside the *palazzo* the Ballroom was draped with magnificent embroidery and with curtains woven with precious stones. Hundreds of great candelabra and candlesticks of gold glittered over the throng of magnificently dressed guests who were dancing, playing cards, filling the supper-rooms and watching a ballet in a miniature theatre.

Sir Harvey pushed his way through the throng of dancers with Paolina following him until, standing talking at the entrance of the card-room, they saw the *Conte*, his height making him easy to pick out even in such a crowded place.

Sir Harvey went up to him. The *Conte* turned with an exclamation of astonishment.

"My dear Sir Harvey!" he exclaimed. "I thought you and your sister had retired."

He took Paolina's cold hand and raised it to his lips.

"The night was dark and empty and suddenly it is sunrise," he said softly.

"We came back," Sir Harvey explained, "because we found a very important communication awaiting us on our return home. It was news recalling me to my own country and it means that we may have to leave Venice immediately. After your kindness we could not be so ungrateful as to depart without saying farewell."

191

"You are leaving Venice!"

It was quite obvious that the *Conte* was stricken by this information. He even seemed to go quite pale.

"I regret the necessity," Sir Harvey answered, "and my sister is desolated that she must leave our new-found friends."

"But you cannot go! It is impossible!" the *Conte* exclaimed. He glanced round him. "Come with me. I must have a word with you. Fortunately, I know this *palazzo* well."

He led them a little way through the crowds to where a curtain of sumptuous brocade embroidered in pearls hung over a partially concealed door. He pulled it aside.

"This is the way to the private apartments," he said. "I know that our host, who is a very old friend of mine, will not mind my inviting you into them."

"My apologies," Sir Harvey interposed, "but I will join you in a few minutes."

He turned away without further explanation and the *Conte* stood back to let Paolina precede him through the door. She gave a last despairing glance over her shoulder. She knew quite well why Sir Harvey had gone and she had an almost irresistible impulse to run after him, to say that he could not do this to her, that wherever he went she must go too.

But she knew he would not listen but would merely be angry with her for disobeying his orders.

Feeling suddenly helpless and utterly alone, Paolina walked through the door and heard the *Conte* follow her and shut it behind them. They were in a small, beautifully furnished sitting-room, lit by only a few candles which shed a soft light on the satin cushions which covered a low couch.

"Come and sit down," the *Conte* suggested.

Numbly, because she somehow felt that she was past all feeling, Paolina obeyed. She sat down, clasped her hands in her lap and waited for what she knew was coming.

The *Conte* stared at her for a minute and then he drew a deep breath.

"I love you," he said. "I think you know that already, and that is why I cannot let you go away. Stay with me here. Stay as my wife. I will make you happy, I swear it."

There was no doubt of his sincerity, and Paolina suddenly felt ashamed because he was offering her so much

192

and she could give him nothing but hypocrisy and deception.

"We do not know each other well," she parried. "How can you be sure you love me?"

"I was sure of it the first moment I saw you," he answered with a little smile.

"We have been brought up in very different ways," she answered. "I am English, you are Venetian. Can we even be sure that our ideas and our interests are the same?"

"Whether they are or whether they are not does not signify," the *Conte* replied. "I only know that I love you, that you are the most beautiful woman I have ever seen in my life."

"Beauty," Paolina exclaimed with a sudden bitterness, "does not make for happiness."

"It does for mine," the *Conte* answered. "To possess you would be a joy and a wonder beyond words."

He bent forward and took her hand in his.

"Paolina, say you will marry me."

"I do not know," Paolina said in a panic. "My brother . . ."

"'I am well aware that it is not correct for me to have spoken to you without asking your brother's permission," the *Conte* said. "But I had always understood that the English put love before convention. That is why I ask you now to marry me; and if you say yes, I will force your brother to agree."

"Supposing he refuses?" Paolina questioned.

"He will not," the *Conte* answered confidently. "When he knows how much I love you and how happy we can be together, I feel sure that he will not stand in our way."

"You know nothing about me," Paolina said.

"I know all I want to know," he smiled. "I have only to look in your face to read the history of your life. I have only to look into your eyes to want, above all things, to teach you the history of love."

She had left her hand in his. Now he raised it to his lips, kissing it passionately, and then drew her nearer to him as if he would kiss her lips.

Paolina gave a little sudden movement and rose to her feet.

"What can be keeping my brother?" she asked.

She was afraid, not only for herself but for Sir Harvey. She thought for one wild moment that he must have gone

193

to challenge the Duke, to do something wild and crazy which might put his life in danger.

Then, even as she spoke, she heard the door which led into the Ballroom open and Sir Harvey came into the room. She would have run towards him, but one warning glance from his eyes stopped her.

"I am sorry to be so long," he said to the *Conte*. "But I became involved in a discussion and could not get away."

"I was glad of that," the *Conte* said simply. "It gave me the opportunity I have been waiting for for some time—to ask your sister to marry me."

Sir Harvey simulated an expression of surprise.

"To marry you!" he cried. "This is quick work. And what about asking my permission?"

"I am doing that now," the *Conte* said quietly.

"Well, I suppose I must not stand in your way," Sir Harvey replied genially. "I have guessed that Paolina found you a very attractive fellow. But I had not expected——"

He stopped.

"But, of course, I had forgotten. It is impossible. I am returning to England."

"Then we must be married before you go," the *Conte* said.

"Oh, but surely," Sir Harvey expostulated, "it would be better to wait? We shall be able to return. Perhaps in three months we will be with you again—at the outside it would not be more than six."

"Six months!" the *Conte* ejaculated. "Ye Gods! But I do not intend to wait that long. If you must go, you go alone. Paolina will remain behind as my wife."

"You will wed each other as quickly as that?" Sir Harvey ejaculated.

"Why not?" the *Conte* enquired. "I am my own master. Marriage settlements can be drawn up immediately. The wedding can take place in my own private Chapel. There is no need for a large crowd to be present—only my immediate relations."

"You seem to have it all cut and dried," Sir Harvey said ruefully.

"I am having to think quickly," the *Conte* said with a grin. "And you know why. Because I do not intend to lose Paolina, whatever happens."

Sir Harvey shrugged his shoulders.

"Well, I suppose the impetuosity of love will have its way," he said philosophically. "Make what arrangements you will. But, I warn you that I must leave for England some time tomorrow."

"We will be married an hour after midday," the *Conte* said. "That will give me time enough to make all the arrangements—both legal and ceremonial."

He looked at Paolina and added:

"You have made me the happiest man in the world."

She did not answer. Her eyes were fixed on Sir Harvey's face.

"Last night I lay awake wondering if I should ever be fortunate enough to arouse your interest in me," the *Conte* continued. "Tonight I can hardly believe my own good fortune."

He kissed Paolina's hand again. She went very white, almost as if she were going to faint, and Sir Harvey said quickly:

"I think it would be wise if now I took my sister home. All this emotion is damned fatiguing, and you, my dear fellow, will have quite a lot of arrangements to make if you really intend to be wed tomorrow."

"I certainly intend it," the *Conte* said firmly. "And you are right. Your sister does look tired."

He slipped Paolina's arm through his.

"Let me take you to the gondola," he said. "You must sleep well. It will be a very quiet wedding; but before it takes place, the Doge and Dogessa must perform the engagement ceremony. I am related to the Doge and he will, I know, make no objections to the haste which is so necessary because of your brother's departure."

The words hardly percolated into Paolina's consciousness, and yet somehow they set the seal to her last hopes that all this was not serious but a dream from which she would be able to awaken.

As she went back with Sir Harvey in the gondola, she tried vainly to find words in which to speak to him, to tell him that she could not do it, that he could not expect it of her. But she knew by the very stiffness of his body beside hers that he did not wish to talk with her. She stole a glance at his profile, sharp and aloof against the dark sky, and felt afraid, almost as if he had turned into a stranger.

"Harvey," she whispered once, beneath her breath. "Harvey."

But he did not seem to hear her.

They arrived at their own steps, said good night to the gondoliers, and Alberto was waiting to let them in. He came up the stairs with them, and when they reached the Long Gallery Paolina waited for him to go so that she could speak with Sir Harvey alone, but he lingered in the background.

"Good night, Paolina," Sir Harvey said, and the tone of his voice was a warning as well as a command.

"I must speak to you, I must!" she pleaded.

But he held open the door of her bed-chamber and almost as if she was mesmerized he forced her, by sheer will power, to enter it.

"Wait! Please . . . please . . ."

"Good night, Paolina."

Sir Harvey closed the door. She heard him call Alberto and walked across the Gallery to his own bed-chamber. And then, because she knew that whatever she did now he would not hear her, she flung herself down on her bed in floods of tears.

She cried, it seemed to her, for hours until finally she rose, taking off her magnificent gown, undressed and took the pins from her hair, letting it fall over her shoulders. She remembered then how Sir Harvey had kissed it earlier in the day, and she felt her tears flow anew at the thought of how happy she had been for so short a time.

"I love you," she whispered, and then crept into bed to lie miserable, unhappy, until the dawn came.

She was so exhausted that it was only then that she fell into a deep slumber until Thérèse woke her at seven o'clock with a bowl of soup and a glass of wine.

"His Excellency's orders, Milady. You are to drink this!" she said.

"I don't want it," Paolina expostulated sleepily.

"But, Milady, it will do you good, and you will need your strength."

"For what?" Paolina asked almost crossly; but even as she spoke, the whole flood of misery and unhappiness came pouring over her. She knew then that Sir Harvey would have told the servants, the *Conte* would have told his friends and relations.

She was to be married. Married to a man she did not love, because there was no alternative.

"The *Conte* is so handsome, Milady," Thérèse was saying. "Everyone admires him. It was known that he was looking for a bride and every noble lady wished him to choose her daughter."

Paolina said nothing, making an effort to sip her soup.

"Of course, there are those who say that he has loved too often," Thérèse went on. "But always married ladies, never girls."

"So the *Conte* has had a lot of love affairs, has he?" Paolina said without interest, speaking merely because she could not help listening to Thérèse and was at the same time trying to keep her own thoughts at bay.

"Oh, yes, indeed!" Thérèse repeated almost triumphantly. "He is a very experienced lover. Me, I like a man who knows what he is about—a man of the world. I have no use for unfledged boys."

Paolina wanted to say she hated them all, men and boys, that all she wanted was one man—only he would not have her.

"There was the Contessa Cattolina Grimaldi," Thérèse chattered. "She loved the *Conte* very, very dearly. When he grew bored with her, she threatened to kill herself. But he did not mind. He told her to go ahead and do it, and so she didn't. She went to Naples instead."

Paolina forced a watery smile to her lips.

"Was that such a terrible fate?" she enquired.

"But, of course," Thérèse said. "The *Contessa* could not stay here where she had been unhappy. Oh, the *Conte* can be very, very hard. But you are so beautiful, Milady, you will twist him round your little finger."

The *Conte* was obviously not quite what she had imagined, Paolina thought. Somehow she did not care. The only thing she wanted was to see Sir Harvey.

"Go to His Excellency," she said, "and ask him if I can speak with him a moment."

As soon as Thérèse had gone, Paolina jumped out of bed, put on a wrapper, tidied her hair in front of the mirror. She looked pale and there were dark lines under her eyes; but she thought with satisfaction, she was still beautiful. Surely, with her hair flowing over her shoulders, wearing the same wrapper in which he had kissed her so passionately yesterday afternoon, he would not be able to refuse her?

Thérèse returned.

"His Excellency is very busy," she said. "He says he will come if it is really important, but only for a minute."

"Tell him it is of the utmost import," Paolina answered.

Thérèse ran from the room. Paolina waited, moving restlessly up and down across the luxurious rugs which covered the floor. The minutes passed and when she was almost in despair for fear he would refuse her altogether, the door was opened and Sir Harvey came in.

One glance at his face told her that he, too, had not slept. He looked pale, even beneath his tan. He shut the door behind him and stood looking at her, at the sudden joy in her face at the sight of him, at the light in her eyes. Her lips were tremulous and her breasts, beneath the thin silk wrapper, were moving agitatedly. The sunshine coming in through the window turned her hair to a halo of gold.

"You have come."

She hardly could breathe the words.

"Yes, I have come," he answered, but his voice was raw. "Why must you crucify yourself and me? Until midday we had best see little of each other."

"I cannot do it, you know that," Paolina said. "And you cannot make me."

Sir Harvey stared at her for a long moment and then he said abruptly:

"I can do no more. And it is true I cannot make you do anything you do not wish to do. But I can make one thing very clear. If you do not go through with this marriage, then I shall leave tonight, without your knowledge, without saying farewell. I shall go out of your life as mysteriously and unexpectedly as I came into it. You can make what explanations you will, but I shall not be here to make them for you."

"How can you do this to me?" Paolina asked piteously.

"Because it is for your own good," he answered. "Do you suppose it is easy for me to give you up? But I am not yet such a cad as to take you and then let you suffer afterwards. This is your one chance, the one chance you have ever had or are ever likely to have, of finding, if not happiness, at least contentment. You will be rich, you will be respected. You will be married into one of the most illustrious familes in all Venice. What does it matter what happens to me after that?"

He stared at her, his face grim.

"Forget that you ever knew me," he commanded. "Forget that Fate, by some strange quirk, sent us into each other's lives for no other reason than to laugh at our torments."

She knew by the sound of his voice how much he was suffering. Because there was nothing she could do about it, nothing she could say in response, she could only cover her face with her hands and feel the hot tears welling up into her eyes and running down her cheeks.

When she looked up again, Sir Harvey had gone. He had closed the door silently behind him and she had not heard him go.

When Thérèse returned, Paolina bathed in water scented with jasmin and dried herself in the soft towels that bore the princely coronet of the owner of the *palazzo.*

She could not help remembering that by tonight she, too, would be entitled to embroider her belongings with such an emblem, and she shuddered at the thought of it. For a moment she thought wildly of going to the *Conte,* telling him the whole truth and saying that she could not be his wife. And then she realized that such an action would do no good. Sir Harvey was going away, and whether she stayed behind with the *Conte* or alone it really mattered little—for without him she was utterly desolate.

She dressed herself mechanically in the exquisite garments that Thérèse brought her—a chemise, beautifully embroidered and edged with real lace; petticoats which seemed as if they must have been made by fairy fingers.

Then the hairdresser arrived and arranged her hair in a very different style from any she had ever worn before. Soft, natural waves framed her little face and made her look young, innocent and untouched.

When he had finished, Paolina saw that on the bed Thérèse had laid an exquisite wedding gown.

"The *Conte's* Aunt sent it to you," the maid explained, seeing Paolina's glance. "It has been in the Ricci family for many generations."

"Why should I wear it so early?" Paolina asked. "I am not to be married until an hour after noon."

"Because it is customary for the Doge and Dogessa to see the bride in her wedding finery when they come to place the pearls around her neck."

"What pearls? What are you talking about?" Paolina enquired.

"You do not know the custom, Milady?" Thérèse asked. "I thought, of course, that His Excellency would have told you about it."

"I know nothing," Paolina answered. "Tell me what happens."

"It is a very, very old ceremony," Thérèse explained.

199

"His Serenity and his wife, seated on thrones, place round the bride's neck the pearls which she must wear for one year after her marriage."

"And where do the pearls come from?" Paolina asked.

"They are usually a present from the bride's Mother," Thérèse answered. "But if she has no Mother, then the bridegroom will make them part of his engagement present. In your country I think you have a ring. But in ours we have a ring called the *ricordino* and the pearls as well."

"It sounds a pretty custom," Paolina remarked, and both Thérèse and the hairdresser vied with each other in telling her what an important occasion it was in the life of a young bride.

The gown was certainly very beautiful and fortunately, with a very few alterations, fitted Paolina perfectly. It was made of silver brocade embroidered all over with pearls, tiny diamonds and lace. She was not to wear her veil until the wedding ceremony, but a huge tiara fashioned like a wreath of flowers in diamond and pearls was set upon her head.

She wondered suddenly whether Sir Harvey would admire her; and even as the thought came to her, she felt her spirits drop miserably to their lowest ebb simply because by the evening it would not matter what she wore or what she said. He would not be there!

"Milady is *bella, molto bella,*" Thérèse kept saying, and then she flung open the door into the Gallery and Paolina walked slowly out to seek Sir Harvey.

He was waiting for her at the far end, looking out on to the Canal. He, too, was dressed with great magnificence in a coat of blue satin. His face, however, was dark and there was a heavy frown between his eyes.

He looked at Paolina and while the servants waited he seemed for a moment unable to understand what was required of him. Then, almost perfunctorily, in a voice devoid of feeling, he said:

"You look very nice. It is time we left."

It was Thérèse who cried out:

"Nice. That is not the right word, Your Excellency. Do you not think she is beautiful? *Molto bella?* As beautiful as an angel in the skies? As beautiful as any Queen, as any fairy princess? Tell us, Excellency, what you really think."

Sir Harvey's eyes met Paolina's. For a moment everybody else vanished and they were alone. She saw deep into his very soul and knew what he was feeling.

"You are very beautiful," he said at length in a voice which seemed to vibrant with pain.

Then, taking her hand in his, he led her down the stairs and out into the gondola.

The *Conte* was waiting for them on the steps of his *palazzo.*

"I can hardly believe your beauty is mortal," he told Paolina as he raised his lips from her cold hand. "Are you a goddess from the sea? I am half afraid Neptune will take you from me."

Paolina did not answer. She only stood stiffly beside him as they waited for the Doge and Dogessa to arrive.

The crowds, sensing that something was about to happen, were beginning to gather in gondolas and in the windows of other *palazzi.*

"Here they come!" the *Conte* exclaimed, and Paolina saw approaching the Doge's magnificent gondola with its crystal glass windows and cushions of crimson velvet. Even though the visit was a private one, the Doge wore a cloak of cloth of gold and gold-embroidered bonnet which proclaimed his office. The Dogessa, who was growing gray and rather heavy in her movements, had also a mantle of cloth of gold with a long veil.

The *Conte* bowed as they stepped out of their gondola and made a formal speech of welcome, while Paolina sank down in a deep curtsy. Then His Serenity and the Dogessa were escorted through the *palazzo* and up into the great reception rooms on the first floor, which were all decorated with white flowers tied with great bows of white ribbon.

Here they were received by the *Conte's* Aunt with a calm, self-possessed dignity, while the Master of Ceremonies brought refreshments on a gold plate. There was wine and sweet biscuits and the special kind of bridal bread. "The emblem of fertility!" the rather sour-looking relative said to the *Conte* as if she doubted the efficacy of it.

Paolina had thought she was too numb to feel anything, but the woman's words sent a shiver of horror through her. How could she bear children to a man she did not love?

When the refreshments were finished, the Doge and Dogessa seated themselves on two high thrones which had been erected at the end of the room. There were velvet footstools in front of them and Sir Harvey came forward and took Paolina by the hand. She resisted an impulse to cling to him merely because she knew that if she made the slightest gesture of affection towards him or he to her, she might break down and disgrace them both.

With her head held high she let him lead her to the velvet footstool, and at the Doge's command she knelt at his feet. The *Conte* handed him a magnificent pearl necklace and he took it carefully in his thin blue-veined fingers.

"May the purity of the pearls of the sea be echoed by the purity in your heart," he said in his kind old voice. "May the years of happiness with the man of your choice be as many as the pearls in this precious circlet."

"I thank Your Serenity," Paolina managed to answer, but as she felt the Doge's fingers fumbling behind her bent head, it was as if he fixed a chain of steel around her neck.

"Pearls mean tears," she thought and remembered that the dead woman in the wrecked ship had brought her tears; but they had also brought her great happiness. Now happiness was gone and this new string, beautiful though it might be, would, she was convinced, bring her tears for the rest of her life. Tears of regret, tears of a yearning for what could never be—for the man without whom all her life must seem utterly empty.

The *Conte* raised her to her feet and slipped a ring on her finger. A huge diamond glittered and flashed in the light of the tapers. Paolina stared at it dully.

"*Basa, basa.* Kiss her, kiss her," the onlookers cried as was customary.

The *Conte* put his arm round Paolina and sought her lips, but she gave him her cheek. As he kissed her, she looked towards Sir Harvey in despair, and saw a sudden expression transfigure his face. There was the red fire of murder in his eyes for one moment; then it was gone.

The ceremony was over. The Dogessa kissed Paolina and then turned to congratulate the *Conte*.

"She is exquisite, Leopaldo!" she smiled. "What a handsome couple you will make! All Venice will want to fête you!"

After that Paolina was introduced to the *Conte's* relations and everyone chatted quite informally until it was time for the Doge and Dogessa to leave.

"You look so beautiful that I cannot believe you are mine," the *Conte* whispered to Paolina, and then his Aunt signalled to him impatiently to attend to some important guests and she found herself standing beside Sir Harvey.

She looked up at him a little piteously.

"I keep thinking that this is a nightmare and I must wake up," she said.

"Look around this *palazzo*," he said harshly. "It is yours. Do you see the pictures? Can you value the furniture? Did you notice the gold plate on which the refreshments were served?"

She shook her head.

"I was thinking how happy and how hungry we were that first meal we ever ate together in Gasparo's little house after we had both been saved from the sea. Do you remember how tough the chicken was and how raw the wine? And yet we enjoyed it?"

"Your gown was shrunk and torn," he answered. "And yet you were even more beautiful than you are at this moment."

"That was because I was happy," she said.

"Neither love nor happiness can survive poverty," he stated positively.

"Who told you that?" Paolina answered. "A woman who had never loved you to begin with? I have often thought that it is luxury, not poverty, that stifles love."

"You have known poverty," Sir Harvey said. "Do you really wish to go back to it? Think of those lodgings you have described to me, in Naples and Rome, in the small towns round the coast. Could you endure them again?"

"With you?" Paolina asked. "They would be Paradise because you were there."

"You are mad," he said angrily. "Look round you and one day you will thank me because I have more sense than you."

"If I live to be a hundred, I shall never forgive you for destroying the only really beautiful thing in my whole life," Paolina answered in a low voice.

"What is that?" he asked almost involuntarily.

"My love for you," Paolina replied.

12

Back at their *palazzo* Sir Harvey sent Paolina to her bed-chamber.

"You have nearly two hours in which to rest and prepare yourself for the ceremony," he said. "I have work to do!"

She knew that what he said was true, but she guessed, too, that he was afraid to be alone with her, afraid not only of her emotions but also of his own.

She lay down on the day bed drawn in front of one of the windows, but knew that rest was impossible. The seconds of her freedom were ticking past like heartbeats. Soon, soon, they would be gone and with them the man she loved beyond her hope of Heaven.

Suddenly she heard a noise outside the room.

She listened and thought she must be mistaken. The sound was peculiarly like a woman sobbing. Curious, she rose, crossed the room and opened the door.

Outside in the Long Gallery a woman in black was standing beside Sir Harvey and sobbing bitterly.

"I love him," she was saying. "I loved him, and now he has cast me away and there is nothing for me but to die."

Impulsively Paolina stepped forward.

"What is the matter?" she enquired.

Sir Harvey turned angrily.

" 'Tis nothing that concerns you," he said. "Return to your bed-chamber."

Paolina would have obeyed him, but the woman took her handkerchief from her eyes and said falteringly:

"Is . . . is this . . . the . . . bride?"

"Yes, I am the bride," Paolina answered. "Why should that concern you?"

In answer the woman flung herself on her knees at Paolina's feet, and taking her hand, raised her tear-drenched eyes.

"Help me! Please help me!" she said. "For I am utterly destitute."

"Paolina, I beg you to leave this to me," Sir Harvey interposed.

Paolina did not move.

"I think," she said gently, "this does concern me."

"You are so beautiful," the woman sobbed. "I can understand him wanting to marry you. But he has loved me for over two years. He has been happy with me, I swear it. And now to cast me off without even a *sequin* with which to bless myself!"

Paolina looked at Sir Harvey.

"Is this true?" she asked.

Sir Harvey shrugged his shoulders.

"She has no right to come here, as she well knows."

"Can the *Conte* really have treated her so shabbily?" Paolina asked Sir Harvey.

"It is the truth, I swear it," the woman interposed. "But I have not come here to make trouble, only to beg that you will intercede for me and ask him at least to support me until I can find another protector, or . . ."

She hesitated for words, and Paolina said softly:

". . . Until your child is born. That is what really worries you, is it not?" She bent down and lifted the woman to her feet. "Come and sit down," she said gently. "We must see what can be done about you."

The woman was pretty. She had a rather sweet and childish face with large lustrous eyes and a full red mouth which trembled now from her tears and made one instinctively wish to give her protection.

"Paolina, you cannot concern yourself with this," Sir Harvey said in a low voice.

"I can," she answered. "For I would not have any woman suffer on my account."

She helped the stranger to the sofa and then, taking Sir Harvey by the arm, drew him towards the window and out of earshot.

"You can go to the *Conte*," she said, "and tell him that

205

if he does not give this woman enough money to tide her over the birth of his child, then he can look for another, bride, for I swear that I will not marry him."

She spoke truculently, for she thought that Sir Harvey was going to argue with her. Instead, the rather severe expression on his face broke into a grimace of amusement.

"Paolina, I adore you," he said in a low voice. "And, dammit, I will give the *Conte* your message with the greatest of pleasure."

He took her hand and raised it to his lips. As she felt his mouth against her skin, she instinctively tightened her fingers on his, and then trembled because she could not help the ecstasy that ran through her at his touch.

"I will not be long," Sir Harvey said.

He walked away down the Gallery, and Paolina heard him calling for Alberto to bring his hat and cloak.

She crossed to the sofa where the woman was sitting.

"Something will be arranged for you," she said soothingly. "If you will just wait here until my brother returns, I am sure that he will bring you good news."

"You are very kind," the woman said, and added with a little sob: "I am ashamed that I should come here and disturb you on your wedding day but I was desperate. My rent is due and I do not know where to turn for money."

"I have been in the same predicament myself," Paolina said.

"You have?" the woman asked with rounded eyes.

Paolina felt that she had said too much, and crossing the room, poured out a glass of wine and gave it into her visitor's hand.

"Drink this and rest," she said. "I must go back to my bed-chamber to get dressed for the ceremony."

Paolina went into her room and closed the door. Thérèse and her hairdresseer were waiting for her. She hardly saw them. Instead, she was looking into the future and seeing other episodes like the one in which she had just taken part. She felt a sudden surge of anger against the *Conte*.

How dare he treat any woman as he had treated that poor creature in the Gallery? How dare he think that women were only playthings to cast aside when he was tired of them?

She wondered what would happen to her when the time came that he grew tired of her, as he undoubtedly would. And then she remembered the great pile of legal documents she had seen lying on Sir Harvey's desk in the Library while they were talking. She would at least be provided for as far as money was concerned. And yet, she told herself with a wry smile that she would always be utterly bankrupt if she were to reckon the amount of her happiness.

The hairdresser had almost finished arranging a coronet of diamonds over a long lace veil which almost covered the dress of silver brocade, when Sir Harvey came into the room. Paolina's thoughts had been dark with misery, and yet, even at the sound of him, she felt her heart leap and she thought the sun had suddenly come out.

"Your Excellency has come at just the right moment!" the hairdresser exclaimed. "I wish you to look at Milady's veil and see if she does not look the very Queen of Beauty. Aphrodite rising from the waves could not be more exquisite."

Paolina saw that it was an effort for Sir Harvey to look at her critically, to inspect the hairdresser's work from both sides. Somehow he managed it, and said:

"An excellent job. I think you have made my sister look really beautiful on this auspicious day."

"No one could make her more beautiful than she is already," the hairdresser said admiringly. "But I am honoured to be allowed to add my small talent to the masterpiece which God has already created."

Sir Harvey gave him a couple of gold pieces and the man bowed his way from the room. With a little wave of her hand Paolina dismissed Thérèse and turned eagerly to Sir Harvey.

"What happened?" she asked.

"The *Conte* was overcome that his sins should have caught up with him," Sir Harvey answered. "I spoke to him very severely. I told him what a bad effect such reprehensible behaviour might have on your affection for him. I even threatened that the marriage would not take place."

"What did he say to that?" Paolina asked, hoping wildly against hope that the *Conte's* fears could be justified.

"He was abject," Sir Harvey answered. "The lady in question is to receive a large sum of money immediately. I waited while he instructed his attorney to take it to her."

"Has she gone?" Paolina asked, looking towards the door.

"As soon as I told her what was waiting for her at home

she hurried off without delay," Sir Harvey replied. "But she was grateful. She said that she would pray for you."

"I shall certainly need her prayers," Paolina said drily.

She turned her face away as she spoke so that Sir Harvey should not see the tears which sprang into her eyes. He looked at her for a moment and then his hand went out towards her.

"Paolina!" he said hoarsely.

The door burst open and they both turned to see Alberto, white-faced and breathless, his eyes almost starting out of his head.

"Excellency," he gasped as soon as he could draw his breath, "we must get away—at once."

"What is the matter?" Sir Harvey enquired.

"I have just been to—the market place to fetch one of your cloaks that was being—repaired," he said breathlessly. "While I was there, I ran—unexpectedly into a cousin of mine. He is in the service of—the Duke."

"Was he surprised to see you?" Sir Harvey asked.

"No—because he told me that he knew—I was here. The Duke knows that I am with you as—your servant. In fact he has known all the time where he could lay his hands on me—and you, Excellency—whenever he wished."

Alberto was obviously so frightened that Sir Harvey walked across to him and put his hand on his shoulder.

"Pull yourself together, man," he said, "and tell me exactly what you heard."

"We are to be killed," Alberto said. "Your Excellency and I. At least, I am to die because the Duke says I am a traitor to have left his service. But you are to be imprisoned in the Castle of Ferrara. Your death will be slow, but nothing can save you. No one has ever escaped from the Castle dungeons."

Paolina gave a little cry of terror and jumped to her feet.

"But, how can he do this?" she asked, walking towards Alberto and Sir Harvey.

"Wait!" Sir Harvey said. "Let us hear the whole story first. What else did your cousin tell you?"

"We are to be taken as soon as the wedding is over," Alberto said. "The Duke will not harm Milady because he is too afraid of the *Conte*. But one of his ships is waiting out in the Lagoon to carry you and me, Excellency, to Comacchio."

"So that is his plan!" Sir Harvey said.

"I am to be killed," Alberto said in a strangled voice. "My throat is to be cut. He has said it and nothing can save me. Even if I run away, they will hound me out!"

"Do not let him make you chicken-livered!" Sir Harvey said sharply. "We will outwit the Duke and live!"

"But, how . . . how will you escape him?" Paolina asked.

She was very pale, her eyes seemed enormously big in the little face she turned towards him, framed with the soft fragility of the long lace veil. Sir Harvey walked backwards and forwards across the room.

"We have got to be clever," he said. "I have no intention of lingering in the dungeons of Ferrara, and you, Alberto, are not going to die. You will live to make a dozen women happy."

Alberto attempted to smile but failed.

"The Duke is very strong, Excellency. Not in himself—for you wounded him—but he has men, many men, who will do his bidding. He is also rich."

"He is also being rather clever," Sir Harvey said. "I have more respect for him at this moment than I ever had."

"How can you talk like that?" Paolina asked almost hysterically. "Do you not realize that your life is in danger? You must go now, at this very moment; quickly, before he expects you to leave."

"I had not thought of that," Sir Harvey said.

"But, of course, it is obvious how you can escape," Paolina said. "He will be quite certain that you will stay for the wedding ceremony; but if you depart from Venice before it takes place, then you will take him by surprise."

Sir Harvey smiled at her.

"What a friend in a tight corner!" he exclaimed.

He put his hand in his pocket and drew out a purse.

"Take this, Alberto," he said. "See that the fastest gondola in all Venice is standing beside the golden one which is to carry her Ladyship to the *Conte's palazzo*. Tell the gondolier that the moment you and I set foot in it he is to carry us out on to the Lagoon to where the swiftest ship that this city can provide must be waiting to carry us to Trieste."

"To Trieste!" Paolina cried in surprise.

Sir Harvey nodded.

"Trieste," he replied. "Once we are in Austrian territory the Duke cannot touch us. And, besides, I have a friend there. We shall need him, for Alberto is holding at this moment the last *sequin* I possess. I can only hope it will be enough."

Alberto was weighing the purse in his hand.

"I doubt it, Excellency," he said ruefully.

Paolina pulled off the pearls that the Doge had fastened round her neck.

"Take these," she said. "Any ship's captain who has sailed the seven seas will recognize their value."

Alberto took the necklace doubtfully.

"The men may be afraid to handle such gems lest they be accused of theft," he said.

"Then make it really worth their while," Paolina insisted, and drew the great diamond engagement ring from her finger.

"What will you say to account for their loss?" Sir Harvey questioned.

Paolina merely shrugged her shoulders.

"Does it matter?" she asked.

"The fastest ships the Mediterranean has ever known will be yours, Excellency," Alberto promised excitedly. The diamond seemed to have swept away his doubts. He hesitated for a moment and then dropped down on one knee. He touched Sir Harvey's hand with his forehead and said simply:

"I will serve you to the end of my life."

Then, before either Sir Harvey or Paolina could speak, he had gone from the room, closing the door behind him.

"He loves you," Paolina said softly.

"Because I am saving his skin for him," Sir Harvey said.

"Must you always infer the basest motive?" she asked. "He loves you for yourself—even as I do. Oh, my darling, take care of yourself."

"I promise you I will do that," Sir Harvey replied. "If I have got to die, I do not intend to give the Duke the pleasure of being my executioner."

"How shall I know that you are safe?"

She hardly breathed the words because they seemed to come through lips that had suddenly grown dry.

Sir Harvey looked at her. She knew in that moment that he was suffering the same agony that she was. It seemed to her that they were standing on either side of a deep river which was growing wider and ever wider until soon there would be no point of contact between them. She saw the despair in his heart, she knew that he must be seeing, too, the desolation in hers.

There was somehow nothing they could say. They could only look at each other until, with a sound that was half an oath and half a sob, Sir Harvey turned, wrenched open the door and went, leaving her alone.

She wanted, then, to sink down on her bed and cry, but somehow she was past tears. She could only stand, dry-eyed, while Thérèse returned with salve for her lips and perfume to place behind her ears and the soft valley between her breasts.

There seemed to be a lot of little things to be done, but Paolina let Thérèse do them. For nearly an hour she sat, almost like a dummy, looking at the past, remembering so many things that had been said and done, so many moments of happiness.

She refused a glass of wine, and then, before she expected it, a knock came on the door and a voice cried:

"It is time to leave."

She knew, then, that the moment when she must say goodbye to Sir Harvey had come. She walked slowly out into the Long Gallery, her veil trailing behind her like a train, her gown, stiff and heavy with the diamond and pearl embroidery, rustling over the polished floor like ghostly fingers.

Sir Harvey was waiting for her, with Alberto behind him carrying a bundle inconspicuously in his arms. The servant's eyes were glittering with excitement and it was obvious that he was anticipating the wild dash that lay ahead of him and Sir Harvey.

There was a bouquet of white flowers in Sir Harvey's hands. He gave it to Paolina and as she took it from him she touched his hand and found it was as cold as ice. She looked up then into his face. It was stern, almost to the point of being expressionless, and yet she could see the agony in his eyes. He did not speak and in silence they walked down the stairs.

"I am going to my death," Paolina whispered beneath her breath. And she knew that it was, indeed, the death of her youth and the death of her happiness. Ahead lay darkness, unendurable misery and an utter, devastating loneliness because Sir Harvey would not be with her.

They reached the steps which led down to the water. The sunshine glinted on Paolina, making the diamonds in her hair and on her gown sparkle and glitter. The crowds that were waiting ouside to see her shouted:

"Good luck! A happy life! God bless you!"

She stood for a moment, almost blinded by the sunshine. Below, rocking a little on the tide, was the vast glittering gold gondola—the ceremonial vessel of a thousand brides. Carvings of cupids and love knots ornamented the centre cabin while the *ferri* at bow and stern represented the goddess Venus.

Beside it Paolina saw there was another ordinary black gondola manned by two strong-armed, tough-looking gondoliers.

This was the moment!

She turned to Sir Harvey and held out her hands. She wanted to say, "God keep you," but somehow the words would not come although her lips moved. Her eyes met his and she felt that in that glance her soul passed from her into his keeping.

"Good-bye, little Paolina!" he said, and then, suddenly, was very still.

It was as if, without words, her whole being pleaded with him. He looked at her; she looked at him. And they no longer heard the noise of the crowd.

"Dammit! Why should it be good-bye?" Sir Harvey asked loudly.

He bent and picked her up in his arms. The crowd cheered more loudly, thinking it a romantic gesture. But Sir Harvey carried Paolina not to the gold gondola with its liveried gondoliers, but to the plain black one which stood alongside it.

He jumped in, dropped her unceremoniously down on the black leather seat, and Alberto followed them.

"To the ship!"

Sir Harvey gave the command, but only the two gondoliers heard him above the cries of the crowd. And then they were away, streaking down the Canal, past the gondolas lining the route that Paolina was to have taken, past the people watching over the balconies and even from the roofs.

They neared the *Conte's palazzo* and saw him waiting on the steps in a coat of gold, embroidered with diamonds and wearing the purple Order of Chivalry across his shoulder. He was talking with various of his friends as elaborately dressed as he was himself, and then someone must have said something, for he turned sharply and saw Paolina in the strange craft.

For a moment he stared, and then went forward a pace as if, unconventional as her approach might be, he was concerned only with greeting her.

The gondola shot past the *palazzo*. Paolina had a sudden glimpse of the *Conte's* mouth falling open in sheer astonishment. She saw the faces of his friends and servants equally astonished, equally ridiculous in their surprise. And then she could look no more.

The Lagoon was in sight. The Doge's Palace lay to their left, and a little way out were several ships, their orange sails vivid against the blue of the sky.

"The ship is ready to sail?"

They were the first words Sir Harvey had spoken since they left.

"Yes, Excellency, all is arranged," Alberto said, but he crossed himself after he had spoken as if to prevent any evil spirit from undoing the plans he had made.

The gondola pulled up alongside a small ship. It was little more than a fishing boat, but the men who helped Paolina aboard had kindly faces, and though they stared at her in astonishment they said nothing until Sir Harvey explained.

"The lady is coming with us. Get under way immediately."

"Aye, aye, Excellency."

Alberto paid the gondoliers and they thanked Sir Harvey and wished him God-speed. Paolina moved across the deck to a small cabin in the stern. She heard the anchor being pulled up, heard commands being given quietly and men running about the deck to obey them.

The sails were billowing out in the wind, the ship was moving. She heard Sir Harvey's voice, and then he came through the doorway into the cabin and she was in his arms.

"I could not leave you behind," he said. "When the moment came, it was too much to ask of any man. Do you forgive me?"

"Forgive you?" she asked with laughter in her voice. "I have nothing to forgive. You have made me so happy. I did not know the world could be so glorious and wonderful."

"It is mad, you know that, don't you?" Sir Harvey enquired, and he held her closer. "It is crazy, insane, a madness that you will doubtless regret. Now it is too late. I will never let you go."

"That is what I want you to say," Paolina whispered.

"You belong to me," Sir Harvey cried almost truculently. "You belong to me as I belong to you. For good or bad our paths lie together."

His arms tightened about her, but still he did not kiss her. He only looked down at her face in infinite tenderness.

"God only knows what sort of life I can offer you, my darling," he said. "You will lie on a hard bed, you will know poverty, perhaps danger. But we shall be together, and one thing I promise you—I shall never stop loving you; not until the end of my life."

"Do you think I want anything else?" Paolina whispered.

He kissed her then—a long, passionate kiss which left her shaking and breathless with her eyes shining like stars.

"I love you! Oh, my God, how I love you," he murmured.

They sat together for a long time, their voices coming only in brief, incoherent sentences, their kisses leaving Paolina weak and yet floating in an ecstasy of emotion and joy which seemed to intensify itself every time he touched her.

It was Alberto's voice that interrupted them.

"Excellency! Excellency! Come and look what is happening," he called, and there was a note of alarm behind his words.

"What is it?" Sir Harvey asked.

He took his arm from Paolina and went from the cabin, and after a moment she followed him. He was standing in the stern of the ship, his eye to a telescope.

Already they were too far off from Venice for Paolina to see anything but the five rounded cupolas of San Marco and the high Campanile which stood beside it, but Sir Harvey was obviously watching something intently through the telescope.

"What do you see?" Paolina asked.

"Activities aboard the Duke's ships," he answered briefly.

Paolina put her hand to her heart.

"The Duke's ships! Are they going to follow us?"

He did not need to answer her question. They both knew that it was unlikely that the Duke would give up without a struggle. It was just a question whether their ship was swifter than his!

"At least we have a start," Paolina murmured.

A moment later they were out of sight of the city and heading for the open sea. It was rough, but the wind was strong and blowing in the right direction.

"Let us hope they will think we are heading south," Sir Harvey said. "That in itself may delay them for a little."

The waves were slapping against the sides; the ship was heeling over. Sir Harvey called for more sail and soon they were running at what seemed to Paolina an almost incredible speed.

It was an hour later they sighted the other ships. There were four of them and when Sir Harvey gave her the glass she could see the Duke's pennants flying from the masts.

"Will they catch us?" she asked.

"They are going to try," he answered.

His lips were tight. She knew then that the danger was very real. She had taken off her diamond and pearl coronet and laid it in the cabin. She had wrapped the beautiful lace veil, which had been worn by generations of brides, over her head and wound it round her neck, and Alberto had taken a cloak from the bundle he had carried aboard and draped it over her shoulders.

Paolina had thought for a moment how incongruous it was that they were standing on the deck of this rough, rather dirty little ship in clothes that had cost a fortune and yet they were both of them without a penny in their pockets.

But it was difficult to think of anything except the ships coming along behind them. It seemed to her that they were drawing nearer. The distance between them was not so great. She turned an anxious face towards Sir Harvey and laid a hand on his arm. He understood without words what she was asking.

"The wind is freshening," he said. "Our real chance lies in the fact that the passage is not a long one—only eight or nine hours at the most."

"They are swifter than us?" Paolina asked.

"They are built for speed," he said briefly.

All through the long, hot afternoon they ran ahead of the Duke's ships. And yet gradually they were drawing nearer. Sir Harvey made Paolina drink a little wine, but when he offered her some black bread, such as the fishermen ate, and a piece of cheese, she shook her head. She

215

was not hungry, she was only anxious as she watched his face and knew by the expression in his eyes what he was feeling.

Once she put her hand on his and said:

"Whatever happens we have had this time together, and I have known that you wanted me. That is what matters more than anything else in all the world. If I have to die, then I shall die happy, knowing that you did not leave me behind."

"You will not die," he said gruffly. "The Duke will see to that."

If he thought to make her flinch, he was mistaken.

"If you die, I shall die with you," she said. "No one can stop me from doing that."

He bent then and kissed her lips, but it was a kiss without passion and it was almost as if the pursuing ships had taken even their humanity away from them.

Hour after hour went by, and yet Sir Harvey strode up and down the deck, urging the fishermen to crowd on more and yet more sail. Paolina sat with her hands folded. There was nothing she could do but wait, and after a time she did not even turn to look at the ships behind them. She was too afraid to see how much clearer they were than earlier in the day.

It must have been nearly evening, for the sun was sinking, when suddenly the Captain gave a little cry.

"There is Trieste," he said, and they could see the long line of coast ahead of them, looking little more than a shadow in the brilliance of the sky.

It was then that Paolina looked back. The ships were little more than two hundred yards behind them. She saw by the tightness of Sir Harvey's jaw that he was well aware of their imminence, and she knew, too, by the terror on Alberto's face, that he thought there was no hope for them.

Paolina could see the grappling irons ready on the decks. She knew that the Duke's instructions were that they were to be taken alive, otherwise the cannon on the bows would have been used long ago.

"Better be dead than the Duke's prisoner," she whispered beneath her breath.

Sir Harvey gave a sudden exclamation.

"Dolt that I am!" he said. "We can run lighter than this. Chuck everything overboard that will lighten the ship. I will pay you for your loss, I swear it—in fact, I will pay you now."

216

He dived into the cabin and came back with the coronet of diamonds and pearls which Paolina had worn on her head.

"Take this," he said. "It is worth a fortune, as you full know. And, now, show a clean pair of heels to those devils behind us."

The men understood only too well what he wanted, and with their eyes on the coronet of diamonds started with a will to discard everything removable. Barrels, furniture, extra sails—all went overboard to float away on the choppy waves towards the ships following them.

Soon, it seemed to Paolina, there was nothing left on board save human beings. The decks were cleared of everything. The cabin was empty save for a wooden bench which was attached to the wall. Even the lantern which had swung from the cabin ceiling was jettisoned with a splash into the sea.

Alberto gave a shout.

"We are pulling away from them!"

Paolina felt it was too much to hope, and yet it was true. The pursuing ships were not so near as they had been. She could see men scurrying about their decks, letting out the sails, but they dared not fling overboard the Duke's property, and the ship which carried Paolina and Sir Harvey was undoubtedly sailing faster now that everything possible had been discarded.

"Another half-hour," the Captain muttered.

It was growing dark. The first stars were appearing in the sky. The wind, which had been so helpful all day, was altering a little, veering southwards but coming back to the west in strong gusts which seemed to sweep the little ship even further ahead of its pursuers.

Paolina suddenly felt very tired. She went back into the cabin and sat down on the hard bench. She was no longer anxious, no longer afraid. She somehow knew that they would win through, that the Duke's ships would not catch them.

It seemed to her that perhaps they had been ungrateful to the Providence that had watched over them for so long to have been apprehensive, even for a moment, that they would not be safe. And yet, as she remembered the Duke's cruel face as he pursued her round his room at the hunting lodge, she knew that he was not a man to give up easily what he most desired.

Italy would be barred to them, she thought, for ever.

And yet, somehow, she did not feel sad even at leaving the country which she knew better than anywhere else in the world. So long as she could be with Sir Harvey, that would be home—wherever it might be, whatever place he chose.

She found herself praying that she could be to him all that he wanted of her and that she could create for him happiness, however meagre their surroundings, however frugal their fare.

And then his cheek was against hers and he was holding her tightly in his arms.

"We are safe, my darling!" he said. "We are coming into the harbour and the Duke's ships are turning back."

She clung to him, wanting to cry because she was so happy. But there was no time for that. She had to thank the Captain and the crew, to say good-bye, to step ashore on to the soil of Austria with the feeling that a new adventure awaited her in this strange land.

Alberto was sent to get a hired carriage. When he came back with one, Sir Harvey helped Paolina into it and then got in beside her.

"Where to, Excellency?" Alberto asked as he opened the door.

"The British Embassy," Sir Harvey commanded.

The door was shut. He put his arms round Paolina and she leaned back against his shoulder in utter contentment.

"Where are we going?" she asked, half sleepily.

"To be married, my darling," he answered. "I cannot wait any longer to make you my wife."

"Two weddings in one day?" she queried. "It is enough for anyone."

"Nothing and nobody shall prevent two weddings taking place," he vowed. His arms tightened about her as he added: "I want to be certain you are mine."

She laughed at that and touched his cheek with her hand. His lips were seeking her mouth and he only released her as the carriage drew up at an imposing mansion.

"What will they think of us?" Paolina whispered in a sudden fright as she saw the powdered footman come running down from the lighted doorway.

"I hope to God they offer us a meal, that's all," Sir Harvey smiled. "I'm famished, and with empty pockets I shall not be particular."

He stepped out first and helped Paolina to alight. The lace veil was still draped over her hair and she looked pale

218

yet very lovely as she walked up the steps and into the great marble hall.

The footman did not seem surprised at their appearance. Only she was conscious of the marks of tar and dust on the hem of her rich gown, that Sir Harvey's white stockings were soiled and there was a streak of oil on the blue brocade of his embroidered coat.

They were shown across the hall and into a large *Salon* lit with glittering chandeliers.

"Sir Harvey Drake!" a footman announced, and a man at the far end of the room who was sitting talking to another man rose to his feet.

"Good God! Harvey!" he exclaimed. "We were just speaking of you."

"I've told you before not to talk of the devil!" Sir Harvey answered. "How are you, Desmond? I hoped you were still here and had not been posted elsewhere. May I present Miss Paolina Mansfield—Sir Desmond Sheringham."

"Your servant, Madam!"

Sir Desmond bowed to Paolina, but turned eagerly to Sir Harvey.

"You were always one for surprises, Harvey. I had no idea that you were coming to Trieste."

"Nor had I until this morning," Sir Harvey answered. "And then I realized that you were the one person who could do me a service, and so here I am."

"What sort of service do you require of me?" Sir Desmond enquired suspiciously. "If you've been duelling again and want a second, the answer's no."

"I want you to marry me," Sir Harvey said. "And at once."

Sir Desmond threw back his head and laughed.

"By gad, Harvey! Isn't that exactly like you? Always the unexpected. You were just the same even when you were a little whipper-snapper at Eton. Time hasn't changed you—has it, my Lord?"

For the first time Paolina and Sir Harvey glanced at the second man who, after their entrance, had stood silent by the fireplace. Sir Harvey held out his hand with a smile.

"Lord Cochrane," he said. "I did not expect to see you. May I present Miss Mansfield, my Lord?"

"Miss Mansfield and I have met before," Lord Cochrane answered. "At my Embassy in Rome, if my memory serves me rightly."

Paolina blushed.

"Yes, my Lord. And you were very angry because my father had lost his letters of credit."

"I cannot believe that I was ever angry with you," Lord Cochrane said with somewhat heavy gallantry.

"You know, Harvey, it is the most extraordinary thing," Sir Desmond said. "Lord Cochrane and I were speaking of you only a few minutes ago. He was asking me if I had seen you and I was saying I had not heard of you for the last five years or more."

"I am flattered that your Lordship should remember me," Sir Harvey said to Lord Cochrane.

"Remember you!" Lord Cochrane ejaculated. "Dammit, man, I have been looking for you for the last eighteen months."

"Looking for me?" Sir Harvey enquired.

"Yes. Heaven knows where you have been hiding yourself. A more elusive fellow it's never been my pleasure to meet. Here am I with good news for you and without an address to which I can deliver it."

"Good news?" Sir Harvey asked. His voice was sharp.

"Good news!" Lord Cochrane replied. "For I have been empowered to convey to you His Majesty's command that you return to England. Your uncle is dead."

"I thank your Lordship for the information," Sir Harvey said formally.

"Apparently, from what I can gather from the official communiqués—which don't tell us overmuch," Lord Cochrane went on, "he confessed before he died to having treated you ill. Anyway, His Majesty is eager and anxious to make amends by pardoning you."

"He will doubtless offer you some ghastly pompous job at Court," Sir Desmond interposed. "It's a dog's life and if you take my advice, you will refuse."

"I shall," Sir Harvey answered. "I am going to retire to the country and live in peace and happiness on my own estate."

He turned towards Paolina.

"Will that suit you, my darling?" he asked.

It was hard for her to answer him. She had realized in this exchange of words just how much the news that Lord Cochrane had given him meant to the man she loved. He spoke casually enough, but she saw the sudden light in his eyes, the little twitch at the corner of his lips which told her what he was feeling.

She had a sudden vision of what lay ahead of them, and the glory and happiness of it almost blinded her. Without thinking she put out her hand and slipped it into his. His fingers tightened on hers so sharply that she almost cried out with the pain. And then, because he was touching her, the thrill and wonder of it made her tingle with an ecstasy that was beyond words.

She felt herself quiver and then realized that everyone was waiting for her reply to Sir Harvey's question.

She looked up at him, her eyes like stars, and saw in his face an expression which made her heart turn over in her breast.

"I shall love it above all things," she whispered.